GRACE AMONG THIEVES

A GRACE MICHELLE MYSTERY

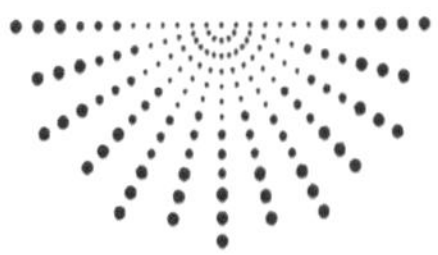

KARI BOVÉE

BOSQUE

PUBLISHING

PROLOGUE

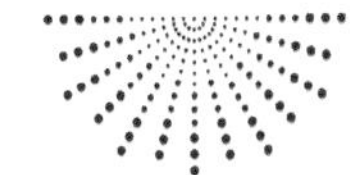

*P*ARIS, FRANCE, JUNE 1924

Marcel Gallois whistled a tune as he walked the streets of the 7th arrondissement of Paris, quite pleased with himself. After seven long years, he'd finally been able to secure a buyer for the treasure. He remembered the night he'd found it like it was yesterday, the night he'd accompanied the Bolsheviks as they raided the Winter Palace in St. Petersburg.

Though originally from France, Marcel and his sister, Madeleine, had been raised in Russia. Their family had lived in privilege, and they were acquainted with the royal family through his father, Bertrand Gallois, an industrialist who owned a highly profitable sugar factory in St. Petersburg. Marcel, unlike his parents, sympathized with the ideas of Lenin and his Bolshevik revolutionaries. Tsar Nicholas II had run Russia into the ground with his weakness and ineptitude. Imperialism was dead, and the new way to freedom was through the Soviet cause.

In the raid, looters had made off with rugs, silver, and priceless objets d'art, and Marcel had been no exception. He'd managed to escape with the treasure held fast to his side beneath his coat. Only when he'd been safe behind the gates of his family's estate had he pulled the jeweled box from under his coat. It had gleamed under the brightness of the full moon.

When he'd finally opened the box, he'd let out a low whistle of amazement, marveling at the prize inside. He'd tilted the box toward the moonlight to better see the intricate design paved with glistening jewels. Tingles had spread through his body, sending a shiver down his spine. It had been a magnificent find, but he hadn't known what to do with it at the time. He had not shared this secret with anyone, especially not his parents. He'd wanted to show it to his sister, who might have been equally fascinated by and excited at the prospect of what the treasure could bring, but before the outbreak of the recent revolution, his parents had sent her back to France. She'd made use of her time there aiding in the Great War.

His parents had insisted they follow her months later, fearing the Soviets would strip them of their riches and drive them into exile. When they'd arrived back in France, he reconsidered sharing his secret with Madeleine but decided against it. What if she, too, had grown to resent the Bolsheviks and their liberation of Russia?

Despite what his parents or his sister might think, Marcel knew his family would need the proceeds from this masterpiece to survive, for they had left their lucrative business behind. Taking the Romanov treasure had turned out to be the perfect solution. But to sell it shortly after their arrival in France in 1917, while the revolution raged on in Russia, would have been foolish. So he had buried it under one of the trees in his family's Parisian garden until he could safely secure a buyer. He had been content to keep it secret and wait. In time, he'd bring back the family fortune.

And that time was now.

He'd finally met with a buyer, and in a few short days, he'd amass a generous sum.

Marcel and his parents had settled in a modest yet stately

home in Paris, and their financial situation was not nearly as bleak as he'd thought it would be. His father had been able to smuggle a great deal of cash into France, so with the money from the stolen objet d'art no longer needed, Marcel intended to use the proceeds to set himself up in business. He also planned to buy a house for his sister and her husband, an American soldier she'd met while caring for him at the *Hôtel National des Invalides*, the well-known hospital for injured soldiers. Unable to stay employed for any length of time due to the ravages of shell shock, his sister's husband could only provide a ramshackle flat for the two of them. A proud man, he'd refused to live with Marcel and their parents. But soon, Marcel would provide the two of them with a lovely home.

When he reached the walk in front of the family's terraced house, something looked off. The front door stood open, and light from inside spilled onto the front steps.

He broke into a jog as he made his way up the path and inside, absently leaving the door open.

"Papa? Mama?" he called to his parents.

From the upper level of the house came the sounds of thrashing, banging, and glass shattering. He raced up the stairs and turned to enter the family parlor when he was met in the doorway by a thickset ox of a man.

Towering over Marcel, the square-faced man had a bulbous nose and a slash of a mouth set in what could only be described as a permanent sneer. Marcel glimpsed beyond the man's beefy shoulder. His parents, sprawled on the floor, lay unmoving.

The man lunged at him and grabbed him by the lapels. "Where is it?"

Marcel blinked, unable to comprehend what was happening. The man pulled back an arm and delivered a hard blow to Marcel's face, knocking him into the wall. He hit his head, and with his vision swimming, he sank to the floor.

The man stood over him. "Where is it?"

Marcel shook his head, trying to clear his vision, his mind spinning. How had anyone found out about his treasure? He hadn't mentioned it to a soul, save for the buyer he'd met earlier that evening.

"Who are you?" Marcel asked.

The man grabbed him by the lapels and hauled him to his feet. He pressed Marcel against the wall. "It doesn't matter who I am. Where is it?"

Marcel again looked to his parents lying on the floor, their bodies inert. Were they dead? His heart wrenched, and he let out a whimpering cry. The man slapped his face hard, and then delivered another blow, this time to Marcel's stomach, making his whole body recoil. He gasped for breath.

"Tell me where it is or you'll end up like them."

A flash of clarity stunned him into the brutal realization. His parents were indeed dead. And it was his fault. His greed had caused this horror. He'd only wanted to help his family, hadn't he? But if he'd never stolen the precious treasure, this wouldn't have happened.

The man raised his fist again, and Marcel put up his hands to stop him. "It's not here. It's somewhere safe," he said, his voice strangled as he fought for breath.

The man pushed him harder against the wall and pressed his forearm against Marcel's windpipe. "Where?"

Marcel slid his gaze over to his parents. He'd be damned if he would let this thug benefit from what he'd done. Obviously, the man he'd met earlier that evening had deceived him and had sent this goon to steal the treasure.

Yes, in that moment, Marcel was willing to join his parents in death rather than give the item over to this animal. "You'll have to figure that out for yourself." Marcel spit in his face.

The man hauled back his fist, and then stars exploded before Marcel's eyes. He sank to the floor, his body racked with pain as the man let go a fury of rage.

"Hello?" an unfamiliar voice rang out from downstairs. "Bertrand? Marie? Are you here? You've left your door open."

Marcel felt the man move away from him and heard his footsteps as he ran down the hall, away from the stairs. A rush of cold air swept over Marcel. The man must have opened the window at the end of the hall and escaped from the roof.

He wanted to answer, to call out, but he could scarcely breathe. He heard the click of the door closing downstairs. Managing to get up on all fours, he half crawled, half dragged himself to the stairway to see who had entered, but no one was there.

"Help! Are you still here?"

Silence filled the air.

Planting his hand against the wall, he struggled to his feet. The floor threatened to slide out from under him, and he leaned against the wall until his head cleared.

Knifelike pain stabbed at the upper right side of his abdomen, and he doubled over. When the wave lessened, he staggered into the parlor. He reached his mother first. Her eyes were wide, staring at nothing, and her mouth hung open.

"Mama," he whispered, and with shaking fingers, he gently closed her eyes.

His father lay a few feet away from her, a large pool of blood surrounding the upper part of his body, his skull caved in.

Marcel let out a howl of anguish, but the effort sent his abdomen into spasms again. He coughed, and a spray of blood coated his hand. In that instant, he thought of his sister. He had to get to the hospital, to her. But first, he had to see the treasure secured. He had to get it out of the country—and he knew exactly where to send it. Then he would explain everything to Madeleine and her husband, and the three of them would follow.

Somehow, Marcel got himself down the stairs and outside to the back garden. His mission to get the treasure as far away from Paris as fast as he could drove him onward. Digging through the soil took a tremendous amount of effort, and sweat poured from his face and down his back. Finally, he reached the small wooden crate in which he'd placed the jeweled box. Carefully, he pried it from the ground and carried it back into the house. He made his way to the washroom, set it at his feet, and turned on the tap.

Glancing in the mirror at his reflection, he gasped. His face, wet with sweat, was a sickening gray color. The blood drained from his head, and his knees buckled. He braced himself against the sink until the wave of lightheadedness passed. His abdomen screamed in pain. He splashed water on his forehead and cheeks, and raked his wet hands through his hair. He grabbed a neatly folded white cloth from a rack near the basin and dried his face.

He picked up the crate and left the washroom. On his way out the front door, he grabbed a piece of paper and pencil from the entry bureau and then made his way gingerly down the steps of the house, wincing in pain. Luckily, a carriage happened to be passing, and he flagged it down.

"*La Poste du Louvre,*" he said to the driver. "*Dépêchez-vous. Hurry.*"

The post office at the Louvre was open at all hours. His eyes kept wanting to close, and he felt himself weakening with every passing minute. He took out the piece of paper and pencil, and he scrawled out a note to the recipient of the treasure, telling her to keep it safely hidden until he or his sister could collect it. He knew he could trust her.

When they reached the post office, he waited for the driver to open the door for him. When he did, the driver's face registered surprise at his appearance.

"*Allez-vous bien, monsieur?*" he asked Marcel with concern in his voice.

"I'm fine. Wait for me here."

He went into the post office and told the postmaster to send the crate to Los Angeles, California. He paid the man, left, and headed back to the coach.

Before he reached it, a pain so fierce took hold of his gut and he doubled over.

The driver was at his side in seconds. "You need to go to the hospital."

"*Oui,*" Marcel agreed. "Take me to the *Hôtel National des Invalides.*"

He only hoped he would get there in time.

CHAPTER ONE

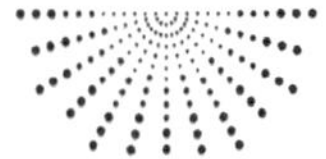

URBANK, CALIFORNIA, AUGUST 1924

I sat in my kitchen enjoying the quiet of the morning. I read over the two telegrams for the one hundred fiftieth and one hundred fifty-first time, I was sure, and still could not completely reconcile their content.

My father was alive.

The first telegram had arrived from Europe about a month ago. In it, my father—if it really was my father—informed me he would be traveling to Los Angeles from New York City via train upon his arrival in America. The second telegram, which had come about a week ago, stated he'd arrived in Los Angeles, and he'd given a phone number where he could be reached.

Even though it'd been a month since I'd received the incredible news that my father was alive, I was still somewhat paralyzed by the revelation.

My sister, Sophia, and I had been told when we were thirteen and twelve respectively that our parents had been killed in a train accident. Our neighbor, who had imparted the news, had alerted the authorities and had told us we would be sent to the orphanage. Fearing we would be separated, Sophia had insisted we flee our family home in Queens County.

We had ended up on the streets of Manhattan. We'd lived in alleyways, or sometimes deplorable rented rooms when we could scrape together enough money, for two years before Flo—or Florenz Ziegfeld, Jr., the Broadway impresario—had found us living in an alleyway near his theater.

Captivated by Sophia's beauty and charm, which had managed to glow just beneath her dirty face and worn clothing, he'd immediately seen her potential for stardom, and so he had taken us in. He'd put a roof over our heads and taught us to sing, dance, and act. He'd made Sophia a star, and he'd encouraged me in my dreams of becoming a costume designer.

But my world had shattered when Sophia was murdered four years ago. Since then, she'd visited me in my dreams—more recently over the last year. While the dreams were always cryptic at first, they'd proven to be enlightening, comforting, and helpful as I'd solved the murder cases of Edward Travis and two of his ex-wives. Sophia had always tried to take care of me, and in many ways, she still was.

Thinking of our time on the streets, a shudder ran through me. We'd rarely had money enough for food, but there had been times when Sophia had come up with the money somehow. She had sacrificed herself to keep us alive. Every time I thought about it, even still, my stomach turned. After *those* nights we'd have enough money to rent a room for a night or two. We mostly spent the time sleeping, and if we were lucky, we'd enjoy the luxury of a bath.

For my part, I'd made doll clothes to sell on the street. Mrs. Taylor, the owner of a dress shop in Chelsea, would supply me with discarded pieces of fabric. I knew my contribution wasn't much, and it didn't take the lasting toll on me the way Sophia's contributions did on her, but in those times, anything helped.

I read the telegram yet again, trying to sort out my conflicted feelings. I had never dared dream that either one of my parents was alive. The news of their deaths had been so final, so permanent, and our lives so difficult after we'd learned of it. I tried to muster up some excitement, some elation, but something made me reticent. Was this person really my father? He'd been alive for the entire twelve years I'd thought he was dead. Why hadn't he reached out before this? Why had he not come home? He'd abandoned us to a life on the streets. A life without support, without family. Sophia had become wildly famous. Surely, he'd read about her.

It occurred to me he could be a fraud, someone who'd recently read about me in the paper, someone in search of notoriety, maybe.

I had been featured in the news after bringing down the serial killer Preston J. Travis, aka James Johnson, for the murder of his stepbrother, the famous director Edward Travis. In addition, I'd also had a small feature written about me as the head costume designer at Ambassador Films. If he was my father, why hadn't he come forward before? I pushed down the hurt that welled up in my heart.

My ruminations were interrupted when Rose, my mother-in-law, walked into the kitchen tying a bright floral apron around her waist.

"Morning, Grace."

After decades of separation, Rose and my husband, Chet, had reunited, and he had invited her to come live and work at our ranch. She cooked and kept house so I could continue to bring in a salary and Chet could focus on running his racehorse rehabilitation business and the ranch.

"You're up and dressed early," she said.

"Morning. Yes." I eyed the clock on the wall, which read 7:00 a.m. "The woman from the Home of the Guardian Angel Orphanage is bringing Stevie over in an hour."

Rose pulled out a cast-iron Dutch oven from a cabinet. "This is the paper boy who just recently lost his parents?" She reached into the grain bin to measure out some flour for bread and then took a whiff of the pasty-gray bread starter she kept on the counter. She'd been nursing it for a couple of years.

"Yes," I said absently, tapping my finger on one of the telegrams lying on the table. "His father. His mother died a couple of years ago from illness." I raised my coffee cup to my lips and took a sip. The taste was bitter in my mouth.

My thoughts returned to my own father. If the person who'd sent the telegrams wasn't really my father, what did he want? And if he was my father, the same question applied. What did he want after so much time? Money? I shook my head and silently scoffed. Chet and I put everything we made, which wasn't a fortune by any stretch of the imagination, into the ranch. We had no money to spare.

"I'm happy to have the boy, but why is he coming here and not staying at the orphanage?" Rose asked.

I took a deep breath, pulling myself away from the telegram.

"He's despondent. Not eating. Fighting with the other children. Sister Margarite, who runs the orphanage, had heard of us and felt the boy would benefit from some meaningful ranch work and a situation where there are fewer children around. Also, he's somewhat familiar with the place, having delivered the paper here for the last year. It only made sense."

After moving to Los Angeles from New York City, Chet and I had purchased the ranch in Burbank, which we'd named *Rancho los Niños,* with the intention of providing a place of refuge for wayward and/or orphaned children. Having both suffered abandonment when we were young—me with the loss of my parents, and Chet when Rose had turned him over to an orphanage when he was just two, unable to properly care for him —we both felt called to help children in need. We'd obtained the necessary licensing from the state and currently had three children living with us: Ida, fourteen years old, Daniel at sixteen, and Susie, now eleven. Lizzy had recently left us to go live with her grandparents in England, and Stevie, at twelve years old, would be a great addition. I'd seen amazing growth in the other kids in recent months, so hopefully, he would find a connection with the children and be able to process his grief through the responsibilities of ranch life and working with animals.

"Well, I'm sure the boy will flourish with time," Rose said.

I smiled at her declaration. When I'd first met Rose, she'd been a sour-faced and stern woman who effused little warmth. In the past couple of years, I'd seen her soften and we had become close. Once pessimistic and skeptical, Rose now saw life in a different way, full of hope and joy—albeit a practical joy.

Susie entered the kitchen in a flurry, her eager face beaming and her strawberry-blond hair askew from sleep. "Gonna go feed the chickens and get the eggs." She grabbed an apple from the bowl on the kitchen table and rushed toward the door on the opposite side of the room to go outside.

"Good morning, Susie," I greeted her with a tone of admonition in my voice. We'd been having a recurring conversation about politely greeting people when entering a room.

She stopped in her tracks. "Oh. Yeah." She placed a finger at her lips. "Good morning, Grace. Good morning, Mrs. R."

Rose gave her a sideways glance and nodded, now busily working up some bread dough on the countertop.

"Thank you, Susie," I said with a smile. "Off you go."

She grinned and then bounded through the door that led to the barnyard, just as Ida entered the kitchen from the living room. She yawned and shuffled over to the cupboard, pulled out a mug, poured herself some coffee, and then plopped herself down in the chair next to mine. Unlike Susie, Ida was practically allergic to mornings and could barely speak until she'd had a cup of coffee.

"Morning," she groaned.

"Sleep well?" I asked.

Ida nodded, placing her elbows on the table. She rested her chin on the base of her palms, and her eyes drooped closed. She jumped when Daniel pushed through the living room door and into the kitchen. Full of vim and vigor, the boy was growing by the day. Over the past few months, his shoulders had filled out and he had lost the gangly look of a stick bug. He, too, grabbed himself a cup of coffee and stood next to the kitchen sink sipping it.

"Hey-yo," he greeted me. He reached over to where Rose had left the bread dough to get something out of the icebox, pinched off a piece, and popped it into his mouth.

I cringed—both at the fact that it probably tasted vile and because it was never a good idea to interfere with Rose's baking. Rose came back to the dough, glanced at it, then eyed Daniel, who was still chewing.

"For heaven's sake!" She playfully slapped him on the arm. "Breakfast will be ready at the usual time, eight thirty. Now go on out of my kitchen and do your chores."

He gave her a brief nod and came over to Ida, gently pulling her out of the chair. "Come on. The horses are waiting."

Ida groaned again.

"Bring your coffee, then." He picked up her cup and handed it to her before ushering her outside.

I turned my attention back to the telegrams.

"What's got you so pensive this morning?" Rose asked as she kneaded the bread dough.

I shook my head and sighed. "I don't know what to do about this latest telegram."

"You've been fretting over that second telegram for a week. What's the harm in calling? Aren't you curious?" She picked up the dough and slapped it on the counter.

"Curious, yes. Among other things." I uttered the last sentence under my breath.

I busied myself with setting the table for breakfast, then

some other mundane tasks while I fretted about whether or not to make the phone call. As it approached eight o'clock, I'd made up my mind.

Before I could think about it any longer, I picked up the telegram and pushed through the door into the living room. Biting a nail, I made my way to the entry hall where the phone rested on the new gossip table and bench I had acquired from one of Ambassador's sets. It was a little rickety but in good condition. I picked up the phone receiver and dialed.

A female voice answered. Startled, I hesitated.

"Hello?" the voice echoed through the receiver.

I cleared my throat. "I, uh . . . I'm looking for Peter Michelle."

"Just a sec," the voice said. The sound of heels tapping against the floor echoed through the phone. Then came a faint rapping, I assumed upon a door. Murmurings. Then more footsteps coming back toward the phone.

"Gracie?" A man's deep voice resonated on the other end.

My breath caught in my throat. No one had called me by that name except Sophia and, on the rare occasion, Flo. My parents had used the name, of course.

"How did you know it was me?" I asked.

"I haven't given the phone number to anyone else."

An uncomfortable silence followed.

"It's good to hear your voice," he said. "You sound so grown up. You must be, what now, twenty-four?"

"Yes." Suddenly, tears pricked at the back of my eyes. I pulled my lips between my teeth. I had so many questions I didn't know where to begin. Was this really him? I still found it so hard to believe.

"I'd like to see you." His voice quieted.

I raised a shaking hand to my temple, and my legs suddenly went watery. I leaned back against the wall. What would it be like to see him again? Would he greet me with outstretched arms, or would his reaction be more reserved? How would I respond?

"Where?" It was all I could manage.

"I'm at a boarding house on Sixth and Alvarado. There's a new diner nearby. I've heard it's pretty good. Called the Kitchen Café or something like that. I don't have a car or I'd—"

"No," I cut him off. I didn't want him coming to the ranch. Not yet. Not until I was sure. I wished Chet hadn't gone out of town. He and Joe Manetti, our neighbor and Chet's business partner, had gone to Mexico to look at some racehorses down there. He wasn't sure when he'd be back. Our farmhand, Ned, was running the ranch in his absence.

"It's okay. I'll meet you there." I was finding my legs again. "But I can't come today. I'm expecting someone. I can meet you there tomorrow after a meeting at work. One o'clock?"

"Yes, that sounds fine, darling."

My heart lurched. *Darling.* The word brought a torrent of memories flooding back, all crashing into one another like toy boats on a stormy sea. Kisses on scraped knees. Stories at bedtime. Laughter. Crying. Raised voices. Fear. Memories I wasn't prepared for. It had been too painful to remember, both the good and the bad times. I hung up the phone and pressed a trembling hand to my mouth.

Rose came from around the corner, drying her hands on a dishtowel. Our eyes locked, and she held out her arms to me and enfolded me in an embrace.

CHAPTER TWO

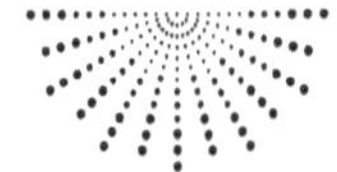

$\mathcal{A}$n hour later, the wonderful aromas of freshly baked bread, scrambled eggs, and bacon filled the kitchen. While Rose made the final preparations for breakfast, I poured the orange juice, my mind still occupied with the phone call I'd just had with my father. I couldn't let it consume me this morning because our new charge would be here at any minute and he would need my full attention.

The sound of knuckles rapping on the front door made me start.

"That must be Stevie." I looked up at Rose as I set the pitcher on the table.

I left the kitchen, and passing through the living room, I ran a hand over my bobbed hair, making sure all was in place.

I opened the front door to see a middle-aged, trim woman with round spectacles and dark hair with streaks of gray shot through it. It was combed tightly against her head and pulled back into a severe bun. She held a leather suitcase in one hand, and her other hand rested on Stevie's shoulder.

I'd always thought the boy looked like a pixie, with a tousled mop of red hair, large and expressive sage-green eyes, and a smattering of freckles that trailed from the bridge of his nose across his cheeks.

"Hello, Stevie." I gave him a bright smile. "It's good to see you."

The boy held out his hand and gave me a firm shake. "Hello." His eyes did not meet mine.

"I'm Celia Groves," the woman said. We, too, shook hands, and then I motioned for them to come inside.

They stepped up into the foyer.

"Come make yourselves at home." I directed my gaze at Stevie. "I hope you're hungry. Rose, our housekeeper, has just made a wonderful breakfast, and the other children will be in soon. They are outside doing their morning chores."

Stevie finally looked up at me with sad, puppy dog eyes. An ache bloomed in my heart.

"I know you've seen the outside of the house many times when you rode your bicycle up to the gate to deliver the paper, but how about I show you around?" I took the case from Miss Groves and set it down.

I held my arm out toward the dining room. "That's where we sit when we have lots of people over. We don't use the room often because we are all pretty casual around here." I pointed to a door. "That goes into the kitchen."

I then turned around and led them to my right. "Here is the living room. We spend a lot of time together here. That door there also leads to the kitchen."

We walked past the staircase and down a wide hallway. I pointed to the room at my right. "This is the den. The children like to play games or do their schoolwork in here. It's really their room. We don't worry about how messy it gets. If it gets too untidy, we just close the door." I chuckled.

Farther down the hallway, I led them into the large sunroom. "This is my favorite room in the house." I took in the room with its white wicker furniture, floral-print cushions, and the large picture windows framing the backyard, which was enclosed by a white picket fence. A large oak provided shade and a couple of swings for the kids. Beyond the yard to the south was an expanse of fields —alfalfa and Bermuda grasses that we cut and baled a couple of times a year. There were more fields to the east of the house.

"Isn't it lovely?" I remarked. Stevie remained silent but gave me a small smile.

"Now, upstairs and your room." I tousled his hair. When we reached the stairs, I pointed to his suitcase still in the entry way. "Might as well bring that up now."

Stevie strode over and picked it up.

The upper floor housed seven rooms, all complete with window seats provided by the gables. At one end of the floor, the west end, there was a large bedroom with an adjoining bathroom for Chet and me. Next to it was a smaller room that I had claimed as a studio where I worked on my own fashion line, which I'd named for my late sister. The other rooms lining the hallway on both sides of the stairwell were for the children. They each had their own room but shared a large bathroom, which caused occasional chaos in the mornings.

I led Stevie and Miss Groves to the east end of the hallway to a closed door.

"And this is your room." I opened the door and smiled, thinking of Lizzy, the last child to occupy this room. I missed her but was comforted by the fact that she seemed happy, even after all the trauma she'd gone through. Like me, she'd thought she'd lost everyone in her family, but through some investigating, we'd found out she hadn't. She had grandparents still living. Lizzy had written from England several times and seemed delighted with her new home and guardians.

Stevie stepped into the room and took a look around. I had replaced the pink floral quilt on the bed with something more masculine. The room was spacious and bright with a wardrobe, small bookcase, and desk that sat next to the window seat.

His eyes slid over to the bed. "I have my own room?"

I smiled. "Yes. All the children have their own rooms. It's important to have your own space—to study, to think, to dream. Don't you agree?"

He nodded slowly and went over to the bed and sat down. "I've never had my own room before. I slept on the screened porch of my parents' house, and at the orphanage . . ." His voice dropped off.

"Well," I said, "this is all yours. Do you like it?"

He gave a vigorous nod. "I'll say."

"How wonderful." Miss Groves scanned the room, beaming. "Sister Margarite told us your home was lovely, but I had no idea. You are so very generous."

I waved the compliment aside. "It's nothing fancy, but it works for us. Come over here, Stevie." I motioned toward the window, and he joined me. "See that little building there?" I pointed to an outbuilding toward the back of the house to the west. "That's the schoolroom. Miss Meyers, our teacher, is wonderfully clever and very nice. The children love her."

Stevie wrinkled his nose, and his lip curled in distaste.

"What is it?" I asked.

He'd gone positively pale and looked up at me with sad eyes. "I'm not that good at school."

I glanced at Miss Groves. She gave me a sympathetic smile and shook her head.

"That doesn't matter," I said, brightening my voice. "I'm sure there are lots of things you are good at. Book learning isn't everything, you know."

He shrugged, still looking peaked.

"Now, how about some breakfast?" I changed the subject. "Will you join us, Miss Groves? Rose always makes plenty of food."

She raised a hand and shook her head. "No, I must get back. But thank you."

We went back downstairs and after I showed her out, I led Stevie into the kitchen, which was alive with activity as the children had come in from their chores. Daniel was at the sink washing his hands while Ida and Susie were seated at the table, giggling about something.

"Take off your hat, young sir," Rose said to Daniel as he wiped his hands on a dishtowel. He swiped his cap off his head and hung it on a hook by the door. All eyes turned in our direction as Stevie and I stood in the doorway. I set my hands on his shoulders for reassurance and made the introductions.

"You can sit by me." Susie lifted her teddy bear off the chair next to hers. "Teddy can sit in my lap."

At eleven, Susie was a little old to be so attached to a teddy bear, but she'd suffered a great deal of trauma in her young life so we let her be. We reasoned she'd eventually grow out of her dependence as she became more confident.

"Want some coffee?" Ida asked.

Stevie wrinkled his nose and shook his head.

"Don't mind her," Daniel said. "Ida only drinks coffee because she thinks it makes her look older."

"Oh, hush!" Ida narrowed her eyes at him.

I led Stevie to the table, and he sat down next to Susie. She gave him a gap-toothed grin.

Rose set a stack of pancakes on the table. Accompanying the delicious-smelling cakes was a jar of maple syrup, another full pitcher of fresh-squeezed orange juice, a bowl of scrambled eggs and potatoes, and a plate of sizzling bacon.

The kids tucked in—all but Stevie.

"Well, go on," Rose encouraged. "Can't be shy around here."

"Yeah," Ida agreed. "You better get it while you can or Daniel will eat it all."

Stevie served himself a modest portion of food. He ate

quietly while the other kids joked, laughed, and teased one another. He sure seemed downcast. Of course, who could blame him? He'd just lost his only parent.

His mood took me back to when Sophia and I had learned of our parents' death. I had been in a state of shock and denial while Sophia had turned to anger. It had been a terrible time.

Now, supposedly, my father was back. And the denial went the other way around.

It can't possibly be him.

I stuck pretty close to the ranch for the rest of the morning to make sure Stevie was settling in all right. I'd alerted my assistant, Clara, to the fact I would not be in to work until the afternoon. We were still waiting on further casting for the picture so my schedule was a bit more flexible at the moment.

An hour or so after the children had gone to the schoolroom for their lessons, I peeked in on them. Miss Meyers, our teacher, was at the chalkboard with Susie working out some math problems while Ida and Daniel sat at the back of the room, both reading. The differences in age among the kids made things challenging for Miss Meyers, but she was an excellent educator and I had no doubt she would rise to the occasion.

I stood at the back of the room near the door and observed. Stevie was watching Susie and Miss Meyers, his elbows on the desk and his chin resting in his hands. Even from where I stood I could see his disengagement. He appeared to be either bored or distracted—I couldn't tell which. Susie, an excellent student who loved learning, paid rapt attention as usual.

I slipped away and went back to the house with a degree of uneasiness fluttering in my chest. It was in my nature to want to make everything all right with the children—and Chet, and Rose, and friends and colleagues. I wanted to fix things for poor Stevie, but I knew he had to work out his grief on his own terms. It was the only way he would heal.

CHAPTER THREE

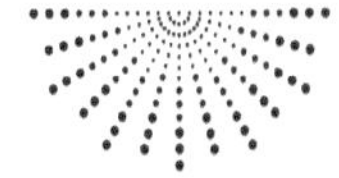

 arrived at Ambassador Films a few hours later.

"Are you all right, Miss Baklanova?" I asked the statuesque beauty who stood before me on the dais in front of a three-way mirror. My assistant, Clara Stapleton, busily pulled straight pins from the seams of the eighteenth-century sack-backed gown the actress donned.

Valentina Baklanova, with her gossamer hair and incandescent emerald eyes, could only be described as a modern-day Aphrodite. She gave me a tight smile, and then her porcelain features crumpled.

"I'm sorry." She blinked and fanned her face with her hand in an attempt to wave away tears. "May I sit down? I'm feeling faint."

Her Russian accent was strong, and I often thought she sounded like her tongue was fighting for purchase around a handful of marbles.

"Of course," I said, taking hold of her hand, hoping she wouldn't collapse with all the pins still in the dress. "Clara?"

"Almost done," she said, working faster.

Clara was a small, eighteen-year-old woman with dark, shortly bobbed hair, curious, bright eyes, and a pert rosebud mouth, and was the niece of Barney and Alice Steinberg, the owners and studio heads of Ambassador Films. She was currently attending Wolfe's Design College, where I'd received my degree, and needed to complete an apprenticeship, so she'd ended up in wardrobe under my tutelage. She was clever and efficient, and was proving to be invaluable to me. I knew she could handle managing the seamstresses and sketch girls on her own, allowing me to spend my time with other tasks, like design and mapping out the wardrobe plot.

At last, the fabric fell away from Miss Baklanova's body, leaving the stomacher, corset, and wide-hooped pannier exposed.

While Clara whisked away the pieces of the dress, I untied the stomacher and tucked it under my arm. I then untied the satin ribbons holding the pannier together and helped the actress step out of it. Quickly, I loosened the stays of the corset at the back, unhooked it along the front, and peeled it off her, leaving her only in a white cotton shift. With my free hand, I helped her over to the club chairs next to the pedestal on which she had stood.

"Would you like some water?" I asked.

"Please," she said, taking in a deep breath. Setting the stomacher and corset on my desk, I grabbed hold of a coffee cup from a side table and filled it with water from the water cooler. I took it over to her.

"Here you go. Perhaps we pulled the corset strings too tight? I'll make sure to be more careful next time."

Miss Baklanova took a sip of water and shook her head. She wrapped both hands around the cup and lowered it to her lap.

"It's not that . . . Well, perhaps it was, but that's not what has me upset."

"Oh, I see." I sat down in the other chair. The two were angled toward each other flanking a side table. "Anything I can do to help?"

"Actually—" her eyes flicked up to meet mine "—I've been

meaning to ask you for last couple of days, but I don't want to bother," she said in broken English. "I know you're very busy with preparations for film."

And I was. As lead designer for the latest project, *Le Coquin*, I was responsible for the design and manufacture of all the costumes. I oversaw the patternmakers, seamstresses, and sketch girls.

Curious, I furrowed my brow. "What is it?"

She looked down at the cup in her hands and then took another sip of water. "It's *moya tetushka*. How do you say . . . erm, my aunt?"

"Your aunt, yes." I nodded.

"She's in hospital. For one week now." Miss Baklanova looked up at me. "She is . . . She is very bad. Getting worse. Doctor says she may never wake again."

"Oh my. I'm so sorry, Miss Baklanova." I reached out and took her hand.

"Please. Call me Valentina." She squeezed my hand. "We are friends, no?"

I squeezed hers back. "Yes. Very well, Valentina."

A brief smile flitted across her face but then vanished, giving way to a quivering chin. "*Moya tetushka* was beaten."

My mouth fell open. "Beaten? By whom?"

"I don't know." Her voice cracked. "I live with her—in her house. When Anton and I—my, I think you say, *fiancé*?"

I nodded my encouragement.

"When we come back from Europe, just one week ago, we go to house and everything was torn apart. Furniture upside down, papers everywhere, kitchen a mess. And *moya tetushka*, she is on the floor, like she's dead."

I gasped. "Oh my goodness! How awful. Did you call the police?"

"Yes. We call right away. They come and bring ambulance.

Ambulance takes her to hospital." Tears quietly escaped from her long sable lashes and fell to her cheeks.

"Have the police found who did this?"

She sniffed and shook her head. "No. They say they are looking but . . . nothing."

I leaned back in my chair, stunned. "That is just terrible, Valentina. Who would do such a thing? And why? Do the police think it was a robbery?"

She looked up at me again with hardness in her eyes. "Nothing was taken."

I leaned forward and rested my elbows on my knees. "Did your aunt have any enemies? Was there anyone who would want to do her harm?"

She vehemently shook her head. "She was—is—kindest woman. Helps the neighbors, reads to children of neighbors, bakes sweets for old people. She is saint, *moya tetushka*."

We sat in silence for a few moments, the only sound the ticking of the clock on my desk. I then remembered she said I could possibly do something for her.

"How can I help, Valentina?"

She pushed herself up from the chair and went over to the silk changing screen. She reemerged carrying her purse and sat down again, quietly opening it.

"I found this in the house a few days ago." She held out a circular bronze pin about a square inch in diameter. The image depicted was of a wreath of wheat with ribbon wrapped around it. At the bottom was a blazing sun, in the center was a globe with a hammer crossed with some kind of farm implement, and at the top was a five-sided star.

"What does this mean?" I asked.

She shrugged.

"And you are sure it did not belong to your aunt?"

"I have never seen this before. Whoever did this horrible thing must have dropped it."

I raised my eyebrows. "It's a clue. The police have to see this. Why have you not taken it to them?"

"I will. I wanted you to see first."

I looked up from the pin and met her gaze. "Me? Why me?"

"You are much skilled at investigation. I saw in newspaper how you found killer of Edward Travis and those women. You proved innocence of that young girl accused of the murders."

It was true. I had found who was responsible for the murder of the famous Hollywood director, and two of the women closely associated with him. In doing so, I had exonerated Lizzy Moore of the crime, the young girl who'd come to live with us at our ranch.

"I want you to find who did this to *moya tetushka* and why," Valentina continued.

"Oh, Valentina, I—" I stared down at the pin and a wave of overwhelm sent my mind spinning. Production of *Le Coquin* was scheduled to begin in two weeks, and I had a ton of work to do. Plus, with Stevie having just arrived at the ranch . . . Needless to say my plate was very full. And I had my own safety to consider. Whoever had done this to Valentina's aunt was obviously violent.

"Please," she whispered.

I met her gaze again, panic rising in my chest. The look in her face nearly broke my heart. But how could I possibly say yes?

"I'm not a private investigator," I explained. "My husband is—well, was. He's retired and running a new and very demanding business. In fact, he's in Mexico right now. I'm sure the police will do all they can to find this person—or people."

"I don't want police. I don't want your husband," she said. "I want you. I trust you."

I pulled my lower lip between my teeth. I wanted to remind her that we'd only met a few short weeks ago.

"Felicity say you don't give up," she continued. "You also found killer of your sister."

Dear Felicity, my very best friend . . . Well, we hadn't started out that way a few years ago back when we met in New York City. She had been the girlfriend of Joe Marciano, a mobster who had kidnapped me to get back at my guardian and manager, Florenz Ziegfeld, Jr. At first, Felicity had been threatened by me, thought I would replace her as Joe's paramour, which couldn't have been further from the truth. The man was a snake. To get rid of me, she'd helped me with my plan to escape. As it turned out, Marciano had nearly killed her for her interference and she had retaliated in a big way. The experience had bonded us and we've been hand in glove ever since.

So when it came to Felicity bragging about me to Valentina, I knew she meant well, but she had really put me in a bind. She knew I was working on this film. She had opted out of the film as a set designer because her interior design business had picked up. And yes, I had found my sister's killer—the same Joe Marciano who was thankfully no longer on this Earth—and I'd also seen to it that his henchman, who'd administered the poison to my sister, was rotting in some prison.

I appreciated Valentina's faith in me, but I simply could not help her. I opened my mouth to protest when she took hold of my hand.

"Promise you'll think about it. Please."

I sighed. I didn't want to give her any false hope but found myself nodding in agreement. I suppose it wouldn't hurt to think about it.

LATER, Clara and I went out for a quick bite to eat. We sat at the counter of Marcia's, a nearby drugstore and eatery. Having lived in Mexico for several years, Marcia specialized in tantalizing Mexican dishes, and the place was a favorite of Clara's. It's café-like atmosphere reminded me of my upcoming meeting with my father and an uneasiness settled in my stomach.

We each ordered a plate of seafood tacos, and Clara tucked into hers with relish. I, on the other hand, picked at the corn tortilla and shuffled my fork back and forth through the rice piled neatly on the side of the plate.

"Not hungry?" she asked.

I shook my head. "No. I have a lot on my mind, I'm afraid."

"About the film? You needn't worry. I've got things in the wardrobe room pretty organized. And I've really got a handle on the fitting schedule. As Timothy casts the movie, I've got time slots set aside for the new cast members. I also—"

I held up a hand to stop her. "I have every confidence in you, Clara. Really. It has nothing to do with the film. It's other stuff. Personal stuff." I picked up a taco and took a bite.

"Oh, I see. Anything I can do to help?"

I set the taco down. "No. It has to do with family."

"Trouble in the marriage?"

I nearly choked mid-chew, surprised at her boldness.

"Sorry," she said, her face coloring. "I shouldn't have asked. I need to hold my tongue. Sometimes things I'm thinking just shoot out of my mouth. Aunt Alice is always telling me to proceed with more caution when in conversation. She's right, but I just can't help it sometimes."

"It's all right, Clara." I said, assuring her. "My marriage is fine. It's my father, actually."

"I see." I could tell she wanted to hear more but was heeding her aunt's advice. I didn't see the harm in telling her about it. In fact, talking about it helped.

"I grew up thinking my parents were dead, and I've recently learned my father is alive."

Her mouth full of taco, she pressed her fingers against her

lips, and her eyes went wide behind the heavy spectacles she always wore.

"Oh my God," she said after swallowing. "You're kidding."

I shook my head. "I'm not. It's pretty surreal. I'm supposed to meet with him tomorrow."

"How exciting!" She wiped her mouth with her napkin and then scrutinized my face. "You are excited, aren't you?"

I smiled. "I'm not sure how I feel. I still can't believe it."

"Wow. And your mom?"

"Still dead, as far as I know." I realized the statement sounded a little callous, but my feelings were all over the place.

Her usually sunny demeanor vanished. "I'm sorry," she said. "My mom died last year."

"Oh no." Though her words sent a pang through my heart for her, it was a bit of a relief to get out of my own wallowing and focus on someone else's feelings for the moment. "I had no idea. I'm so sorry."

"She worked in a hospital. She contracted the flu, and it killed her."

I laid my hand over hers. "Clara, that's awful."

"Yeah." She stared at her second, half-eaten taco, her appetite seeming to go the way of mine suddenly. "Aunt Alice and Uncle Barney really stepped in to help my dad. He's been a bit of a mess. Has always been a bit of a mess, really. He isn't that interested in me. Never has been. My mom was my rock. We were very close." Her eyes welled with tears.

I thought of my relationship with my own mother but couldn't conjure up feelings of closeness. Sophia had filled that mothering role for me most of my life, even though she had been only a year and ten months older than me.

"I'm glad your father is alive," she said, taking off her glasses to wipe away the tears that had settled on her cheeks. She used her napkin to dab at her eyes.

I smiled at her. She'd probably give anything to have her mother back. Why didn't I feel more grateful? More elated?

"What was the matter with Miss Baklanova?" Clara asked, changing the subject. "She seemed upset."

"Oh, she's having her share of family troubles, too. Like the rest of us, it seems." I didn't feel comfortable divulging all Valentina had shared with me, nor her request that I help find whoever had nearly killed her aunt. Aside from not wanting to betray a confidence, it was too much to contemplate with everything else on my mind. I shouldn't have said I'd even think about helping her.

~

MY RETURN to work presented me with the uncomfortable opportunity to turn her down. After I'd attended a meeting with Timothy and the writers, I went back to the wardrobe room.

As I walked in, Clara caught my gaze and came over to me. "Miss Baklanova is waiting to see you." She tilted her head in the direction of my office. "She has a man with her." She arched her brows at me like this news was of some importance.

"She's back?"

Clara nodded.

When I walked into my office, Valentina was sitting in one of the club chairs by the three-way mirror, accompanied by a strikingly handsome man sitting in the other. I guessed him to be about ten years her senior. He wore a finely tailored navy-blue suit with a crisp white shirt and maroon tie. A gray homburg rested on his knee.

"Hello." I entered the room and placed my handbag, sketch pads, and notebook on the desk.

Valentina and the gentleman rose to greet me.

"Grace Michelle, this is Anton Belsky, my fiancé," Valentina said, laying a hand on his arm.

The man, not much taller than Valentina, strode over to me and took my hand.

"How do you do?" I extended my hand for a handshake but was instead given a brush of his lips across my knuckles. His waxed mustache felt stiff against my skin, and heat rose to my face at his forwardness.

"It's a pleasure to meet you." He made direct eye contact. His heavy-lidded eyes were large and brown. "Valentina has spoken highly of you."

Although not as marked as Valentina's, I could distinctly hear the same warbling quality of a Russian accent in his voice.

"Same," I said with a nod of my head.

"I've read about you in the papers." He smiled at me, running the brim of his homburg between his fingers. "Quite impressive. And you are a skilled designer, as well."

"Oh, well—" I stammered, never comfortable with compliments.

"Valentina says she would like you to help her find the criminals who assaulted poor Anna Ivanova, her aunt."

I swallowed, hating what I was about to say. "Well, yes, she has. It's a horrible thing that has happened to Miss Ivanova." I turned to Valentina. "But I think you'd be better off with the police. I really don't—"

Mr. Belsky cleared his throat. "I'm prepared to pay you. Handsomely." He considered Valentina with admiration in his eyes. "Anything for my intended." She smiled up at him and then directed her gaze at me.

Anxiety welled up in my chest. If I could, I would gladly help without being paid, but I simply couldn't. I did not have the time, nor the energy. I had other, more pressing responsibilities and a long-lost father to contend with. Although, Chet and I could use the money. We had enough to get by, but our budget was tight.

No, that didn't matter. We'd be fine. We always were.

"But, Miss Bakla—Valentina," I said, my gaze sliding over to her, "told me the police are already looking into the matter."

"Yes, apparently they are," he said with dubiousness in his voice. "But it seems it is not a priority for them. We want extra help. We have every faith you can find these brutes."

I shook my head, shocked at their utter confidence in me. I was not a professional. The cases I'd solved had a direct impact on me and the people I loved. I'd done it purely out of fierce protectiveness. This was something else altogether. It was too much.

"I'm so sorry, but I really must decline," I said to Mr. Belsky. "Your offer is very generous, but I—"

He held up a hand. "No need to explain, Miss Michelle. I understand, but the offer still stands if you change your mind."

I suppressed a sigh. He was not making this easy. I looked at Valentina, and my heart wrenched at the disappointment on her face. I gave her an apologetic smile, and she returned it with a slight, sad upturning of her lips. She really would be better off working with the police on this. I hoped she would come to see it.

She turned to Mr. Belsky. "Grace and I have meeting with Timothy and the Steinbergs about the film. Pick me up in one hour?"

He wrapped an arm around her shoulders. "Of course, darling." He then turned his attention to me. "Miss Michelle. It was a pleasure to meet you."

"I'll walk you out." Valentina took his arm.

I watched them leave the office with a heavy heart, but at least the matter was settled.

CHAPTER FOUR

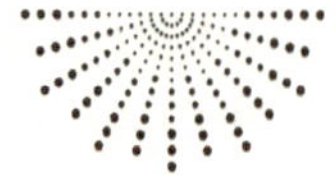

The next day, I drove my Birmingham four-door sedan down Sunset Boulevard on my way to the Kitchen Café, my heart in my throat and my stomach doing flip-flops. I drove slowly, my mind racing with thoughts of what the meeting with my father would be like. I glanced in my side-view mirror and noticed a dark-green car with a dent in the right fender following me very closely. The driver must be in a hurry. Without thinking, I pressed my foot harder on the gas pedal to speed up a little.

I was probably driving so slowly because I was filled with trepidation at meeting this man who claimed to be my dad. Would I even recognize him? How had he changed? I remembered him as tall—all wiry with dark-brown hair that he wore parted in the middle and slicked back with pomade. His hazel eyes, more gold than green, had flecks of brown in them, and the skin at his temples crinkled merrily when he smiled. But I couldn't recall his voice, or his laugh, or if he had been moody or consistently cheerful. Many memories of him—or really, of my childhood at all—had been locked away.

Through the dreams I'd had of Sophia over the past several

months and my informational yet always disquieting experiences with the spiritualist and medium, Lenora Lange, I'd learned that I'd experienced a great deal of trauma in my early life that I had repressed. The most chilling realization was that, in a fit of madness, my mother had come after me with a knife. The fated "weekend getaway" Sophia and I had thought our parents had been taking when they'd left that fateful Friday afternoon had turned out to be my father taking my mother to an asylum to have her committed. I'd buried those memories deep in the vault of my mind. No stranger to childhood trauma himself, Chet reasoned I had done so to protect myself.

What I did remember of my father was that he often had been absent. But on the rare occasions he was home, he would join in the fantastical games Sophia and I played in the yard. He'd chase us, growling like a bear, and we'd squeal in delight as we tried to get away from him. Whenever he caught us, he'd lift us into his arms, sometimes together, and swing us round and round until we were dizzy.

My favorite memory of him was when he'd read to me before tucking me into bed. In those few remembrances, he had made me feel so safe, so secure—like nothing could hurt me. And in the end, he had protected me from my mother. He had stepped in front of her when she'd gone after me with the knife, preventing her from striking me.

I squeezed my eyes shut at the recollection.

When I popped them open, a car whooshed by in front of me from out of nowhere, speeding along on a perpendicular street. In that split second, I realized I was about to run a stop sign. I slammed on the brakes, looking into my side mirror. The car following me had dropped back and, thankfully, was not in danger of hitting me. My car jerked to a stop, my arms braced against the wheel and my heart racing with adrenaline. I shook my head, rattling my imaginings free. I had to pay attention.

I turned right and headed down Alvarado toward Sixth, my

eyes focused on the road and my surroundings. Diligently, I again looked in the side mirror. The same green car was still behind me. I let go a rattling breath. The person behind the wheel must think me a horrible driver.

Finally, I reached Sixth Street and turned left. I was familiar with the area, as one of the seamstresses who worked at Ambassador lived near here. She'd also told me about the new diner. I spotted the marquis above the restaurant on the opposite side of the street. I had to park half a block away, but I didn't mind. It would give me a little more time to collect myself before meeting my long-dead father.

I parked the car and then opened my handbag to retrieve my powder compact. Once I had it, I raised my head to see the green car that had been following me pass by slowly and then pull into a parking spot on the next block. A feeling of unease bloomed in my gut, but I didn't know if it stemmed from the nervousness at meeting my father or from the green car. I took a deep breath. Of course the anxiety came from the fact that I was about to come face-to-face with the man who, with his passing, had left a hole in my heart as wide as the Hudson River.

I opened the compact and took a quick look in the mirror. I dabbed some powder onto my nose, my forehead, and my chin. Staring into the reflection of my green eyes, the compact shaking in my trembling fingers, I summoned an image of Sophia for strength. The vision I conjured of her—her curly auburn hair lit by the sun and swirling around her head and a serene smile of assurance on her face—melted my shoulders and instilled in me the courage I needed.

"Well, here goes nothing," I whispered, straightening my favorite burgundy cloche hat to perfection. I took another deep breath, dropped the compact back into my handbag, stepped out of the car, and made my way across the street.

I opened the door to the diner and went inside. A long counter with about twelve stools stood to one side of the rectangular room, and a row of wooden booths graced the other. A man at the farthest booth rose, his eyes riveted on me.

My heart stuttered when he gently raised his hand in greeting. It was a familiar gesture, something he always did when posing for a photo, as if saying hello to the camera. Sophia and I used to tease him about it. He was more stooped than I'd remembered, and his frame seemed smaller. His face, though bearded, had a gauntness to it that was startling and unfamiliar, but I was still some distance away. Unable to believe my eyes, my mouth went dry and my feet rooted to the floor, but at the same time, my knees weakened as if they would give way and send me to the ground. My breath hitched in my throat.

Oh, Sophia. How I wish you were here to see this.

He gently beckoned me over. My feet were like lead, and the short walk to the end of the room felt like miles. I kept my eyes trained on his face, afraid he would vanish into the air like a puff of smoke. He held out his hands to me.

"Gracie," he whispered. His eyes, darker than I remembered, were rimmed with moisture. Cautiously, I placed my hands in his.

"You are so beautiful," he said. He pulled me toward him and planted a dry kiss on each cheek, the roughness of his beard tickling my skin.

I swallowed, feeling as if I were in a dream.

In slow motion, he motioned to the booth where he'd been sitting. It was only then that I noticed a woman was sitting there.

She had dark-blond hair, delicate features, and eyes the color of cornflowers. My eyes were drawn to the beauty mark slightly above the corner of her mouth. She scooted out of the booth and stood next to my father. She was diminutive, petite. They glanced at each other with a look that could only be classified as adoring.

"This is Madeleine," my father said. "My wife."

She held a hand out to me. "It's such a pleasure to meet you, *ma chérie,*" she said.

I stared at her, a little startled she'd use such an endearment having never met me.

His wife. But my mother was his wife. The sinking feeling came back into my knees, and I grabbed hold of the back of the booth for support. My father lurched forward and took my other elbow to steady me.

He had a wife. How long had they been married? Thoughts of him living a wonderful life, falling in love, remarrying, and living in comfort while Sophia and I had suffered on the streets of New York soured in my stomach. I swallowed down the bile that threatened to come up.

"Sit down, Gracie."

I sank into the booth and rested my forehead in my gloved fingertips.

My father was alive. And he left us alone.

The muscles in my jaw tensed. I raised my eyes to see that they had both sat down again.

My father looked at me pensively. "This must be a shock," he said. "You've gone quite pale."

Mute, I merely nodded.

He motioned for the waiter to attend us. "Please bring some water," he said when the man arrived. "And more coffee."

The waiter nodded and left.

"I'm sorry," I finally croaked. "I just— How did you— How long—"

He reached across the table and patted my hand. "I'll explain," he said.

～

MY MIND WAS full of so many questions. The waiter brought my water, and Madeleine's and my father's coffee, and asked if we wanted anything to eat. My stomach was in knots and my chest reverberating with a slow burn of outrage so I declined, but they each ordered a sandwich.

I sipped the water, intently watching my father's face as he spoke to the waiter. I suddenly recalled that although he was a presence larger than life in my child's memories, he had always been soft spoken, his words measured and thoughtful. He'd often pause mid-sentence as if making sure his words conveyed his meaning accurately. And he did so now. But his appearance was so altered. He must have been, what, forty-five years of age? But he looked a decade older and his eyes flitted about with nervousness.

When the waiter left, he focused his attention on me and opened his mouth to speak when I stopped him.

"Why now?" I blurted. "Why have you contacted me now and not when I really needed you? When Sophia needed you. She's dead, you know." My jaw tightened again, and my throat constricted, causing a pain that was difficult to swallow.

His gaze dropped to the coffee cup in front of him, and his hands started to tremble. He balled them into fists to quiet them. "I read about Sophia," he said quietly.

"You knew," I scoffed. He knew, and yet he hadn't reached out to me—to comfort me, to mourn with me. "I don't understand," I ground out.

He held his trembling hands up as if to placate me. "I think I need to go back to the train accident," he said. "I hope to help you understand."

I crossed my arms at my waist and shot a look at Madeleine. This woman, this stranger who had replaced my mother. She gave me a weak smile but couldn't hold my gaze.

"Do you know why we left that weekend?" he asked me.

A pain stabbed through my heart. "Yes. It was Mother. You were taking her away. She was sick. Mad."

He nodded. "Yes. She had put you girls in danger. Especially you. I couldn't have that." His eyes softened when my gaze met his. I wanted to stay in my anger, but instead, sadness overtook it at the memory. My breath hitched in my throat, and I swallowed.

"They thought I was dead." He dropped his gaze to the table. "The medics who arrived at the scene of the train accident. But, apparently, as they were moving me, they noticed I was alive, but barely. I was unconscious for many months in the hospital. After I regained consciousness, they kept me there for a little over a year. I had to learn how to eat again, speak again, care for myself again. For all intents and purposes, I should have died."

Madeleine reached over and laid her hand on his.

"When I was released," he continued, "the first thing I did was set out to find you and your sister. But it was as if you'd vanished from the Earth. I had no money—all our savings had been spent on bringing me back to life—and I had no employment so I couldn't hire anyone to help me."

His gaze traveled to the counter and then met mine. "I don't know if you remember, but the house we lived in was not ours. We were renting while saving to buy. So I didn't even have the house to sell for any kind of income." He sniffed and cleared his throat. "Anyway, I was heartbroken. Despondent. I started drinking—heavily. There are spans of time I don't remember. What I do remember is that I wished I was dead. And I believed that wherever you girls were, you were better off without me."

I took in his words but distanced my mind and heart to them. They were too painful to absorb completely. *Better off without him?* I knew he meant he'd loathed himself, that he thought he wasn't good enough to be a parent to us, but it rang of an excuse. Outrage threatened to break my resolve to listen, but I squelched it down.

He closed his eyes, shaking his head. Shame emanated off him in waves, and I felt my anger give. But only a little.

He blinked his eyes open. "I took what little money I had and went to Europe, to join the war effort over there. This was a couple of years before the United States entered the war."

He stopped to sip his coffee. My arms ached from holding them so tight against my torso. I released my grip, folded my hands, and settled them on the table.

Then he carried on. "It seemed as if I would be granted my death wish, as I was injured in 1917. Gravely. Again, I was confined to a hospital. This time in France. I had endured a spine injury, and—" He winced as if remembering the pain.

Madeleine reached up and put an arm around his shoulder. He took in a deep breath and then let it out slowly, comforted by her touch.

"Suffice it to say, I remained in the hospital until 1922. It's where I met Madeleine. She is a nurse." He looked over at her, and they shared a smile.

I watched in fascination. That he could seem to love someone so dearly—aside from my mother—was strange to me. It gave me an uneasy sensation in my stomach, as though I'd just received a punch to the gut. He had found happiness. Love. Comfort. But where had that left Sophia? She'd been broken by hardship, by survival, by heartbreak. She hadn't gotten a second chance—or a third as in his case. The tension returned to my neck and shoulders.

"When did you find out about Sophia?" I asked, still wanting explanations. "She died in 1920." My words came out clipped and hard.

He nodded, indulging me. "Her fame was known in Europe, although to my knowledge she never traveled there."

"She didn't," I informed him curtly.

"News of her was often in the papers. Her death was a terrible tragedy."

A tragedy? I leaned forward and looked him squarely in the eyes, my blood pressure rising. "She was murdered." I said the words slowly, emphatically.

"Yes," he said. "And you found her killer. You gave her justice. You made me proud, Gracie."

I blinked, and my mouth fell open. He was proud of me? He had no right to enjoy that privilege. Had he not given up on us, on himself, we wouldn't have had to endure such hardships. Sophia might have still been alive.

"Believe me," I said, my voice trembling with anger. I tried to keep it in check. "I felt no pride in the act. I was nearly killed myself." I pointed my finger at him, ready to deliver a torrent of what had transpired. He had known about her—about us—and yet, he hadn't reached out? It was incomprehensible. Reprehensible. "You have no idea what—" Suddenly, a warm and tingling sensation oozed over the top of my right shoulder. A vision of Sophia standing next to me, her hand resting there, flashed through my mind, and I gasped.

"Grace?" Madeleine leaned over the table toward me. I glanced over at her and could see genuine concern in her eyes.

I shook off the sensation. "I'm fine." I settled myself again but couldn't say more in the moment. A thousand emotions held my tongue. Or was it Sophia?

The waiter came over and set their sandwiches on the table.

Grateful for the momentary reprieve, I struggled to gather myself. The waiter left, and the silence continued. I took another sip of my water and then set the glass down slowly.

"You knew of Sophia's death," I said. "You knew of me, knew where I was. Why did you not reach out to me?" I implored, still not understanding, not accepting his excuses.

He gave a sigh of resignation. "I am sorry. Truly, I am. I—" His hands started to tremble again. He reached up and rubbed his fingers over his forehead as if it pained him. "I'm not right—not fit. I'm not right in my head."

Madeleine laid her hand on his arm again and looked over at me. "It's shell shock. He suffers greatly."

"I felt I was not fit to be a father, that I would only bring you pain. You and your sister had made something of yourselves. You did that without me, without your mother. I felt it was better if I remained dead to you. I didn't want to hold you back," he said, his eyes brimming with moisture again.

I leaned against the back of the booth, his words finally sinking in. A sudden wave of compassion and understanding rolled over me. I was not a parent, biologically speaking, but I would do anything I felt was in the best interest of the children in my care. He had thought he would be a burden to us. He'd figured he was doing us a favor, sparing us from further anguish. He had been wrong—oh, so wrong—but he'd felt he was doing the right thing. He really was broken.

"I see." It was all I could manage to say, but my anger had melted away, leaving only pity in its wake.

Suddenly, the sound of a glass shattering on the floor echoed in the café. My father's eyes went wide and wild, and the color drained from his lips. His hand gripped the side of the table, and the minor trembling in his body turned to violent shaking. He seemed about to jump up from his seat when Madeleine grabbed hold of his arm. She set her handbag on the table and glanced over at me. "There is a syringe in there. Please get it out," she said quietly but with urgency.

My father's nostrils flared, and his jaw flexed with the clenching of his teeth.

I rifled through the bag until I found the syringe. I handed it to Madeleine. In a swift motion, she jabbed the needle in the upper part of his arm, right through his shirtsleeve. I stared in amazement.

Within a few seconds, the expression on his face softened. He closed his eyes, and his body relaxed. Madeleine patted his arm and put the syringe back into her purse.

"Is he all right?" I asked, mystified by this experience.

She nodded. "He will be, but we will have to go. He will need to rest."

"What was that? That you gave him?"

She looked at me with sympathy in her eyes. "It's morphine. I'm afraid he's quite dependent on it. I have been trying to ween him off it, but with the weeks of travel and the anticipation of seeing you, and . . . Well, he's been under some duress."

Morphine. I quickly looked around, hoping no one had seen her give him the injection.

"You realize that's illegal in this country," I whispered. I had no idea if it was legal or not in Europe, but here, the government was really cracking down on the use of opiates.

Her face paled. "We—um—we've found a doctor. He prescribed it for pain." She hastily put the syringe back in her purse.

My father opened his eyes, and they were filled with a placid serenity.

Madeleine motioned for the waiter to come to the table. "May we take the sandwiches with us, please?" she asked.

"Certainly," he said. "I'll get them wrapped up for you." He took their plates away.

"I'm sorry." She smiled at me. "We will have to continue the visit another time."

"Of course." I glanced at my father again. His eyes focused on nothing, and there was an eerie vacancy in his expression.

Madeleine opened her handbag and pulled out a dollar bill. She set it on the table and added two nickels for the tip.

"Can I give you a lift?" I asked. "My automobile is just—"

She shook her head. "No. The boarding house where we are staying isn't far from here. The walk will do him good."

Chet had told me of many soldiers' dependence on various drugs—cocaine to keep them awake and energized for fighting, and alcohol and other depressive drugs to calm them or help them sleep. I said a quick prayer of thanks that Chet, as a soldier, had never fallen victim to a dependence on these things. In fact, he had never even smoked and rarely drank alcohol.

My father gave me a broad smile. His head moved wobblily on his shoulders, as though he'd had too much to drink and it would snap off his neck.

"Gracie." He pointed at me. "You are just as beautiful as—" he hesitated, as if collecting his thoughts "—as I remembered."

Tearing my gaze away from my father in his inebriated state, I glanced at her. "I can give you a ride, it's no trouble."

"Really, it's best if we walk."

The waiter appeared with a brown bag. Madeleine handed him the dollar and ten cents. He nodded with a smile and left the table.

"Come, Peter," she said. "Let's get you back to the house so you can rest."

Picking up the bag from the table, she then nudged him out of the booth, and I scooted out myself.

"Well, this has been—" I started, suddenly feeling very awkward. How did I say goodbye? Did I shake his hand? Give him a hug? He answered my quandary by taking hold of my elbow and giving it a squeeze. Perhaps he felt the same awkwardness.

"I'd like to see you again," he said, his words coming out slow and even more measured than before, as if he had trouble wrapping his tongue around them. "I'd like to see where you work. With all those movie stars. And your husband. He's a private investigator?"

"Retired. And yes, that would be nice," I agreed a little reluctantly.

Madeleine smiled warmly at me. "We'll be in touch."

I hung back a moment as she guided him down the aisle, around the busboy who was sweeping the broken glass into a dustpan. I followed them to the front door.

Madeleine and my father stepped out onto the street, and I watched them go, my mind and my heart full of conflicting thoughts and emotions. Madeleine, with her arm through his, turned and gave me a small wave. They walked away leaving me with the feeling that this meeting, this new reality of my father alive and walking the Earth, had all been a dream.

I went to the door and happened to glance down at a nearby table with a newspaper and dirty dishes on it. The paper was opened to an interior page. My eyes locked on the photo, and a zing of adrenaline shot through me. A headline above it read, Murderer Preston J. Travis, aka James Johnson, Escapes from Prison, Injures Guard.

Gasping, I grabbed the paper and looked at the photo more closely. A chill rushed down my spine as I stared into his cold eyes. How could this have happened?

I set down the paper, unable to look at the photo any longer, a sense of foreboding taking hold of me. It was never good to wish ill upon anyone, I knew, but in this instance, I wished James Johnson was dead.

CHAPTER FIVE

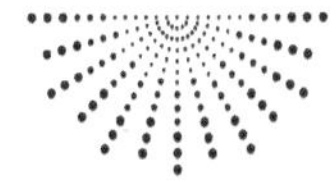

"You're serious?" Felicity said, her dark-blue eyes wide as she stood in the doorway of her cottage at the mansion property. A white scarf, gathered in a bow behind her right ear, encircled her head. The contrast of white against her dark skin had a stunning effect. That was the best word for Felicity in general. *Stunning.* She had no idea how beautiful she really was, and it made her even more charming. "He escaped?"

I pressed my lips together and nodded.

"Come in, come in." She ushered me into the house and picked up the newspaper, still tied with string, sitting on a chair in her entry. She pulled off the string and opened it.

"Page two." I wasn't in the least bit offended that she hadn't taken my word for it. This was something that had to be seen for oneself.

"Heavens to Betsy! I don't believe it," she said, reading the headline. "It says he was set to hang in three weeks."

"I know." I shook my head in dismay. "Do you think Florence is in danger? She was to be his latest victim."

Felicity let out a breath between pursed lips. "I don't see

how. She left last week for a photo shoot on Long Island for some hoity-toity magazine. She said she'll stay out there for a few months for some R & R. I got a telegram from her yesterday."

"Do you think he would go after her?"

Felicity's brows came together. "How would he know where she is?"

I bit my lip. "You're right. He wouldn't know. But what about you? What if he comes back to the mansion looking for her? You're not safe here. Have the repairs been done on your bungalow? Can you go there?"

She scoffed. "They fixed the roof, only to find problems with the foundation. The place has been condemned."

"Well, then can someone stay with you?"

"The maid and the groundskeeper live on the property. I'm not alone, Grace. Please don't worry about me. You're the one who needs to be careful. You were responsible for putting him in jail."

The green car I'd seen earlier that day flashed in my mind. Had I been followed to the café?

"I'll be careful," I said, a niggle of worry at the edge of my words.

Felicity reached out and laid a hand on my shoulder. "You've gone quite pale, dear. Would you like some tea?"

"That sounds wonderful," I said with a sigh of gratitude. I was feeling a bit shaky. "I can't stay long, though. I need to get back to the kids."

We walked into her sunny kitchen, and she filled the teakettle with water and put it on the stove. I tossed my handbag on the table and took a seat in one of the white-washed French farm chairs.

"You came all the way over here to tell me about James Johnson? I'm glad to see you, but why not just call, sugar?" she asked.

"I wasn't quite ready to go home. I needed some company. I met with my father today."

Pulling out a chair to sit down, she froze. "Oh my. You finally did it. So, tell me, was it really him?"

I nodded. "I'm pretty sure, although he was a little different from what I remembered. He used to be so robust—or so I thought. But he's faced some real hardships since the day he and my mother left."

"Oh my goodness." She sat down and took hold of my hand. "You've had quite a day. No wonder you seem so rattled. Tell me about it."

I recounted all that he and Madeleine had told me.

"He's remarried? How does that make you feel?" she asked when I was done.

I shrugged. "I'm not really sure. I'm still reeling that he's even alive. Of course, I want him to be happy . . ." I said the words, not sure if I truly meant them. Sophia and I had suffered so much in his absence, and all the while, he'd been living in Europe, finding love again. It didn't seem fair.

"What is she like?"

Felicity's question brought me out of my reverie. The teakettle whistled, and she got up to turn the burner off and make our tea.

I fiddled with the spoon in the sugar bowl. "Pretty. Much younger than him. Attentive. She's a nurse," I said quietly. It didn't seem right to mention the incident with the morphine. Besides, I was still processing that bit of information. "They seem to adore each other. I know I should feel happy for him, but—"

Felicity brought over our teacups. Steam floated off them in curving swirls. "You sound sad, sugar."

I shrugged. "I don't know what I am. Sad, angry, and confused, I guess. He's known about Sophia and me for years. Yet, he never contacted us. Said he felt we were better off without him. How could he have just given up on us like that? And then when Sophia died—" My voice broke.

Felicity reached across the table and laid her hand over mine. "You just need time. Don't rush yourself, honey. This is a lot to take in."

I flicked away a tear that had escaped onto my cheek.

"You just need to get reacquainted is all," she soothed. "You've been separated—for whatever reasons—for over a decade. It will take a while to get to know each other again."

"I wish I could remember more about my childhood." I took a sip of my tea. I hadn't had any use for those memories before, since, by all accounts—with a mad mother—they were generally not good ones, but now I wished I knew more about my parents.

I sniffed and smiled at Felicity, glad I had come over. She always knew what to say to make me feel better.

There was a loud knock on the door.

Felicity rose from the table. "Probably Consuela, the cleaning lady. She's bringing the key back from the mansion. I'll be just a sec." She patted me on the shoulder as she walked by.

I spooned some sugar into my tea and then sipped it, savoring the sweet bergamot flavor. A strange voice from the entry hall wafted into the kitchen. It didn't sound like the house-maid. It sounded male.

I got up and made my way to the door. Felicity was speaking with a hefty man in a suit and an officer in uniform.

"We've had reports that a man matching Johnson's description was spotted down near the border of Mexico, but we just wanted to see if he'd been around here at all in the last day or so," the man in the suit said.

"I haven't seen him," Felicity said.

I moved closer and stood at her elbow. The man in the suit tipped his hat to me. Thick, heavy eyebrows, like two fat cater-pillars dancing over his eyes, dominated his features. "All right, then." He pulled a card out of his coat pocket. "If you hear anything, you let us know."

Felicity took the card and scanned it. "Will do, Detective Baptiste."

He tipped his hat again, and then he and the officer turned and walked away.

Felicity quietly shut the door. "Sounds like we might not have anything to worry about after all, if he's headed for Mexico."

"Let's hope that's the case," I said, not sure I felt any hope at all.

I GOT BACK to the house right about the time Rose was putting dinner on the table. I set my handbag and gloves on the gossip table as Susie and Ida filtered into the dining room.

"Why are we eating in here?" I asked them.

"Mr. Chet and Mr. Manetti are on their way home," Susie said, bouncing up and down on the balls of her feet, her teddy bear secured under an arm.

"Oh, thank goodness." Relief swept through me. With Stevie's arrival, in addition to my father being in town for an undetermined time, preparations for a new film underway, and now the news of James Johnson's escape, I was eager to have Chet back. Besides, even though he'd only been gone a few days, I always missed him terribly when we were apart.

Rose pushed through the door from the kitchen to the dining room with her backside, her arms laden with a pot roast.

"Chet's coming home?" I asked.

She nodded, setting the roast on the table. "Called while you were gone. Said they were about two hours out. He should be walking through the door any minute." She beckoned to me with a tilt of her head to follow her back into the kitchen.

After the door swung shut behind us, she turned to me with fists on her plump hips. "We've had a bit of an afternoon," she said, her voice lowered.

At her tone, a flutter of alarm rose in my chest. "Oh? What happened?"

"Stevie and Daniel got into it out in the barn. Ned broke them up, but I'm afraid Daniel's a bit worse for wear."

"What?" My hand flew to my throat. "A fight?"

She nodded. "Daniel's got a black eye."

"Oh no," I groaned.

Rose raised her hands in the air. "Gotta hand it to the kid. He showed some real maturity by not cleaning the boy's clock."

Just then, Ned came into the kitchen. He swiped his hat off his head when he saw me.

"Grace." He nodded. At twenty-one, Ned was a handsome, strapping young man with dark hair and chestnut eyes that always had a glint of mischief in them. He'd proven invaluable to us as a dedicated farmhand, and Chet was grooming him to be a farm manager.

"What's this about a fight today?" I asked him.

Rose went about getting the potatoes and vegetables ready to take into the dining room.

He walked over to the sink and began to wash his hands. "Yeah. That Stevie is one angry kid. From what I gather, Daniel said something to him about being a paperboy, and the guy flew off the handle. Gave Daniel a shiner. I was surprised Daniel didn't hand the kid his hat. Not sure that would have happened even six months ago."

Daniel was a good four years older than Stevie and probably outweighed him by twenty pounds. Daniel had arrived at the ranch angry and detached himself.

"Yes," I said, pleased with Daniel's restraint. "Where are the boys now?"

"Daniel should be coming in at any moment. He was just finishing up filling the horses' water tanks in the fields."

"And Stevie?"

"Been up in his room ever since the fight," Rose said. "Haven't seen hide nor hair of him." She looked over at Ned. "Made some chocolate icebox cake for dessert. Your favorite."

Rose had a soft spot for Ned. She said he reminded her of Chet, and I couldn't disagree. They did look very similar. Chet was taller and broader across the chest, but Ned could pass as his younger brother.

He gave her a warm smile. "Thanks, Mrs. R., but I've gotta go right after dinner. I'm taking Ruth to the pictures. Save me some?"

I was glad Ned had found such a sweet girlfriend in Ruth. For a while, his attentions had been bestowed upon me, which made for an awkward situation. Chet hadn't seemed too concerned, but it had made me uncomfortable. Now things were much easier between Ned and me.

"You bet, kid." Rose winked at him and took the other two dishes out to the dining room.

I was just about to follow her when Daniel came in through the kitchen door. I frowned when I saw his bruised face.

"He's got a mean hook," he said with a lopsided grin. I was glad to see he hadn't taken the blow too much to heart.

"Oh, Daniel, I'm so sorry that happened." I pushed the hair away from his forehead with my finger, inspecting his left eye more closely. It was a little bloodshot and the dark moon under it looked painful, but the area around his eye wasn't swollen, which I supposed was a good thing.

"Aw, it's okay. I shouldn't have ribbed him about his paper route. I didn't think he'd get so angry about it."

I smiled at him. "I'm afraid Stevie is quite fragile at the moment. But that's no excuse for hurting anyone. I'll have a talk with him."

"Don't be too hard on him. I know how he feels. Like he's lost everything."

I cupped Daniel's cheek with my palm, impressed and moved by his compassion for Stevie, despite what the boy had done to him.

"I won't. That's quite kind of you, Daniel. I must say, you've made me proud."

His cheeks flushed, and he cast his gaze to the floor. To think that he, once angry and headed into a life of crime, could see Stevie's pain and identify with it made me realize that perhaps we truly were giving these kids a life filled with hope and promise.

Daniel was fiercely loyal to those he considered his friends, and I felt sure he'd win Stevie over in short order. My heart swelled with gratitude. "Go on and get some dinner before it gets cold," I said, changing the subject to ease his embarrassment.

His eyes met mine. "Aren't you eating with us?"

"Yes. But I'm going to go check on Stevie first."

I followed him out of the kitchen and detoured down the hallway and up the staircase. When I reached Stevie's door, I knocked.

There was no answer. I knocked again. Still nothing. Carefully, I opened the door. "Stevie?"

He was sitting on the bed, his suitcase beside him.

I walked into the room and sat down at the desk chair across from him. "You haven't unpacked."

He shook his head. His freckled face was mottled with blotches of color, and his eyes were red rimmed and swollen.

"I understand you had a difficult day," I said gently.

He rolled his eyes and looked away from me, making it perfectly clear he wasn't thrilled with my presence.

"Do you want to talk about it?"

"I don't want to be here. I'd be fine on my own." He slowly turned his head to face me.

I nodded. "I see. Where would you live?"

He shrugged. "Down by the tracks."

"You mean, like a hobo?"

He shrugged again.

I leaned forward and rested my elbows on my crossed knees. "It's not as easy as it seems, living on the streets."

His lips turned up in a sneer, and he scoffed. "How would you know?"

I fixed him with a firm gaze. "Experience."

His eyes narrowed, and he looked at me as if I'd fallen from the moon. "You?"

I arched my brows at him, pressing my lips together. "I was exactly your age when my parents died." I intentionally left out that my dad had just returned to me. That would be a conversation for later. What happened today had no bearing on what I had lived through then.

"My sister and I ran away. We didn't want to be separated, and we didn't want to live in an orphanage."

His expression softened from anger to curiosity, but he didn't say anything.

"It was really tough. Sophia was the oldest, so she felt it was her responsibility to keep us alive." I refrained from mentioning the gritty details of our existence at the time but hoped he got my meaning. "I was willing to help her with the burden, but she wouldn't hear of it. I helped in my own way, but it was hardly the kind of sacrifice she made.

"Living on the streets was awful. Terrifying. We never knew when we were going to eat, where we would sleep. This was in New York City, too, and the winters were harsh. Beyond cold. Not like here where the sun shines most of the time and it rarely freezes. Those winters were the worst." My voice trailed away, and I closed my eyes to shut out the memories.

I opened them again and met Stevie's gaze. He blinked at me in astonishment, taking in my tale of woe. I hoped I'd gotten my message across: running away from anything was never a good idea.

"He said my paper route wasn't real work," he said finally.

"Daniel did?"

The muscles in his jaw twitched, and he screwed up his mouth to keep his chin from trembling. "But the money I made helped me and my dad. It bought us some bread and canned meat when Dad wasn't working."

I nodded. I had learned from Sister Margarite that Stevie's father had trouble holding down a job due to bouts of melancholia. I remained quiet, encouraging him to continue, glad he wanted to open up.

"Dad could be a real pain in the neck sometimes when he was down in the dumps, 'specially after Mom died, but I could always make him smile when I brought home some food, or the *Times*, or some sweets. He said sometimes it was the only thing that kept him going. And then—"

I pulled in my lower lip. "He died?"

His eyes teared up. "If only I could have made more money . . . Then I could have got him a doctor, and—" His posture slumped, and he held his hands over his face, his shoulders heaving with his sobs.

I sighed, commiserating with the enormity of the responsibility the boy must have felt to keep his father alive. It was irrational, yes, but he believed it to be true. I rose from the desk chair and sat down on the bed next to him.

I wrapped my arm around his shoulders. "It wasn't your fault, sweetie."

No wonder he'd acted out when Daniel had made the comment. How many times since I'd remembered my mother had come after me with a knife had I questioned whether or not there had been something I could have done, or not done, to make things right for her? And I was a grown adult. The guilt had buried itself deep. It was inescapable, woven into the fabric of my being.

"We're not so different, you and I, Stevie." I leaned my cheek on the top of his head. "I know you're angry, and you're sad, and you don't want to be here, and that's okay. But it's better than being on your own. Believe me."

He sniffed and then wiped his eyes. He lowered his hands and then looked down at them on his knees.

"Can I keep my paper route? Mr. Stanford said I could come back if the orphanage would let me, but they wouldn't."

I gave his shoulders a squeeze. "I don't see why not. I'll ask Ned if you can do your chores in the afternoon so you can spend the mornings on your route."

"Thanks," he said with another sniff. "Can I call Mr. Stanford tomorrow?"

"Of course."

His shoulders relaxed, and I could almost detect an upturning of his lips.

"Oh, and I really like the horses."

I smiled and released his shoulders. "Me too. Are you ready to come down for dinner?"

"I don't mean to be impolite, ma'am—" He looked up at me with doleful eyes.

"Grace," I said.

"Uh, Grace, but I'm not hungry."

I patted his knee. "I understand. Would you like me to bring you a plate? Maybe for later?"

"If it's not too much trouble."

"It's not."

"Thank you." He pressed his lips together in an attempted smile. "Guess I'd better unpack."

I left the room, my heart lifted and breaking at the same time.

CHAPTER SIX

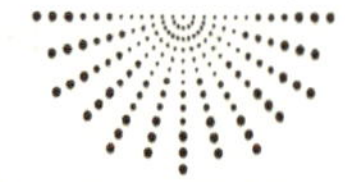

Chet arrived just as I came downstairs. "I'm so glad you're here," I said, greeting him in the hallway. "I have so much to share with you."

"It's good to be home. Something smells wonderful." He took me in his arms and gave me a long, lingering kiss. "Besides you." He nuzzled his face into my hair. He smelled good, too, like citrus and spice. He often wore the Italian cologne I'd given him for Christmas two years ago, Acqua di Parma.

"Your mother made a pot roast," I said, pulling away from him. "Why don't you wash up? I'm going to fix Stevie a plate to eat in his room."

Chet's eyebrows pinched over the bridge of his strong, straight nose. "But we don't let the kids eat in their rooms."

I took in a deep breath. "I'm making an exception, just for tonight. I'll fill you in later."

He kissed my cheek and then went into the downstairs powder room to wash up. I entered the dining room to find the children, Ned, Rose, and Miss Meyers noisily enthralled in laughter and conversation. The sound made me smile. We were indeed providing a happy home for these children.

"Where's Stevie?" Ida asked, taking one of Rose's home-made rolls from the breadbasket.

"He's feeling a little out of sorts. I'm taking him some dinner." I took a plate from an empty seat, gathered utensils and a napkin, and asked Rose to please serve it up for me.

"But you never let—" Susie started.

I fixed her with a glance. "It's only for tonight. You all go ahead and start eating. Chet and I will be with you shortly. "

Susie lifted a shoulder in nonchalance and tucked into her meal.

Rose handed me the plate, and I took it upstairs to Stevie. He had finished unpacking and was putting his suit-case under the bed. He held a book in his hands. I placed the plate, the utensils and napkin, and a glass of milk on the desk. He gave the food a sideways glance and then sat on the bed, his back resting against the headboard, and opened his book. I thought about asking him if he wanted to talk some more, but he'd started reading so I turned to go.

"Ma'am— I mean, Grace?" he said.

I stopped with my hand on the doorknob and looked over my shoulder. "Yes?"

"Thanks."

I smiled at him. "You're welcome." I quietly closed the door behind me, reasoning that a good night's sleep and some privacy would do the boy a world of good.

By the time Chet and I made it to the table, the kids had finished eating and were taking their plates to the kitchen. Rose, Ned, and Miss Meyers were finishing up and sat quietly talking while Chet and I enjoyed our dinner. As usual, Rose's magic in the kitchen did not disappoint.

After we'd finished, Rose brought us coffee. Miss Meyers picked up her plate with thin, delicate fingers. She was a slip of a woman with long features—long nose, long neck, long arms and legs. Not attractive in the conventional way, she had a kindness in her eyes that made one instantly comfortable.

"No coffee for me tonight, Rose. I'm going to my room to prepare for tomorrow's lessons," she said, rising from the table.

"I guess I'd better get started on the kitchen." Rose gathered her plate and a serving dish.

"May I help?" I asked, about to get up from my chair.

She shook her head. "Thank you, no. It's easier if I do it myself."

I knew she wouldn't let me help—she never did—but I still liked to offer. Tonight, though, I was grateful she'd waved me off. I wanted to fill Chet in on what had happened over the past couple of days.

"Have you seen the paper today?" I asked him.

"No. Haven't had the chance." Chet sipped his coffee.

"James Johnson escaped." Saying the words made my stomach fold in on itself.

His eyes popped open wide. "What?"

"I know. I can't believe it. I'm worried, Chet. The police came by Felicity's today, asking if he'd come to the mansion. The detective said someone had seen a man that looked like him at the border of Mexico, but what if it wasn't him?"

Chet nodded. "You're right to be worried. We'll have to be careful. Stay alert."

I took in a deep breath and let it go, trying to quell my anxiety. "I didn't want to say anything to the others until I spoke with you. We will have to tell them so they can keep an eye out, as well. But I don't think we should tell the kids. I don't want to scare them."

"Agreed," said Chet.

I then told him about my conversation with Valentina and Mr. Belsky. I wasn't quite ready to bring up the meeting with my father.

"Anton Belsky, you say?" Chet asked.

"Yes. Do you know him?"

Chet shook his head. "No. He's quite the successful business-man. Owns Pacific Savings and Loan."

"He did make quite an impression," I said, remembering his fine clothes and polished demeanor.

"Anyway, I didn't know what to say to Valentina. I felt terrible turning her down. She seemed quite distraught—rightfully so."

"Doesn't sound like a routine robbery." Chet leaned back in his chair and stretched out his long legs. Fatigue settled around the corners of his light-gray eyes.

"It wasn't, apparently. Whoever broke in didn't take anything." I took a sip of my coffee and pressed my fork into the crumbs of chocolate cake on my plate.

"Might have been looking for something."

"Maybe. It all sounded very strange." Then I remembered the pin Valentina had shown me. "She found something at the scene. It was an elaborately decorated pin with a hammer and some other thing—some kind of implement with a curved blade."

"Hammer and sickle?" Chet's eyebrows rose. "Did you say she is Russian?"

I nodded. "But she's been here in America for quite some time."

He narrowed his eyes in thought. "That's the symbol for the new Soviet Republic. That *is* strange." He rubbed his eyes with his thumb and forefinger. "Well, I know you want to help, but you've got enough to keep you busy."

"Yes, I do."

I then told him about Stevie and the altercation with Daniel.

"He'll come around in time," Chet said, stifling a yawn. He looked positively beat. I thought about bringing up the meeting with my father, but then thought again. That was a conversation that could wait 'til morning. Besides, I still hadn't fully processed the encounter. If I was honest with myself, I didn't really want to think about it at the moment, either. I just wanted to crawl into bed with my husband, curl up in his arms, and fall into oblivion. But how could I with a murderer on the loose?

I AWOKE the next morning with a new perspective in regard to my father. I had dreamed about him throughout the night. Memories of moments with him and me together were reawakened.

One of the memories was of the two of us walking along a meandering pathway in a park. Sophia and my mother hadn't been there with us. We'd stopped at a nearby stream and watched the fall leaves float and dance along the water as they worked their way through the rocks. He had explained the different kinds of foliage, the cycles of the moon, and shared with me the wonders of the nature surrounding us. There were other scenarios, too. All of them tranquil. Peaceful. Safe.

Like many of my nighttime illusions, the dreams of him were vivid and clear, but when I awoke, reality, reason, and pragmatism oozed their way into my psyche, causing confusion. Throughout the past year, it had been Sophia who'd visited me in my slumber, and through those visits, she'd helped me save Lizzy. I hadn't understood it at the time, but Sophia had guided me to the truth, and I'd learned to trust those dreams. But I was uncertain about the feelings prompted by last night's visions. Yet, I felt lighter, buoyant, and dare I say, elated.

My father is alive.

I turned over to say something about my visit with him to Chet, but he was gone—probably checking in on the horses and seeing to the kids and their chores.

I glanced at the clock on the nightstand. It was nearly eight o'clock. A jolt of adrenaline shot through me. How had I slept so late? I needed to be at Ambassador in two hours, and I had some things to do around the house and my studio first.

I shot out of bed, washed my face, ran a comb through my hair, and got dressed.

In the kitchen, Daniel and Stevie were sitting at the breakfast table, their heads bent together, their attention focused on something in Daniel's hand. He was telling Stevie about it. To my relief, they'd seemed to have worked out their differences.

I reminded myself to speak with Ned about afternoon chores for Stevie and to mention to Rose that he would be using the telephone today. She didn't like the children talking on the telephone without permission, said the phone was only to impart and receive information, not to while away the day chatting with friends. And we had a party line so we needed to be courteous of the other two families that shared it.

I took a glass from the cupboard and poured myself some fresh orange juice just as Chet, Ned, and the girls came in for breakfast. They scattered to go wash up, Chet staying in the kitchen to use the kitchen sink.

I walked up to him and stood on tiptoe to give him a kiss on the cheek. "Why did you let me sleep so late?" I whispered.

His gray eyes regarded me with affection as he dried his hands on a dishtowel. "You looked so peaceful, I didn't want to disturb you. You'd been tossing and turning all night."

His words surprised me. I had awakened rested and calm. "Really?"

"Yeah. I even tried to wake you up once, but no cigar."

I shrugged. "I had very vivid dreams. About my father."

"Have you decided whether or not you are going to call him?" He leaned his hip against the counter and folded his arms.

I indicated with a tilt of my head for him to follow me into the living room. We passed through the swinging kitchen door.

"I saw him yesterday," I said, my voice barely above a whisper.

Chet's eyes opened wide in surprise. "How did it go?"

"It was interesting," I mused. "He's remarried. She's a nurse.

French, I think. She cared for him after he was injured in the war."

"Did he look like you remembered?"

I shrugged. "My memories of him are a little hazy, but yes—I think so. He has a beard now, and he looks aged, more aged than he should be, but I suppose with what he's been through . . . He's also much thinner than I remembered. I remember him being robust, but I suppose that is a child's memory. I was also smaller then."

"When can I meet him?" Chet asked, raising an eyebrow.

I hesitated. "Soon, I—"

The phone rang, making me jump. Chet sidestepped me and went to the entry hall. I followed him.

He picked up the receiver. "Hello?" He listened, and then he handed the phone to me. *Your father,* he mouthed.

My heart stuttered, and I took the phone from him. "Good morning," I said, trying to sound cheerful, like no time had passed at all, like he wasn't a total stranger to me.

"You must help me," he said, his voice ragged and frantic.

"Goodness. What's wrong? What's the matter?"

"It's Madeleine," he said. "She's gone. I went to the market for just thirty minutes to get— And then when I came back— Oh God! She's gone."

My heart raced. "What do you mean 'gone'?" I didn't want to say the words, *Is she dead?*

"She's not here. Those bastards—"

I shook my head, uncomprehending. "Who?"

"Please, just get here as fast as you can. 239 Alvarado. Hurry!" There was a click on the other end.

"He hung up," I said to Chet, placing the receiver back on its cradle.

Concern swept his features. "What'd he say? What's going on?"

"It seems his wife is missing. He sounds very distressed—said he wants me to come over. Now."

Chet placed a comforting hand on my shoulder. "I'll go with you."

The kitchen door pushed open, and Rose peered around it. "Did you get the phone?" she asked.

Chet nodded. "Yes. It was Grace's father. We need to go see him."

Rose looked mildly affronted. "But you haven't had breakfast yet."

"It's rather an emergency, I'm afraid," I said, my heart pounding.

Rose's annoyed expression morphed to compassion. "Oh dear. Well you better go, then."

I went to the hall closet and pulled out a sweater and my burgundy cloche. Chet picked up his coat and hat from the gossip chair, and we scurried out the front door. We hopped into the car and sped down the long driveway that led away from our ranch.

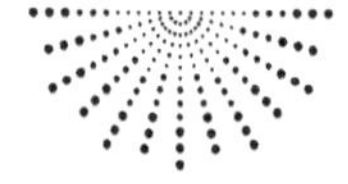

CHAPTER SEVEN

We pulled up to the large brick house on Alvarado. A sign in front of it read, BOARDERS WELCOME.

We got out of the car, climbed the dozen steps that led to the front door, and rang the bell. A woman in an apron answered. She was plump, with fat, rosy cheeks. Her brows were pulled down over her small eyes in consternation.

"You must be Grace," she said. "I'm Nancy Wilkins—owner of the place."

"Hello. Yes, I'm Grace. And this is my husband, Chet."

"He's in such a state." She opened the door wider to let us inside. "I'll take you to his rooms."

She led us into the entryway and then down a hall. She pointed to a door. "Right here. If you'll excuse me, I have a pie in the oven." She went back the way we had come.

I rapped on the door. Inside, footsteps approached. The door opened, and my father stood there, his eyes wild and his hair a disheveled mess, like he'd been running his hands through it. His body trembled, shaking from head to toe. He motioned for us to come inside and then paced the floor, his hands going in and out of his pockets. I shared a glance with Chet as he closed the door behind us.

We had stepped into what looked like a small apartment. It was modestly appointed with older, worn, but good-quality furniture. A musty tang mingled with the odor of cigarette smoke. A burning cigarette lay in an ashtray on a side table next to the sofa. From the living area, there were three other doorways—all open. The doorway in the center led into a bathroom.

"What's going on, Dad?" I asked, the word *Dad* sounding strange coming out of my mouth and making me feel somewhat uncomfortable. But *Father* didn't feel right, either, and I certainly couldn't bring myself to call him by his name, Peter.

"She's gone. Gone!" Still pacing, he kept his attention riveted on the floor. "They've taken her."

"Who's taken her?" I asked.

He stopped and finally looked at us in earnest. "You're the private investigator." He pointed at Chet.

"This is my husband, Chet," I said. "Chet, this is Peter Michelle, my . . . father."

He came over and shook Chet's hand, then continued pacing like an animal in a cage. He suddenly went to the couch, slumped onto it, and proceeded to run his hands through his thinning hair.

I went over and sat down next to him. I remembered how Madeleine had calmed him down before. "Do you have your medicine?"

He shook his head. "Have to stay sharp."

"Mr. Michelle, do you have any idea who would have taken your wife?" Chet asked.

My father turned to me, not answering the question. "You work with Valentina."

I pulled my chin back, shocked at his strange and inappropriately timed declaration.

"Valentina Baklanova? Yes. Why? How do you know her?"

His eyes glazed over, and he looked right through me. "We have to get to Valentina. She knows."

I glanced at Chet in confusion, as if he could somehow explain what my father was talking about. My father shot up from the couch and started to pace again.

Chet stepped in front of him, blocking his way. He held up a hand. "Mr. Michelle, sir, you need to tell us what you are talking about in order for us to help you."

My father ran his hands down his face as if he didn't know what to do with them.

"Mr. Michelle?" Chet prodded.

"What does Valentina have to do with this?" I questioned.

He grabbed the sides of his head with both hands, as if trying to shut out our questions. It was clear we weren't going to get much more out of him if he continued to be this agitated.

"Where is your medicine?" I asked him.

He pointed toward one of the doorways, and I took his cue. I walked into the bedroom. It was a small room with a double bed and two nightstands on one wall, and a wardrobe on the opposite wall. I spied a medicine vial on one of the nightstands, and next to it was a syringe kit. I picked them up and carried them out to him. He took the items from me, went into the bathroom, and closed the door. Chet gave me a puzzled look.

"Morphine," I said. "He fought in the war and was severely injured. Madeleine said he is quite dependent upon it."

Chet nodded in understanding. "It's the bane and savior of many a soldier."

"She said they found a doctor here who gave him a prescription, but—"

"The Harrison Narcotics Tax Act of 1914. The government is really pressuring doctors not to prescribe it anymore," he stated.

"Right. Seems a little suspect."

Chet casually moved through the apartment, looking it over. He went to the desk, picked up a framed photo of my father and

Madeleine, studied it, and put it back down. He then sifted through some papers strewn across the desktop. I went into the kitchen. It, too, was small but tidy. Nothing seemed out of place. There was the faint smell of coffee in the air. A Dutch door, the upper half a paned window, stood next to the range, providing the apartment with its own entrance.

I returned to the living area as my father walked out of the bathroom looking like a different man. He had even combed his hair and tucked in his shirt.

"Thank you," he said to me.

I smiled at him. "Tell us what happened."

"Let's sit down." Chet motioned toward the couch.

My father and I went to the sofa. Chet sat in the armchair that was positioned perpendicular to it.

My father cleared his throat but didn't speak. Finally, he took in a deep breath and let it out slowly, then proceeded. "I got up early. Went to the store to get us some breakfast items. Madeleine isn't a morning person." He ran a hand over his mouth in anguish.

"Did you leave through the kitchen door?" I asked.

He nodded. "Yes. We've been using it exclusively. Anyway, I came back and went to wake her, but she was gone."

"Perhaps she took a walk?" I tried.

He shook his head. "Her clothes and shoes are all here—but her night dress and robe are gone."

That did sound strange.

"What makes you think someone took her? Why would they take her?" Chet asked.

"They are looking for something." My father held up his hands in impatience. "They think she knows where it is. Please, I have to speak with Valentina."

"How do you know Valentina?" I asked.

"I don't." He let go an exasperated sigh. "Valentina is the niece of Anna Ivanova, and Anna Ivanova worked as a housekeeper for Madeleine's family for a short time while the family lived in Russia. Madeleine never met her, though. The family employed her after Madeleine returned to France."

I blinked in surprise. "My, what a small world."

"Marcel Gallois, Madeleine's brother, came to possess an item that once belonged to the Russian royal family," he continued.

"The Romanovs?" Chet asked.

My father confirmed with a single nod of his head. "Their family—Madeleine and Marcel's parents—were closely associated with the Romanovs through business connections. Prior to the revolution, Madeleine's father knew it was coming. He sent Madeleine back to France where she pursued a career in nursing. After the revolution, the Kremlin seized the family's business. Luckily, Marcel and his parents were able to leave Russia and return to France. At that time, Anna Ivanova moved to the United States. Apparently, she kept in touch with the family. They still had some means—quite a lot by anyone else's standards—but their fortunes were greatly diminished."

He reached over to the end table and took a cigarette from a silver case. His hands trembled as he lit it, but he was decidedly calmer. He took a deep drag and then released a pointed stream of smoke. "Marcel, who had kept the item safe, decided it was time to sell it. He found a buyer, and they made plans to meet the following day, but that night, someone—we think it was henchmen working for the buyer—broke into the house and tortured his parents in an attempt to find out where this item was hidden. Marcel returned to the family home to find the intruder in the house and his parents dead."

"How awful," I said, my voice barely a whisper.

"The intruder turned on Marcel, and they had quite a brawl. Marcel ended up dying from his injuries, but somehow, he managed to get to the post office. He sent this item to Anna Ivanova—Valentina's aunt—for safekeeping."

He swallowed hard, his Adam's apple bobbing beneath his unshaven neck. "Then, he went to the hospital where Madeleine worked. He was in a really bad way. He'd told her where he'd sent the item and instructed her to flee the country. Told her to sell it so that we could live out our days in comfort in America. He said once we sold it, we would be safe. Then he died in her arms."

I listened with rapt attention to this fascinating tale, and slowly, something occurred to me. Valentina's aunt lay in the hospital. An intruder had turned her house upside down.

"Oh my god," I said, looking from my father to Chet. "Valentina. This is what I was telling you about, Chet."

His brow furrowed. "You mean when she asked you to help find the person or people who had hurt her aunt?"

"Yes! But Valentina didn't know why the house had been broken into. She and her fiancé were in Europe at the time. Maybe whoever did it was looking for this item."

My father glanced over at me. "Valentina spoke to you of this?"

I explained what she had asked me to do. "But she didn't know why her aunt had been attacked. She may not know about this item," I said. "She certainly didn't mention it."

He stood up and started pacing again, sucking furiously on the cigarette that was now nearly just ash. "They must not have found it," he said, with something like hope in his voice. "Or why would they have taken Madeleine?"

Chet turned to my father. "What is this item? When was it sent?"

He took another drag of his cigarette and raked his hands through his hair again, making it untidy once more. His eyes darted between me and Chet, and his mouth twisted as if struggling to make the words come out. The smoke streamed in a burst from his nostrils like a dragon.

"Marcel sent it shortly before we came into the country—

about a month, maybe five weeks ago. This buyer, or his thugs, must have tracked it down."

"And what is it?" I prodded.

"We don't know," he said finally. "Marcel died before he could tell Madeleine. All he said was that it was worth a fortune and that we had to leave the country. Perhaps these people followed us. Hell, they might have gotten to US soil before we did three weeks ago. I have to speak with Valentina." He turned to me. "Can you arrange it?"

I blinked up at him, another realization hitting me, this one wrenching my heart in two. My father had come to Los Angeles three weeks ago in search of some expensive treasure, not necessarily to see me. He'd read about me in the papers. He knew I worked at Ambassador and that Valentina did, too. Of course I would have access to her. And he also knew that I had found both Sophia's and Edward Travis's killers. He knew my husband was a private detective. The awareness sunk in like a weighted stone upon my chest.

I stared at him with a mixture of sadness, pity, and bewilderment. "I suppose I can," I said, my words coming out soft and low, my heart still stinging with the knowledge that I was merely a means to an end to the man I had once adored and admired.

"We have to find it!" My father turned on me and raised his voice. "They will—" He shook his head, tears pooling in his eyes. "They tortured her parents to get the information." He clenched his teeth and banged his palm repeatedly against the side of his head. "I never should have left her alone! I didn't protect her!"

Unable to watch this self-flagellation any longer, I rushed over to him and took hold of his arm. His body sagged, and his knees buckled. Chet and I got him back over to the sofa.

"We will find this package—and we will get her back. I promise," I said. I looked up at Chet, and he gave me a thin-lipped smile, compassion written in his eyes. I only hoped it was a promise we could keep.

I wrapped an arm around my father, my hurt feelings forgotten as I witnessed the brokenness of this man who was once so strong and hearty.

"She is my life," he sobbed.

My father, once again in a state of agitation, went into the bathroom and shut the door.

Chet came over to the sofa and sat down next to me. "Are you okay?" he asked.

I took a deep breath, not quite sure how to answer, a million different emotions coursing through me. "He's so . . . different from what I remembered."

Chet put a hand on my knee. "War does terrible things to people. It changes them. Forever."

I looked into his eyes. Chet didn't speak much about his time in the war. It was as if there was a two-year gap in his life, and I could only imagine what horrors filled that gap. Both of us had lived through unspeakable traumas, so speak of them we usually did not. Only now, I was faced with the reality of one of my traumas come back to life and I had no choice but to deal with it.

I laid my hand over Chet's, still on my knee. "We really should contact the police," I said.

Chet didn't respond, but I could see the wheels in his head turning.

"What?" I asked.

He rose from the sofa and went into the kitchen. I followed him. He took a cursory look around. "No sign of forced entry," he said, opening the exterior door. He examined the doorknob fixtures and windows. "And whoever took her—if she was taken—wouldn't have used the interior door to the house. Too risky."

"What do you mean, *if* she was taken?"

Chet ran a palm over his chin. "Something seems . . . off.

You sure things were okay between him and Madeleine? Perhaps they got into a fight and she left."

"But her clothes," I added. "My father said there weren't any missing except her nightclothes, which she would've been wearing."

"Yes, but—" Chet walked over to a trash bin next to the sink and opened the lid. He started to rummage around in it and then paused. He lifted out a silk, floral dressing gown smeared with blood. His gaze shifted to meet mine.

I raised a hand to my throat. "Oh god."

We heard the bathroom door open. Taking the gown, Chet made a beeline for the living room, me on his heels.

My father was staggering toward the bedroom.

"Mr. Michelle," Chet called out to him.

My father slowly turned around. His face had gone slack, his eyes droopy and unfocused. He faltered and grabbed on to the sofa for support. He'd doubtless taken more of the morphine. A lot more.

Chet held the dressing gown out in front of him. "Is this Madeleine's?"

My father, his eyes glassy, raised his hand in the air, and then sloppily swatted downward as if he were shooing away a fly. He was out of his mind on the drug, unable to respond. He turned and shuffled into the bedroom. We followed him and watched as he fell face down onto the bed.

"What do we do now?" I asked Chet. "Should we call the police?"

He took in a deep breath and let it out slowly. "If we do that, your father will be implicated in Madeleine's disappearance. We might want to see if we can find out more first."

"Implicated. Because of the blood on the dressing gown?" I lowered my voice to a whisper, thinking the unthinkable. "Do you think he hurt her? Or worse?"

He pulled his upper lip between his teeth, considering. "It's possible."

"Maybe we should at least check with the hospitals, then?" I offered.

"Not a bad idea." He stuck his bottom lip out and then scratched at it. I could see those wheels turning again. "And the story about this valuable item that's supposedly worth a fortune . . . Do you buy it?" he asked, doubt in his eyes.

"Gosh," I said, shaking my head. "It is quite the fantastic story. But why would he lie about something like that?"

"Could be delusional. Did your father or Madeleine mention anything about this item when you met them at the café?"

"No. Why don't you believe him?" I was a little confused by Chet's reaction.

"He doesn't even know what this thing is," Chet said matter-of-factly. "What is its true worth? Has it been appraised? We also have to take into account that it might have been stolen. He said Marcel 'came into possession of' this item. During the revolution, the Bolsheviks raided the royal family's residences. Many items were stolen. If it was taken from the Romanovs during the siege of the palaces, it belongs to the Kremlin. If he and Madeleine intend to sell it like Marcel wanted them to, your father would have to sell it on the black market—and that's quite a dubious underworld."

I shuddered to think of my father partaking in criminal activity. I could hardly imagine it. Then again, my knowledge of him was from the perspective of a twelve-year-old, and how well does a twelve-year-old really know their father—his past, his ghosts, his fears, his weaknesses? As well as I could remember, I had always revered my father because he had never given me reason to do otherwise. But I could not say with confidence that I knew the true inner workings of his psyche.

Still, I wanted to give him the benefit of the doubt.

"But he said Madeleine's family was acquainted with the

Romanovs. Perhaps the royal family *gave* them this treasured item—maybe it wasn't stolen. And what about the break-in at Valentina's aunt's house? Don't you think that's a strange coincidence?"

Chet pressed his lips together. "Yes, but we have to consider it could be just that, darling. A coincidence. Are the police working on that case?"

"Yes, that's what Valentina said."

"Good."

"Do you think maybe Madeleine went to Valentina's of her own accord? Maybe that's where she is," I said.

Chet raised an eyebrow. "Maybe. But your father said Valentina and Madeleine didn't know each other. That's why they needed you—to introduce them to Valentina. And that wouldn't explain the blood on the dressing gown."

"Right," I said absently, trying not to relive the hurt at this new revelation.

I looked at my watch. "Speaking of Valentina, I've got a meeting with her and Timothy at the studio in thirty minutes. I can ask her about this package and if she knows of Madeleine." I ran my hands over my hair, wishing I had time to fix up a little. "Can you drop me off there?"

"Sure. How long do you think you'll be?"

"A couple of hours probably. I can get a taxi home."

"All right."

"Maybe Valentina will have information that can help us to find Madeleine." I said the words with hope in my heart, but my mind was filled with doubt. Valentina had made no mention of a package or an item having anything to do with her aunt's attack.

"Sounds good," Chet said. "I'd like to hear what she has to say."

I took another look at my father, who was now heavily asleep, before we walked out of the bedroom.

"What should I do about him?" I asked.

"Leave him a note. Tell him to call you at the studio when he gets up."

I took a notebook and pen out of my purse, scrawled out a message, and set it on the desk. My gaze landed on the photograph of my father and his wife. They stood arm in arm, their heads tilted together, smiling at the camera. I didn't recall ever seeing a photo of my mother and dad together, and a pang of sadness stabbed at my heart. I picked up the frame and put it in my handbag. The photo might come in handy in our search for Madeleine.

CHAPTER EIGHT

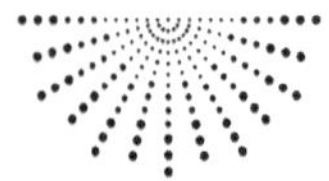

I arrived at the studio five minutes late for the meeting. As luck would have it, Valentina had not yet arrived. I breezed through wardrobe and headed toward my office when Clara approached me.

"Hello, Grace. Timothy said he'd be here in a few minutes." She looked up at me through her round-rimmed spectacles.

"Great," I said with a sigh of relief that he and Valentina were late, as well. I motioned for her to follow me into my office. "Do you have the sketches for the Pierre Moreau character? Timothy has been asking for them. And also for the brother character? I wonder if he's been cast yet. I heard Howard Graves was in the running." I'd never worked with him before but heard he could be difficult.

"Rumor has it United Artists is clamoring to get him for one of their pictures," she said.

"Oh, well I guess we will just have to wait and see, right?" I flopped my handbag and coat on my desk chair and started to go through the sketches out on my desk.

Cantigny, a voice whispered in my ear.

I looked up at Clara. "Did you say something?"

She lifted a shoulder in a shrug. "No."

The hairs on the back of my neck rose, and I shook off the tingling sensation that had bloomed in my hands. It wasn't the first time I'd heard things. Knowing about my mother's slow decline into madness, I often wondered if that would be my fate, as well. Had her insanity started with voices and unsettling dreams?

Clara came over to my desk. "Can I get you some coffee?"

I was aware she'd asked me a question, but the image of my father sprawled across his bed in a drug-induced stupor popped into my thoughts. Coming to terms with both my parents' disabilities—my mother's slide into insanity and now my father's mental problems, as well as his addiction—was sobering and a bit terrifying. My father's state of mind had, for all intents and purposes, been brought on by the war. My mother, on the other hand, well, I had no idea what had fractured her mind. She had never spoken of her family, and I had never met any of her relatives. When I thought of Sophia and her dalliances with drugs and alcohol, it was almost too much to bear.

I turned my attention back to Clara. "I'm sorry, did you say coffee?"

She blinked up at me and nodded.

"Yes, that would be wonderful. And I have another, rather off-topic task I'd like you to do for me, if you wouldn't mind?"

"Sure," she said, eagerness in her voice.

"Would you please call the hospitals in town and ask if a Madeleine Michelle has been admitted?"

Her mouth dropped open. "Oh dear. Is she a relation?"

I waggled my head back and forth. "In a manner of speaking." I didn't offer anything more, not wanting to get into the details.

"Of course," she said, clearly bewildered by my request. "I need to call Emily's Embroidery Shop to check on Helen's gown

first. It proved a little too detailed for my skills. I hope you don't
mind that I sent it over there."

I pulled myself away from the sketches again and met her
gaze. "Emily is one of the best. I'm impressed with your initia-
tive. It shows you want only what's best for the picture, and
that's worth gold."

She pushed her glasses up on the bridge of her nose with a
beaming grin and let out a sigh of relief. "Oh good. I'll call her,
and then I will get right to calling the hospitals." She hesitated a
moment. "I hope everything is okay," she said cautiously.

"Me too."

I hated to be so cryptic, but I really couldn't get into the situation with her. I could barely grasp it myself.

She left my office just as Timothy strode in. He gave me a
tight-lipped smile and walked straight over to the club chairs
next to the three-way mirror. His cinnamon colored hair, often a
tangle of curls, had grown long, giving him an even more impish
and boyish air, save for his thick, closely cropped beard. Irish to
the core, Timothy exuded charm and levity, but today he looked
like he carried the world on his shoulders.

"You okay?" I asked. Timothy and I had become good
friends having worked together on *The Queen of Whitehall*,
despite the fact that it had never hit the silver screen. We had
high hopes for our current film, but I didn't like his defeated
demeanor.

"Sorry, lass." He raised a hand in apology. "We just lost
Howard to United." He slapped his hand on his knee. "He was
bloody perfect for the role."

I sighed. "I'm so sorry." And I was sorry for Timothy and
the film. Sometimes the production delays in this business could
be infuriating, and it coming on the heels of *The Queen of
Whitehall* put pressure on everyone working on the picture. But
there was a part of me that was silently relieved, considering
what I had going on in my personal life. Yes, I was expected to

be at work, but until I had more people to costume and fit, I had more time to spend with Chet, the kids—especially Stevie—and now my father, who desperately needed my help. Not to mention the fact that James Johnson was on the loose. It would be of great benefit to stick closer to matters at home, that was for sure.

"Well, there's nothing to be done about it, darlin'. So where's Valentina?"

"Should be here any moment."

He stood up and came over to my desk. "Show me what you've got."

I showed him some of the sketches, and he perused them with intensity. Timothy had a great eye for costuming and how the clothing made the characters come to life.

"These are good," he said, nodding. "They show her feistiness. Maybe a bit more jewelry to show her power?"

I grabbed a pencil and decorated the drawn character's neck and earlobes with opulent jewels. I then pushed the sketch toward him. He leaned over the drawing to get a better look.

"Aye, yes, lass. Perfect."

Our attention was pulled away from the papers as the energy in the room changed. Electricity seemed to bounce off the walls. I turned to see Valentina and her beau, Anton Belsky, standing there, and beside them was Lenora Lange, the famed psychic medium. My senses always went into overdrive in her presence.

"You brought an entourage, darlin'," Timothy said, a tinge of irritation in his voice.

Valentina removed her dark, turban-effect hat with red feathers cascading down the side, and pushed aside the blond waves that had fallen against her cheek. "We have plans to go to lunch after the fitting."

"We'll stay out of the way." Mr. Belsky placed his hands behind his back and stuck out his chest with an authoritative air. An uncomfortable silence filled the room.

"This is my fiancé, Anton Belsky," Valentina introduced him to Timothy.

Mr. Belsky proffered his hand. "Pleased to meet you, Mr. O'Malley. Valentina has spoken quite well of you."

Timothy's shoulders relaxed, and his face eased into a smile. He took Mr. Belsky's hand.

"And you know Miss Lange," I added.

Timothy took her hand and brushed his lips against her knuckles. Miss Lange looked at me and blinked slowly, the way she did when she was receiving some kind of message from the otherworld. Goose bumps rose on my arms. Was it Joshua, her collective of souls, who was speaking to her? Or perhaps it was Sophia, who always seemed to come through when Miss Lange and I were together. While I had received accurate messages from the beyond before through the medium, the whole idea still made me a little uneasy, and her presence, as usual, unnerved me. I always had the sense she could see right through me and knew my innermost secrets through her communications with Sophia—like she could see all or read my mind. I shook off the eerie sensation.

"Well," I said, pulling my gaze away from hers, not wanting to get into any kind of metaphysical discussion at the moment. "Please take a seat." I gestured to the two club chairs. "I'll just go into the wardrobe room and find another chair for—"

"I'll get it," Timothy said with a smile. I was glad to see his mood lift.

Valentina and I went behind the screen in the corner, and I helped her get into all the layers of the French Revolution–inspired costume. Sometimes it took more than one person to help her as the redingote gown was quite voluminous and the actress often had to be wrestled into the corset, bustle, skirts, and tight-fitting coat. I didn't envy these poor actresses who had to go back into the dark ages of fashion just to be authentic in a film role, but art was art, after all.

She did not bring up the situation with her aunt, nor did I—for the moment. As I was tightening the strings of the corset, I pondered how I would approach the subject.

"I know you have plans to go to lunch," I said, keeping my voice low, "but I wanted to speak with you about something after the fitting. I don't want to take up Timothy's time to discuss it right now. He has a lot on his plate with trying to cast the role of Pierre."

"Certainly," she said and let out a squeak as I pulled the strings taut.

"Too tight?" I released them a bit.

"*Niet.* I just wasn't ready," she said. "But the corset feels good right now. Will the coat fit over it if you leave it this way?"

"We can let the seams out of the coat a bit, if necessary," I acquiesced.

"Let me see how it moves." She held her arms out behind her for me to help her into the coat. I slipped it over her shoulders and then came around to fasten the buttons.

I stood back and surveyed the fit. "See, it's fine."

"I'll walk," she said.

I stepped away, allowing her and the voluminous skirt room to come out from behind the screen. She walked straight past the mirror and practiced sitting, standing, bending down, reaching, and so forth. It looked quite effortless, and I smiled. One of the pleasures of dressing Valentina, I had recently discovered, was that she was not concerned with how the garment looked on her. She was more interested in how it worked from a practicality standpoint and if it made her feel connected to the character. This, in my opinion, was the mark of a true artist.

She stopped and stood in front of Timothy for his inspection. He got up from his chair and circled her, his eyes riveted on the gown, his arms crossed, and his demeanor pensive. He raised his hand to his chin and further perused.

He glanced over at me. "From my standpoint, it's perfect," he said.

I grinned, thrilled with his assessment.

"What do you think, Valentina, darlin'?" he asked, touching the lace at the bottom of her sleeve.

She placed her hands at her waist and moved the skirt back and forth. Finally, she stepped up onto the dais to look at herself in the mirror and then did the same thing again. She turned and surveyed the back of the dress, which had a short train.

"*Da,*" she said, raising her chin. "Perfect."

From his chair, Mr. Belsky clapped his hands together, delight on his face. I couldn't decide if he was thrilled with the dress or excited about the idea of going to lunch. I hoped he would be patient while Valentina and I talked.

"All right, then," Timothy said. "If you don't need me for anything else?"

"We're done," I said.

He nodded and then left my office.

"What did you want to speak with me about?" Valentina asked, stepping down from the platform.

"Oh, well, would you like to change out of the dress first?" I asked.

"*Niet.*" She shook her head. "I will stay in it as long as possible. I like to feel it is a part of me, you know?"

Mr. Belsky cleared his throat. "Will this take long?"

I shook my head. "No. It's about Valentina's aunt."

Mr. Belsky sat up straighter in his chair.

"She is between worlds," Miss Lange interjected, startling me with her smooth, ethereal tone. Her words sounded like threads of silk being moved through fabric. I shivered.

"Oh no. Did she . . . ?" I uttered, worried she'd passed.

"She clings to life," said Miss Lange, "but is pulled toward the light."

I glanced over at Valentina, who gazed back at me with sadness in her eyes. I gently touched her elbow. "I'm so sorry."

"What is it you wanted to say?" Mr. Belsky asked.

I wasn't quite sure how to begin. "Valentina, do you know anyone by the name of Marcel or Madeleine Gallois?"

She looked up and blinked in surprise. "*Da.* Well, I knew *of* them, of the Gallois family. *Moya tetushka* worked for them."

I gave her a brief rundown of my conversation with my father.

"The family are dead? Murdered?" Valentina asked, a horrified look on her face.

"As far as I know," I said. "And now Madeleine, Marcel's sister, is missing. Whatever was in this package, the Gallois family died for it. And we think Madeleine's disappearance might have something to do with it. Do you have any idea what it might have contained?"

Her eyes brimmed with tears. "I know nothing of this. I do not know about this package." Suddenly, the color drained from her face. "*O moy bog! Moya tetushka,* perhaps she received the package when I am out of the country."

My thoughts exactly.

"And now she is— She cannot speak."

I hated imparting this disturbing news to her about Marcel's family, but if the story was true, it might explain what happened to her aunt. Valentina needed to know. "Madeleine is in danger. I'm afraid you may be in danger, too."

Valentina placed her hands at the front of the corset as if she suddenly had trouble breathing. She reached for the back of the chair. Seeing her distress, I unbuttoned the coat and she let me take it off for her. I then loosened the stays of the corset.

She took a deep breath. *"Spasibo."* She thanked me and sank down into the chair, the costume giving her no option but to perch on the edge of it.

"We need to get to the bottom of this," Mr. Belsky blurted, jumping to his feet.

"Have the police had any luck finding who was responsible for the attack on your aunt?" I asked.

"Niet," Valentina said quietly. "I go to them yesterday. They say they are still investigating but have nothing. I show them the pin."

"The police are incompetent," Mr. Belsky added. "They don't care about Valentina or Anna Ivanova. They think all Russians are communists. Please, Miss Michelle, won't you consider helping us now? My offer still stands. I will pay you for your services as an investigator."

I swallowed hard, not sure what to say. If the story my father had told me was true, and if Madeleine had indeed been kidnapped, I was already involved. How could I refuse to help my father? But, truth be told, I had no idea where to begin.

"Please," Valentina implored.

My gaze slid over to Miss Lange, who considered me with ice-blue eyes, her fingertips steepled at her lips. She delicately raised her brows in encouragement.

Did she sense something? Know something? The woman was such an enigma. I shuddered again.

I heard, or rather sensed, someone just outside the doorway. I walked over and peered around it to find Clara standing there. Startled, she looked up at me with her big hazel eyes. How long had she been lurking in the doorway?

"What is it, Clara? Why didn't you just come in?"

Flustered, she blinked up at me. "I . . . I didn't want to interrupt."

"Oh. Well, what is it?" I repeated. "Have you had any luck with the hospitals?"

"No."

I looked at her expectantly, waiting for her to tell me what she had come for. Finally, she said, "I . . . I, um, was coming to get the dress from Valentina."

"She wants to keep it on for a few minutes. I'll bring it to you when we're done."

"Okay," she said and then quickly walked away. I had a feeling there was more she'd wanted to say, but I'd talk to her later.

I went back into the room. Valentina and Lenora Lange were speaking in whispers.

"Well, Miss Michelle?" Mr. Belsky had lit a cigarette and exhaled a stream of smoke in my direction. "What do you say? Will you help us?"

I clasped my hands together at my waist, stalling for time. I was already deeper into this than I wanted to be on account of my father. "I will help you, but I'm not a licensed investigator. I can't take your money."

"You are very generous," Valentina said with a smile. "Thank you."

I smiled back. "You're welcome. In the meantime, Valentina, can you stay with someone?"

Mr. Belsky placed his hands on her shoulders. "She'll stay with me."

She looked up at him adoringly. "I've been staying there since we've returned from our trip, anyway. My home is so . . . empty without *moya tetushka*."

"Good," I said, wondering what in the hell I was getting myself into.

AFTER VALENTINA and Mr. Belsky left, I went in search of Clara. I had been dismissive of her and wanted to apologize. I found her at her desk in the corner of the wardrobe room, working intently on a costume sketch. When I approached, she looked up at me and smiled.

"Was there something you wanted to tell me?" I asked. "I'm afraid I was a little preoccupied when you came into my office earlier. I apologize."

"No need to apologize," she said. She reached for a newspaper lying next to her sketchbook. "I thought you'd be interested in this."

She handed it to me. I stared at the headline: MURDERER JAMES JOHNSON FOUND DEAD AT SANTA MONICA PIER.

A numbing buzz started in my head. I blinked at the words, not quite able to take them in.

"You were involved in the case of Edward Travis's murder, weren't you?" she asked.

"Yes, yes, I was. I read only yesterday that Johnson had escaped from prison."

"Well, he's dead now," she said matter-of-factly.

I read the rest of the article. He'd been found in a burned-out car in the parking lot of the Santa Monica Pier. His remains were unrecognizable, but some of his effects were found at the scene, namely a partially melted medical insulin kit that was spotted on the floor of the car. It was known that James Johnson was diabetic, and that knowledge had tipped me off to his role in the murders. There had also been a partially burned hat with his name in the hat band.

"You all right?" Clara asked.

"What?" I glanced over at her. "Yes, yes, I am. Quite relieved, actually."

I handed her the paper, still in a daze from the news. James Johnson was now one less thing I needed to worry about.

CHAPTER NINE

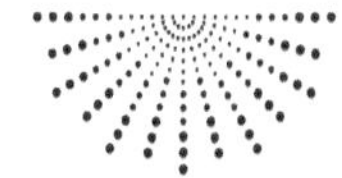

$\mathcal{D}$iscouraged that Madeleine had not been found at one of the hospitals, I thought back to the bloody dressing gown and Chet's insinuation that my father might have something to do with her disappearance. I didn't want to believe it, or even consider it, but what did I really know of their relationship? What if he had been out of his mind with some wartime flashback and had attacked her? Or perhaps they'd gotten into a terrible fight while he was in one of his drug-induced stupors? Or both?

I supposed it was possible, but it was hard to imagine he would ever physically hurt her, as he had seemed so distraught at her disappearance. He'd said she was his life. I wish I understood more about his character, but I had been so young when he'd disappeared from my life.

Could she have left of her own accord? Had she discovered where this valuable treasure was and then left him? Maybe she had used the bloody dressing gown as a ruse? But she seemed so devoted to my father. However, given his addiction and his afflictions, maybe it had all been too much for her. Perhaps she was with him out of a sense of duty. Did she truly love him, or had she felt sorry for him?

I made my way to the front gates of Ambassador Films to get a taxi. There were usually a few out front waiting to get a fare with some famous actor or actress. I spied two of them. I approached the first one and got in. I told the driver the address of the farm, and he pulled out of the lot.

As we drove down the road, I took the picture frame with the photo of my father and Madeleine within it from my purse. I studied the photo, trying to glean from it what I could of their relationship, their body language. My father, with a playful expression on his face, had her in a firm grasp. Her smile was broad. Almost too broad. Was it a bit forced? Perhaps it was actually a grimace?

If she had intended to leave my father, where would she go and how would she get there? Would she leave Los Angeles? If so, I imagined she would take the train. Le Grande Station on Second Street and Santa Fe Avenue was the closest station to the boarding house. It was a bit out of my way, but I thought it was worth a shot to see if any of the workers there might recognize her from the photograph.

"Driver," I said, leaning forward in my seat, "I've changed my mind. Take me to Le Grande Station please."

He nodded and turned down the nearest street to change our route.

We made our way to Hollywood Boulevard and then turned onto Sunset. I assumed, correctly as it turned out, we'd take Sunset all the way to Broadway.

The driver pulled up in front of the station about thirty minutes later. I paid him, thanked him, and then got out. I hustled up the steps and headed inside.

The place was teeming with people. Seeing how busy it was I suddenly felt foolish in this most likely vain attempt.

I spotted a row of five ticket windows with attendants inside.

If I wanted to find out if Madeleine had purchased a train ticket, I would have to stand in line and speak to each one and show them the photograph.

I picked the first line to my right, which was the shortest line, about seven people deep, and settled in. Luckily, it seemed to be moving pretty fast. I scanned the other lines. They too were moving along nicely.

The interior of the station was a pleasant, open, and airy space with potted palms and other greenery attractively arranged throughout. Honey-colored oak benches with wrought iron finishes were lined up in the center of the high-ceilinged room. A buzz of electric energy hummed with all the people and activity.

My attention was drawn to a couple with two children, a girl and a boy, probably aged at around eight and six respectfully, standing near one of the potted palms at a doorway, obviously waiting to board their train. The girl, holding her father's hand, and the boy, holding his mother's, jumped up and down with joy, probably excited about riding the train. An older woman stood behind them beaming at the children, clearly amused at their enthusiasm.

Then my gaze was pulled to a man standing near them. He wore a gray, rather rumpled-looking suit that was a bit large for him. His hat was pulled down low on his head, concealing the upper part of his face, and a cigarette dangled from his lips. An extremely tall and well-dressed woman wearing a wide-brimmed hat stood next to him, arms crossed at her waist.

Go, a woman's voice whispered.

I turned around and was startled to see a man behind me. "Excuse me?" I said.

He was short and round faced, and he smiled warmly at me. He nodded, indicating the space in front of me. The line had moved, and there was a big gap between myself and the person ahead of me. I hurriedly moved up. In seconds, I was at the window.

"Where to?" the ticket master asked. He had deep smile lines at his temples and wore a patent leather–brimmed cap like all the other uniformed attendants.

"I'm not traveling today," I said. "I need to know if you remember selling a train ticket to a woman with a large beauty mark on the left side of her face, right above her mouth?" I showed him the photograph. "She would have been here this morning."

He gave me a dubious look. "I see hundreds of people every day, ma'am."

"I realize that." I smiled. "She's very pretty, blond, petite, and she has a French accent."

He pressed his lips together and shook his head. "I'm sorry, ma'am. It's not ringing a bell."

"Thank you," I said, a bit discouraged. But what could I expect? The place was full of travelers and was probably this busy every day.

I walked over to the next line, and my eyes drifted back to the children who were growing louder and more animated by the second. I wondered why their parents did not tell them to settle down. I certainly would have.

The older woman behind them had lost her amused expression. Her lips were now pursed in disapproval. I glanced at the man with the suit, and he quickly diverted his gaze. He'd been watching me. I took in a deep breath and shook back my shoulders, trying to shuck off the eerie sensation. I thought of James Johnson, but then remembered the newspaper article Clara had shown me earlier.

I supposed it wasn't terribly unusual for a man to regard me with some interest, I reasoned. Perhaps he found me attractive.

Go, the voice whispered again.

Icy fingers played upon the back of my neck. I looked around me. The sound was distinctly female, but no woman was close enough for me to hear her. Was this another voice in my head or the same one I'd heard earlier at work mentioning that strange word—*Cantigny*. Was it Sophia speaking to me from the grave as she had on occasion before? And, if so, what did it mean?

I chased away the thought, lest I started to dwell on the fact that I might be going mad.

I settled into line behind a woman carrying a small dog wearing a coat of green velvet. A papillon, if I wasn't mistaken. The woman's own fur-collared wrap coat was finely made and of the highest quality. She exuded an air of wealth and poise, and I wondered if she was an actress. I knew of most of the actresses in Hollywood, but there were always more coming from all over, flooding the southern coastline.

I proceed through all the lines with no luck. No one had seen Madeleine, or at least they hadn't remembered her. Feeling defeated, I headed out.

When I emerged from the building, I noticed the man with the rumpled suit standing up against the wall. How strange. I'd thought he had been waiting to board a train. Maybe he'd just been seeing someone off—like the tall, elegantly dressed woman, I reasoned. But an uneasiness settled in my gut so I quickly descended the steps toward the line of taxis waiting for fares. I walked briskly to the first cab.

I got in, tossed my handbag on the passenger seat, and closed the door. As we drove past the station, I looked up to the top of the steps. The man was still there, looking onto the street, his face still hidden by the brim of his hat. I couldn't see his eyes, but I had the distinct feeling he was watching us leave.

I tried to shake off the disturbing sensation. I guess I had been spooked by the voice in my head, and now my imagination was running away with me. At any rate, I was leaving and the man leaning up against the building made no effort to get into a car and follow us.

Since I was in such close proximity to the boarding house, I decided to pay my father a visit. "Two thirty-nine Alvarado please," I said to the driver.

He hadn't called me at Ambassador as I had asked in my note. A niggle of worry persistently pervaded my thoughts, swirling like an agitated butterfly in my stomach since Chet and I had left him earlier that morning. Truth be told, thoughts of my father had been consistently lurking in the corner of my mind since I had gotten that first telegram informing me he was alive. Thoughts of Sophia crept into the periphery of my mind, as well. The words *Cantigny* and *go* played in my thoughts. I assumed the former was a French word, but it made absolutely no sense to me. Madeleine and her family were French, though. Did it have something to do with them?

These whisperings were not a new phenomenon. Lenora Lange had told me they were messages from the beyond, but I still worried I might be cracking up. The messages left me feeling unsettled and confused, as they were never complete, never cohesive. Miss Lange had insisted I was being guided or consoled or informed about troubling matters in some way. It was just up to me to figure out what the messages meant.

I pulled my attention back to the taxi, silently observing the view out the window, attempting, with a modicum of success, to clear my mind. About ten minutes later, we pulled up in front of the boarding house. I told the taxi driver to wait for me.

"Meter's still running," he said without turning around.

"I know. I won't be long."

As I made my way up the walk, I noticed a green car drive by, and a niggling feeling crept into my bones. Was that the same car I'd seen near the café?

I couldn't determine the make or model, nor could I tell if there was a dent in the fender as I watched the car turn onto an intersecting thoroughfare. My gaze settled on a black Ford Model T on the opposite side of the street. A man was sitting in the driver's seat reading the newspaper. He must have sensed me

observing him because he turned from the paper and gave me a
nod in greeting. He didn't look familiar to me. I thought it a
strange place to be reading the paper, but maybe he was waiting
for someone. Could his presence have something to do with
Madeleine's disappearance? And, if so, why was he just sitting
there?

Thoughts of my father passed out on his bed overtook me,
and I continued toward the house. I considered entering his
rooms through the door in the alleyway, but that didn't feel quite
right, so I went to the front door of the house and rang the bell.
The landlady answered and motioned for me to come in and go
to my father's rooms.

He answered when I knocked, looking as frantic as he had
been earlier that morning. "I'm so glad you're here." He grabbed
me by the sleeve and pulled me into the apartment.

"What's going on? Are you all right?" I asked, alarmed by
his agitation. He went over to the desk, picked up an envelope,
and handed it to me.

"It's in there," he said. He fumbled with a pack of cigarettes,
pulled one out with shaking fingers, and lit it. His pacing ritual
began.

I took the letter from the envelope and unfolded it. In typewritten letters, it read: *Your wife says you don't have the egg.
FIND IT or she dies. Await further instructions.*

"Egg? What does this mean?"

He didn't answer but continued pacing. The corner of
another piece of paper peeked out from the envelope, and I lifted
it out. It was a photo of Madeleine tied and gagged. A dark
bruise stained the upper part of her right cheek under her eye.
My stomach clenched at the sight of her.

I scanned the note again. The letters were faded, as if the
typewriter ribbon had been running out of ink. Also, the letter *a*
hung below the others, making the words look jumbled.

"They will torture her," my father said, his voice shaking.

"That's what they did to her parents. Marcel said they died from the torture."

I shook my head in dismay. "We have to get the police involved. This is proof she's been kidnapped."

"No!" my father shouted, making me flinch. Seeing how he'd startled me, he raised his hand in apology, ash from his cigarette falling to the floor. "These men are professionals. They get one whiff of police and she's dead." He took a deep drag of his cigarette, his hand trembling so hard I was afraid he'd drop it. I wondered when he'd need to reach for the morphine again.

"We can't get the police involved," he repeated.

"Dad, the police are much better equipped to handle this kind of thing. We—"

"I cannot involve the police!" he yelled.

"Why?" I countered, my hackles raised at being treated this way. I was trying my best to help him.

"It's my medicine."

"What?" I asked, confused.

He sighed. "The morphine. I obtain it illegally." He crumpled, looking as if he might pass out, and then he righted himself. "I'm sorry to tell you about this. I'm so ashamed."

"But Madeleine said a doctor prescribed—"

"She lied. To protect me. I don't have a doctor here."

"Oh my god," I said, shaking my head.

"If we get the police involved, they might find out about the morphine. I could be sent to prison, don't you see?"

"Then get rid of the morphine!" I raised my voice. Wasn't that obvious?

He closed his eyes as if fighting for control. "I can't. You don't understand. How can I expect you to understand? I cannot function without it. Not now, not while I'm torn apart with Madeleine missing."

I stared at him, open-mouthed. He was right. I did not understand the power of his addiction, nor that it had such a grip on him he would not give it up for the sake of involving the police to find his wife. What kind of man had he become?

"And these men who have taken her, they will kill her if we get the police involved," he repeated, his voice calmer.

I sighed, acquiescing . . . for the moment.

"The item—" he said, changing the subject.

"An egg?" I interrupted, my eyebrows raised. The idea was preposterous.

"The item," he continued with thinly veiled impatience in his voice, "was stolen from the Russian royal family during the siege of the palace in St. Petersburg. Madeleine's brother was a Bolshevik sympathizer."

My heart fell to the pit of my stomach. *Stolen?* Chet had been right. This was turning out to be an even bigger nightmare than it had seemed already.

"Why didn't you say so before?"

"Don't you see? If the police find it, they will return it to Russia, and then Madeleine will die." His voice hitched with emotion. "These goons are part of a much larger operation, I'm sure of it. If we don't find it, they will kill us all." His voice ended in a high-pitched squeak, and his whole body shook so violently I thought he was going to collapse. I took hold of his arm and led him to the couch, trying to control my own trembling at this new information.

He sat down, and I stood over him, staring at him, unable to fully take in what was happening. This predicament was much, much bigger than he'd first explained.

"Why would an egg cause such danger and turmoil?" I thought out loud.

"It's a Fabergé egg," he whispered.

I folded my arms across my waist, growing impatient with this convoluted conversation. "I thought you said you didn't know what it was."

He looked up at me with sheepish eyes. "I—"

"You lied. When are you going to start telling the truth? How can you expect me to help you—"

"Please, please," he said, his voice wavering. "No more lies. I promise. I'll tell you everything. We have to get her back."

My jaw tensed, but an overwhelming surge of pity swept through me at the desperation on his face. He was a complete mess.

I let out a sigh. "What's a Fabergé egg?" It sounded completely ludicrous.

"They are jewel-encrusted gold and silver eggs created by the esteemed House of Fabergé for the Russian royal family since 1885. Each one is worth a fortune."

So it *was* an egg. And a very valuable one at that. I sank down on the sofa next to him.

He rested his elbows on his knees and raised his quaking hands to his face. "We have nothing," he said between his fingers, and then he lowered his hands. The skin on his face had gone pallid and gray. "We spent everything we have coming over to this country. I'm down to my last fifty dollars. We needed this egg—to sell it—to have a future," he continued. "I can't work anymore, Gracie. Marcel intended to send the egg to Anna Ivanova, for her to keep it for him. He planned for the three of us to follow as soon as possible. He was going to set us up here in the United States, but when he realized he wasn't going to make it, he begged us to come anyway, to find the egg, sell it, and live comfortably for the rest of our lives. Once we were settled, Madeleine was going to help me get off the morphine. We had it all planned, and now—"

He shook his head. "But now the fortune doesn't matter. Only Madeleine matters. We need to find this egg. We need to get her back. I can't lose her."

I wrapped my arm around his bony shoulders, my mind whirling. It was becoming increasingly clear he was in no condition to be left alone. And it was also glaringly obvious he was most likely in danger. What if these people came back for him, tortured him to get information, killed him? As broken and flawed as he was, my father had just been returned to me. How could I lose him again?

"You're coming with me," I said quietly but with conviction.

He met my gaze, confusion in his eyes. "What? Where?"

I gave his shoulders a squeeze. "Get your things together. You're going to stay with me. We have room in the bunkhouse."

"But what about Madeleine?" His eyes filled with fear. "We need to wait for further instructions."

"We'll continue to check on the place. Are you paying weekly here?"

"Yes." He raked his hands through his hair.

"Very well." It was the middle of the week so we had a couple of days. "I'll take care of next week's rent, but you aren't staying here until we get this situation figured out."

He shook his head. "I don't know—"

"Dad," I said with a little more zeal, "we are family. That is what families do. They help one another, take care of one another."

"All right," he said reluctantly. "I'll just be a minute."

"I'm going to call the farm to let Rose and the others know we have a guest. May I use the phone in the hallway?"

He nodded and then went into the bathroom, I assumed to take a dose of morphine. That, too, needed to be dealt with, but now was not the time.

I went into the kitchen and checked to make sure the door was locked, then came out through the living room again and went out into the hallway. I made my way to the phone and picked up the receiver. I hesitated before dialing. I hoped I was doing the right thing. It was clear my father could not remain here alone, but taking him to the ranch might put us all in danger. But what choice did I have? He was my responsibility. I needed to take care of him.

I informed Rose of the situation and asked her to have Chet pick us up. She said she'd send him on his way and we hung up.

Then it dawned on me. There was one more person I needed to call.

I dialed the number.

"Hello, Joe? It's Grace. I need a favor. How would you like to come to dinner tonight?"

CHAPTER TEN

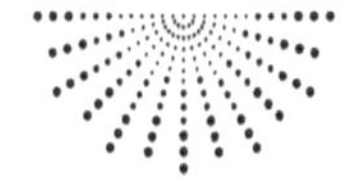

I paid and dismissed the cab driver who was still waiting for me on the street, and Chet arrived thirty minutes later to retrieve us. My father was still in the bedroom when Chet knocked on the kitchen door. I answered it and started to tell him the new version of Dad's story and showed him the note and the photo.

"This is far more serious than we'd thought," I said. "Dad told me this precious item was a Fabergé egg. Jewel encrusted, worth a fortune. It was stolen from the palace in St. Petersburg."

"That's what I was afraid of," he said on an exhale.

"These people are obviously dangerous. I don't want to put the kids in jeopardy." The man who had been sitting in the car reading the paper flashed in my mind. I told Chet about it. "What if he's being watched?"

"There is no one out there right now," Chet said. "I'll make sure we aren't being followed on the way back to the ranch."

I nodded, feeling a little bit better. I thought about the strange man at the train station. There was no indication he'd followed me here. I also reminded myself he hadn't made a move to get in a vehicle to do so and couldn't have possibly followed us on foot. Then I remembered the newspaper headline Clara showed me.

"James Johnson is dead." Saying the words eased my disquiet at the idea of being followed.

Chet nodded. "I saw the newspaper. Hell of a note. At least he won't be a threat to anyone anymore. But you are right. Your father shouldn't be left here alone."

"I've called Joe to enlist his help. "

Joe Manetti, our neighbor and Chet's business partner, was a confirmed bachelor and had plenty of experience with all kinds of personalities—law abiding and criminal included. A veritable tough guy, Joe had been raised on the wrong side of the tracks and had made good in his life. I had every confidence he would help us keep the ranch secure and stave off any kind of trouble that might come our way because of my father.

After a somewhat circuitous route to the ranch, we arrived about an hour and a half before dinnertime. Chet parked the car, and then we walked Dad over to the bunkhouse, which was situated behind the barn. Ned, Daniel, and Stevie were mucking out the stalls as we passed and stopped working when they saw us.

I motioned for them to come over, and then I made the introductions. "He's going to be staying with us for a while," I said. "In the spare room in the bunkhouse." I swung my gaze over to Ned, who nodded in agreement.

"It will be nice to have a roommate," he said, smiling at my father.

Dad didn't smile back but gave a curt nod.

Chet laid a hand on my dad's shoulder. "I'll show you your new digs and get you settled in." Carrying my father's small suitcase, he led him into the bunkhouse.

"He looks sad," Stevie said, leaning against the muck rake in his hands.

"He is." I didn't see the point in sugarcoating anything, but I also didn't feel the need to explain to Daniel and Stevie. At least not yet. "We'll have to go out of our way to be kind to him." I smiled and then turned my attention to Ned, giving him a tilt of my head. "Can I speak with you?"

He handed his rake to Daniel. "Sure. You boys continue. I'll be back in a minute."

"I need to do my paper route," Stevie said. He and Miss Meyers had arranged to get his route back, and as it turned out, the newspaper needed him for both morning and evening deliveries. It had only been a couple of days since his arrival, but so far, he was doing a good job of juggling his paper route, schoolwork, and chores.

We walked several yards away from them and stopped under the great oak tree that canopied the backyard and the area leading to the barn. I gave Ned a brief rundown of the situation.

"We are going to have to keep an extra close eye out for any strangers who might appear here at the ranch. Also, it might be nothing, but I've seen a green car with a dent in the right fender a couple of times. I've called Joe, too. He's coming over tonight for dinner. I'm going to ask him to help keep a lookout."

Joe's ranch butted up against ours, and the road that led to our ranch was actually part of his property—he'd just allowed an easement for us to share it. Anyone coming to our ranch would have to pass through his.

"Sounds good." Ned sank his hands into his pockets. "I'll be sure to keep my eyes peeled."

"Thank you." I smiled. "I'm going to ask Rose to serve us dinner in the dining room tonight. I've also invited Felicity. The kids can eat in the kitchen."

After I'd called Joe, I had called Felicity. I figured I'd best assemble a team to help find this egg, or Madeleine, or both. We needed all the help we could get. But I didn't want the kids privy to this information until I could figure out what exactly they needed to know. I wanted them to be careful but not afraid, which would take some finessing.

"I'd like for you and Miss Meyers to join us for dinner, as well. Were you planning to eat here tonight?"

"Yeah. Ruth is spending some time with a friend."

"Good. Thank you, Ned."

"You got it," he said with a firm nod. "Well, I better finish up. See you in a bit."

Stevie strode over to us. "I need to go now," he said. "If I don't, I won't finish before dinner."

My heart stuttered at the thought of him leaving the ranch, but I reassured myself that we had not been followed. His paper route meant so much to him.

"All right," I said. "But, Stevie, no talking to strangers."

TWO HOURS LATER, we were all sitting down to dinner. Rose had prepared a creamy Waldorf salad and hearty rabbit stew. Next to me, my father slumped in his chair, his mood sullen. I couldn't decide if his tamped-down appearance was due to worry, depression, irritation, or another dose of the morphine —or perhaps it was the addition of two gin rickeys he'd helped himself to before dinner. We normally didn't have alcohol in the house in these days of Prohibition, but we'd had some stashed away from the party Edward Travis had hosted in our home earlier that year. Chet had felt the nerve-racking occasion called for it, and my father had already had the lion's share.

Felicity, usually able to charm and engage anyone in polite conversation, tried in vain to connect with him. After another attempt, she shot me a look and I gave her a brief shake of my head, indicating her efforts would be to no avail.

"Thank you for joining us tonight," Chet said. "We have a situation we'd like to discuss with you and to enlist your help with."

All eyes turned to us, and Chet gave me a nod. I explained what we were up against.

"How can we help?" Felicity asked, eagerness in her tone.

Cantigny, a voice whispered. It was Sophia's voice. I was certain this time. She repeated the word. What did it mean?

"Grace?" Felicity looked at me with a furrowed brow.

I snapped out of my reverie. "Yes, sorry. We need to find this Fabergé egg, or we need to find Madeleine. Preferably both. But we don't have much time."

"I'd like to get my hands on these hoodlums," Joe said, leaning forward in his chair.

"We need your eyes and ears here, Joe," Chet said. "We are going to rely on you and Ned to keep this place as secure as possible. We have to protect the kids at all costs."

A brief flicker of disappointment crossed Joe's face. He probably wanted a more active role, but he quickly complied. "Will do," he agreed.

"So where do we start?" Felicity asked. "Seems like finding a needle in a haystack. We have so little to go on."

I took a deep breath. "I agree. Tomorrow, we can start with Valentina's aunt's place. Go over it with a fine-toothed comb, see if we can find any clues as to the whereabouts of this parcel. Maybe the police missed something."

"We should also probably canvas the hotels." Chet took a bite of his stew. "These men most likely aren't American—either French or Russian. We should ask hotel staff or guests if they have encountered any foreigners."

"I can do that," Felicity volunteered.

"We should also question the neighbors of the boarding house," I said. "Ask if they've witnessed anything or seen anyone unusual in the area."

"I'll take that," Chet said.

"Okay, then we have a plan."

I looked over at my dad. He'd straightened his back, and

the life had come back into his eyes. His expression had brightened, and instead of staring at his plate as he had been the entire time so far, he made eye contact with the others. I'm sure our conversation had instilled a little bit of hope in his heart.

He cleared his throat. "Thank you," he said, addressing all of us. "I really appreciate your helping Madeleine." As he said her name, his voice hitched. He cleared his throat again. "I only hope it isn't too—"

I laid my hand on his arm, stopping him. "We can't think like that, Dad. We need to move forward. Are you with me?"

He nodded, but the worry in his eyes returned.

The sound of the front door opening and closing captured my attention. From where I was sitting, I could see Stevie heading toward the staircase, his newspaper tote slung over his shoulder. I took a quick look at my watch. He was later than usual.

"Excuse me." I got up from the table and followed him up the stairs. His door was left slightly ajar, and I gently knocked.

"Stevie?" There was no answer so I pushed the door open. He lay on the bed, his eyes closed.

"Stevie, are you all right?" I sat down on the bed next to him. "Rose saved you some dinner. It's rabbit stew. Are you hungry?"

He opened his eyes and shook his head. "I just want to sleep."

"Did everything go okay on the paper route?" I asked, wondering if something had happened to bring about this melancholy and fatigue.

"Yeah, it was fine." He turned over onto his side, facing away from me. I reasoned these mood swings were due to his grief. In my own experience, the rollercoaster of emotions associated with grief sometimes came out of nowhere when you were least expecting it. The only thing that lessened the heartache was time.

I sat there wondering what to say next to comfort him, but

he'd made it clear he didn't want to talk. I got to my feet and left the room, a heaviness settling in my chest.

THE GROUND IS thick with mud, and my shoes are heavy with it as I slog my way over the terrain. Gunshots ring out through the air. I stop and stand over a large trench dug out of the ground. It stretches as far as I can see, winding around like a ribbon over the land.

Sophia, who is dressed in a white, flowing, Chiffon gown, holds my hand. She points to several men in Army uniforms, hunkered over a tiny fire trying to warm their hands, their rifles perched across their knees. Snow falls softly around us, and our breath freezes in crystalized droplets that fall to the ground.

Two of the men, their heads bent together, talk in hushed tones while others sleep or sit quietly smoking cigarettes. One of two men in conversation is my father, but he looks different to me. The sudden shouts of more men in the distance fills the air. The men in the trench jump into action.

"Cantigny," Sophia whispers. And then she is gone.

I opened my eyes and sucked in a breath. It had been a few weeks since I'd dreamed of Sophia, aside from the waking dreams and whispered messages I had experienced of late. Was she trying to tell me something, or was this just the fractured musings of my imagination and broken memories?

I thought of my father and wondered how he'd fared the night in the bunkhouse. He must be sick with worry over Madeleine. As much as I struggled with the reality that my mother had been replaced in his heart, I could see the deep love he and Madeleine shared, how necessary she was to him and his well-being. Had he slept, or had he spent a restless night in a new and strange place tossing and turning? Or, worse yet, had he rendered himself unconscious with morphine?

I closed my eyes again and said a silent prayer that we find Madeleine and that eventually we be able to bring my father back to himself, free from the chains of his memories and the drug.

When I opened my eyes again, dim light filtered through the window. Chet stirred beside me and then sat up and reached for his robe on the bedpost. He quietly put it on, padded across the floor in his slippers, and walked out of the room.

My thoughts drifted to Stevie—another sad and broken being. His pain was so palpable I could feel it sink into my heart every time I looked at the boy. Grief was a force so powerful it was difficult to penetrate and break apart. And it never really left you, I knew that for certain. There would always be that piece of sadness in the periphery of my soul.

I got out of bed and reached for my own dressing gown on the opposite bedpost. I wrapped the silk around me and breathed in its scent, the aroma that lingered in my imagination reminding me of Sophia. The robe had once belonged to her. In reality, I knew the fragrance of her favorite perfume no longer remained in the fabric, but the memory of it was so fresh in my mind I could actually smell it every time I put on the gown.

The dream that had awaken me bloomed in my mind again. What did it mean? Did it have something to do with the turmoil that had arisen from Madeleine's disappearance? Perhaps I should arrange a reading with Miss Lange. As uneasy as she made me, she'd been helpful in pointing me to James Johnson when I'd been trying to vindicate Lizzy of Edward Travis's murder.

I slid my feet into my slippers and made my way down the hall to Stevie's room. Slowly, I turned the doorknob and pushed open the door. The gray light of early morning filled the space. He slumbered heavily, his breathing steady and slow. I pulled the door shut and went downstairs, telling myself he was okay. He would be okay. He just needed time.

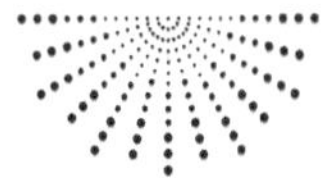

$\mathcal{I}$ arrived at Ambassador within the hour. I wanted to get as much work done as possible as early as possible so I could continue to work on the case. I knew Valentina would be at the studio, as well, since we were scheduled to do a costume screen test that morning. Perhaps we could go to her aunt's house to search for clues when we were done.

I made my way to the fabric room in search of a textile appropriate for another actress's costume. I scanned the cubbies looking for the perfect fabric.

"Morning," Clara said from behind me.

I turned to face her. "Good morning, Clara. You're in early."

"So are you," she said with a smile.

"Well, I'd like to leave early this afternoon." I sifted through the rolls of fabric, and I finally found one that might work. I pulled it out and examined it. It was a heavy, dark-brown velvet brocade. "There we are. This is perfect for Helen's ball gown, don't you think?"

"It's gorgeous," she said absently. Her mind seemed to be elsewhere.

I turned my full attention to her. "You okay?"

She nodded. "I was going to ask you the same thing. You seem so distracted lately."

Her statement surprised me. I thought I had been doing a fine job compartmentalizing and separating work from the case.

"I'm fine," I said, shaking it off.

"Does it have something to do with Madeleine? Who is she?"

I set the bolt of velvet down on the table. "She's— Well, she's my father's wife. She's missing, and I'm trying to find her."

"Oh. I guess it's good she isn't in the hospital, right?"

I swallowed, wishing she was in the hospital as opposed to being held captive by greedy murderers.

"Yes," I said, not wanting to elaborate.

Clara laid a hand on my shoulder. "Please let me know if there is anything I can do to help." Her smile was warm and exuded sympathy.

"Thank you." I reached up and patted her hand. "I will."

Our attention was drawn to the doorway when someone lightly knocked. It was Valentina.

"Oh good. You're here," I said, glad she was punctual. The sooner we could get her dressed for the screen test, the better. She'd have to do a few costume changes, and I wanted to be as organized as possible to ensure a smooth shooting session. I handed Clara the fabric. "Let's get the pattern laid out on this and get it cut. Take it to one of the seamstresses, maybe Marie," I instructed. "Then come to my office and help Valentina get dressed." I turned to Valentina. "I need a word. Come to my office?"

"Sure," she said.

We stepped inside my office, and I indicated she take a seat in one of the club chairs. I sat in the opposite one.

"Madeleine has indeed been kidnapped," I said. "My father received a note from her captors demanding we find this parcel or—"

Valentina's eyes widened. "What is this thing?" she asked, exasperated. I knew the feeling.

"It's . . . Well, it's— I can't tell you. It will put you in danger."

She pulled her chin back in dismay. "*Moya tetushka* could die because of this item. It was sent to my home. Am I not already in danger?"

I bit my lip, considering whether or not to tell her. She was right. She was in deep, too.

"It's a jeweled egg that's worth a fortune." I felt that was sufficient information.

"An egg?"

"Yes." I also didn't want to tell her how Marcel had come to possess the egg, that he'd actually stolen it and now it belonged to the Kremlin.

"But, please, Valentina. You mustn't tell anyone what it is. Not even Mr. Belsky. Anyone who knows will be in danger."

"*Da.* I will tell no one."

I let go of the breath I hadn't realized I was holding. "Thank you. These men, whoever they are, have made it clear they are willing to kill for it. We have to find it. I'd like to search your aunt's house for any kind of clue as to its whereabouts."

"Of course," she said. "I am meeting Anton there, to get more of my belongings. He didn't want me to be there alone, even though I have driver. He's very protective."

"That's wise," I said, touched at his concern.

"We can go after screen test."

"Wonderful." I breathed a sigh of relief. "Let's get you dressed."

Right on cue, Clara walked in with the first costume. I felt confident that things were going to run right on time this morning.

AFTER THE SCREEN TEST, Valentina and I met in the actors' parking lot. Having never learned to drive, Valentina employed a chauffeur to drive her white Rolls-Royce Silver Ghost. She introduced me to Max, a gentleman of considerable age, as he held the back door open for me to get in. Now I understood Mr. Belsky's interest in meeting Valentina at Anna Ivanova's. Max would be no match for violent criminal heavies. I slid across the seat to make room for Valentina, and she gracefully climbed in after me.

Fitting her exotic persona, the automobile she owned was anything but understated with red rims and whitewall tires. The leather interior, also red, was soft as butter. Like Valentina herself, this machine turned heads. The traffic on the street allowed us through like the parting of the Red Sea. Drivers and passengers on the road gawked at us like rabid fans. Uncomfortable with the attention, I had to force myself not to sink down in the seat to hide myself.

"Where is your aunt's house?" I asked instead, diverting myself from my feelings of exposure.

"Beverly Hills."

"Oh!" I couldn't hide my surprise. In my mind, her aunt was a little old lady who'd immigrated to this country with nothing but the clothes on her back, like so many people of foreign descent did.

She gave me a smile of understanding. "I bought house for her. Anna Ivanova raised me. My mother died when I was very young. I have six older siblings. My father could not take care of all of us so *moya tetushka,* my mother's sister, took me in. She never married. It's always been just two of us. I missed her so much when I left Russia. When the Gallois family moved back to Paris, I sent for her here." Her chin quivered.

"I see," I said. "You must love her very much."

Overwhelmed with emotion, Valentina nodded.

We rode in silence until Max swung the big machine onto a long driveway that climbed up a sloping hill.

"Here we are," Valentina said, her voice brighter having had some time to collect herself.

We drove through a grove of eucalyptus trees. Citrus trees dotted the hills around us, as well. Valentina rolled down her window, and the soft, peppery fragrance mingling with the tang of lemon floated in through the open window. She breathed in deeply, closing her eyes and relishing the experience. It was heartwarming to see her appreciation of the natural world—quite the contrast from all the material trappings surrounding her.

Finally, we approached a single-story, California ranch-style house—white stuccoed with a Spanish tile roof. I noted several chimneys. I didn't really know what I had expected, but even though the house was large, it was modest in appearance—not like a mansion but like a home.

Max opened our doors for us, and we got out. My senses came alive with the fragrant aroma of roses filling the air. To the side of the house was an enormous rose garden filled with both vibrant red and soft pink blooms. The smell was intoxicating.

I followed Valentina through the front door. I was half expecting a butler to greet us at the foyer, but there was no one there. Light flooded through tall windows lining the U-shaped interior that surrounded a tranquil courtyard. A large, tiered fountain sat in the middle of the courtyard.

"This is lovely, Valentina," I said in amazement.

"It is—*was*—my little paradise. But now—"

I could see how what had happened here with her aunt could turn her feelings toward the place.

"Well, let's get started," I said. We didn't have time for melancholia at the moment.

"Please," she said, "what are we looking for?"

"Anything that might lead us to this package—any kind of

clue to its whereabouts. What time does the mail delivery come?"

"I believe mail comes in the early afternoon. One or two o'clock. Why?" She held out her hand for my handbag and set hers and mine down on a large, rectangular entry table.

I looked at my watch. It was nearing two. "I'd like to speak with the mailman. See if he remembers the package."

I turned around to face the front door and looked for a mail slot, but the door, rustic in design, appeared too heavy and too old—like antique old—to ruin with a mail chute. "Where does the mailman deliver the mail?"

She opened the front door and pointed to a patinaed cast-iron mailbox sitting atop an ornate cast-iron pedestal near one of the exterior windows. I hadn't noticed it when we'd driven up.

"And the packages?" The box looked rather small for large deliveries.

"He brings them to front door. *Moya tetushka* is usually home. She only went out to market, and she worked at church sometimes, but that was in morning."

"I see. Can you keep an eye out for the mailman and let me know when he arrives?"

Valentina nodded.

"Okay, then. I'll get started." I smiled at her, hoping to give her some assurance.

Standing in the center of the house, I turned to the right to cover that part of the residence first. Because of its U-shaped design, the interior of the home seemed to be one big window-lined hallway with rooms on the opposite side.

I started down the Saltillo-tiled hall and found my way first to a modestly furnished bedroom. I went to the wooden bureau and started to go through it. The drawers were empty. I went to a large wardrobe and opened it. Empty, as well. Must be a guest room, I reasoned.

I scanned the floor, looked under the bed, and peered into the fireplace, which was devoid of anything except a grate and three unburned wooden logs. As it was late August, it was not quite cool enough for a fire.

I went back into the hall and found another room, this one much larger with books lining the walls. A library.

A musty odor floated on the air and mingled with the smell of old books and dust. Between two floor-to-ceiling windows sat a substantial Victorian mahogany desk. I walked over to it and sat in the leather chair. I ran my hands over the surface of the dark, smooth wood, then went through the drawers. Everything within them was tidy and organized. If the intruders had gone through this desk, someone had set it back to rights, which was a little unfortunate because whoever did—I assumed Valentina or a member of her staff, if she had one—might have missed or inadvertently disposed of a clue.

I leaned back in the chair to think and closed my eyes. Immediately, a vision of Sophia appeared. She was standing in a beautiful garden. Her hair swirled around her head in the breeze, and the leaves of the trees rustled and swayed with the movement. I could hear the deep, resonating sound of bells—like those of a cathedral.

Unable to reconcile the vision, I opened my eyes and shook away the image. I slid open the middle drawer of the desk again, and my gaze settled on a stack of papers. There were a few bills marked *Paid* in ink—one from a grocer, one from a hardware store, and one from a landscaping company in the amount of one hundred fifty dollars. A note under the total read, *Fr. Michael.*

A priest. Church. Or was it a cathedral? Why had I heard cathedral bells? Was Sophia trying to tell me something?

I slid the drawer closed, came out from behind the desk, and scanned the room. In every corner a chair and side table invited one to sit down and read. In accordance with every other room of the house so far, light flooded through the windows. It was an ideal reading room and evoked the feeling of luxury and time.

And this room, too, had a fireplace. It shared a chimney with the room I'd just left, but something was different about this fireplace. It had been used. I knelt down to peer inside. A single lonely log, singed black, hadn't completely burned, but there was a pile of ash underneath it.

I spotted a fireplace poker to my left and used it to sift through the ashes. I noticed what looked like a partially burned piece of paper toward the back of the fireplace. Setting the tip of the poker on it, I dragged it forward. It was the corner of some kind of bulletin or advertisement that had eluded the flames. It read, *Weekly Bulletin M—San G—* The rest of the words had burned off. Why had this missive been tossed into the fire and not just thrown in the trash?

"Grace?"

I turned to see Valentina in the doorway with Anton Belsky. I hadn't been aware he'd arrived.

"I think I may have found something in *moya tetushka's* bedroom. Tucked under some items in bedside table."

They entered the room, and I nodded a greeting to Mr. Belsky. Valentina held out her hand. Resting on her palm was a small key.

"It is a safe-deposit box key," Mr. Belsky said.

"Oh my goodness." A cascade of chills raised goose bumps on my arms. I took the key and examined it. It looked exactly like the safe-deposit box key Chet and I had. "It would only make sense that she would put something so valuable in a safe-deposit box in the bank. This is wonderful, Valentina! Do you know where your aunt did her banking?"

She looked over at Mr. Belsky and then turned her gaze back to me. "Pacific Savings and Loan. Anton's bank."

"Of course," I said, feeling a little silly. Why wouldn't they do business at Anton's bank? Valentina had agreed not to tell him what was concealed in the package, but if it was in his bank and we found it, wouldn't he want to know its contents?

Wouldn't he expect Valentina to open it? I decided to wait to see how things played out. Actually finding the egg would be a good problem to have. "Well, let's go, then."

~

VALENTINA HAD TAKEN a few moments to put some things in a suitcase, and then we set out to leave. As we were walking out of the house to the cars parked out front, a vehicle was making its way up the drive. It was a postal truck.

"Oh good," I said. "We didn't miss him."

He parked the truck and got out with several envelopes in his hand. He had a stout physique, with thick legs and a pudgy middle. His round face sagged with age, and his eyes drooped in the corners, giving him the look of a basset hound. He tipped his cap to us.

"Miss Baklanova," he greeted her.

"Hello, Sam," she said.

"How is Miss Ivanova?"

She shook her head. "She is not doing so well."

The mailman pressed his lips together. "I'm awful sorry to hear that. Such a nice lady. She doesn't deserve what happened to her."

"Hello, Sam," I broke in. "My name is Grace, and I wanted to ask you a question pertaining to Miss Ivanova's attack."

He tipped his hat to me. "Don't know if I can help, but fire away."

"Do you recall delivering a package to the house about a month ago?"

He gave a slight chuckle. "Do you know how many packages I deliver in a month?"

"I know," I said, "but this one was sent from Europe. Does that ring any bells?"

He pressed his lips together, and then his eyes brightened.

"Yes. Yes, I do remember. There was a package postmarked from overseas. Heavy thing, about yea big." With his hands, he indicated roughly two feet long by one foot high—larger than I had imagined.

"Must have cost a small fortune to send so far," he continued. "I took it to the door and rang the bell. Didn't want Miss Ivanova to have to lift it. She answered the door, and I set it inside the house for her."

"Thank you, Sam," I said, encouraged by the news.

"You bet." He tipped his hat again. "Better be off. The mail waits for no one." His gaze traveled from me to Valentina. "I'll keep your aunt in my prayers."

As he got back into his truck, I turned to Mr. Belsky. "The package he mentioned seemed rather large for what my father described. Do you have safe-deposit boxes that big?"

"Yes," he said. "We have a couple sizes of safe-deposit boxes. What Sam described would fit, but perhaps this item is not as large as you think if you account for the container that might have been used for an overseas delivery."

"Yes, you're right," I said. "Well, shall we?" I was anxious to get to the bank. If the egg was there, we could get Madeleine back and then report the incident to the police.

CHAPTER TWELVE

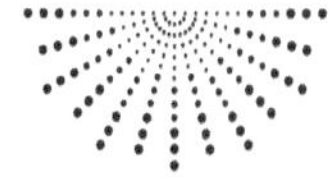

On our way to the bank—Valentina and me in her automobile with Max at the helm, and Mr. Belsky in his gleaming white Mercedes with sweeping fenders and glimmering wheels—Valentina explained to me that Pacific Savings and Loan was a private bank, and at the moment, there were two branches. One was in Los Angeles and the other in San Francisco.

"Anton comes from large banking family in Russia," she continued. "He immigrated ten years ago. Settled in San Francisco where he started his own banking company."

"How interesting," I said, always curious about how people from other countries settled in America. "And did you know each other in Russia?"

"No." She shook her head. "I met him in San Francisco. We were only acquaintances at first, but we kept seeing each other at parties. We became friends."

"I see."

"I got film role in Los Angeles soon after we met so I moved here."

"Did you keep in touch, then?"

"No. But when he moved here two years ago to open Los Angeles branch, I ran into him at country club. He asked me to dinner, and we see each other ever since." She smiled at the recollection.

"How lovely." It was nice to see her without the troubled expression she'd been wearing of late, consumed with worry for her aunt.

Max slowed the Silver Ghost. Other cars lined the curb in front of Pacific Savings and Loan so he had to park a little ways beyond it.

Mr. Belsky waited for us at the huge double doors leading into the building. As we entered the bank, the guard at the door greeted Mr. Belsky, and he ushered us inside. We swept past the customers in line. The tellers, all wearing black suits, straightened their backs at seeing Mr. Belsky and did their best to greet customers in a friendly and efficient manner.

The guard led us through a door and walked down a hallway, going deep inside the building. We reached another set of doors to the right. Mr. Belsky waved the guard away and took a set of keys from his pocket and opened the door. We entered a room with walls lined with green metal boxes, all with bold numbers soldered on them and each with two separate key holes.

The boxes on the bottom row were larger, about the size of a milk crate. Embedded in the center wall was a large metal door that I assumed led to a walk-in safe. A large table sat in the middle of the room. The air was thick and cold, and the atmosphere sterile. The thought of being locked inside this room sent a chill down my back.

"Which one?" I asked.

Mr. Belsky picked up a leather book from another, smaller wooden table next to the door. He started to flip through the pages. "Ah," he said, his face grim with concentration. "Here we go. Anna Ivanova. Number two hundred fourteen. Wait here while I get the other key."

I started to peruse the numbers on one wall while Valentina scanned the other two. After a few seconds, I found it, and a surge of disappointment swept through me. It was one of the smaller boxes.

"Here it is." I pointed. "But I don't think we'll find what we're looking for."

Mr. Belsky came back into the room, strode over with the bank's key and inserted it. He nodded to Valentina and she took the one she'd found and opened the box. He pulled the box from the wall and carried it over to the table. Valentina eagerly started to go through it. She sifted through some papers and set them on the table.

"May I?" I asked her, setting my hand on the papers. She gave a quick nod.

I studied each one. There was a deed to the house, two birth certificates—Anna's and Valentina's—and some other legal documentation that I couldn't read as it was in another language, which I assumed from the symbols was Cyrillic. There was also a receipt for a fairly substantial donation to the Mission San Gabriel Arcángel.

The burned paper I'd found in the library fireplace flashed into my mind. The letters I had been able to make out were *M* and *San G.*

"Valentina, does your aunt attend this Mission San Gabriel?"

She nodded. *"Da."*

"There was a receipt in the desk drawer of the library made out to a landscaping company with the name Father Michael written at the bottom. He is from the mission?"

"He was. He died last year. *Moya tetushka* paid for church's courtyard to be landscaped. It had fallen into disrepair. She worked with Father Michael on it. They made it beautiful," she said wistfully.

But, again, why burn the bulletin?

I also found it curious Anna Ivanova was Catholic. I would

have assumed she would have belonged to the Russian Orthodox Church. I had never been religious myself, but once, while living in New York, I had attended a Catholic church with Helena, one of the Ziegfeld showgirls. I had been fascinated with the pomp and circumstance and somber rituals of the Mass.

I pulled my attention back to the papers and sifted through the rest of them. I found nothing of significance.

Valentina then produced a small wooden box and opened it. Four velvet boxes were nestled inside—the kind used for jewelry. She opened each one. Two of them contained delicate gold necklaces, one a diamond ring, and the last one a silver bracelet. She snapped them shut.

"Only trinkets," she said.

"Mr. Belsky, is there a way to find out when Miss Ivanova last accessed the box?"

He went back to the book and opened it up. "March 1923."

"Well before Marcel sent the package," I said, trying not to let my discouragement show.

Feeling we were at a dead end here, I looked at my watch. "I need to get back to the ranch and see to the children. I'll give Felicity a call and find out if she had any luck at the hotels."

Mr. Belsky put all the items back into the safe-deposit box and returned it to its slot in the wall. He locked it with both keys and handed Valentina one of them.

"And I must get back to work," he said. He placed his hand on Valentina's back. "Are you all right?"

"Yes. I will take Grace home now. Then I go to hospital to see *moya tetushka*."

"Until later, then." He planted a kiss on her forehead.

Valentina and I said our goodbyes to him and then walked back down the hallway, through the door, and into the lobby. There were even more customers than before. Then I remembered it was the fifteenth of the month—payday.

We skirted the lines and walked out the front door. As we

descended the steps, I noticed a man sitting on one of the lower steps smoking a cigarette. As we passed by, he pulled his hat lower on his forehead, which I thought strange and oddly reminiscent of the man at the train station. Could it be the same man? A shudder escaped down my spine.

We continued down the street toward Valentina's automobile, and my feeling of unease only increased. I turned my head to look back at the bank. The man had stood up and was watching us. I quickened my pace and surged a little in front of Valentina. I thought about telling her to hurry up, but I didn't want to alarm her.

We finally reached her car. As I was about to get in, I spotted a dark-green Oldsmobile parked on the other side of the street. It looked exactly like the car I had seen driving by the boarding house. I had been concerned about the man in the black car parked across from the boarding house, but now that seemed like a coincidence. But the green car that had driven by . . .

My gaze flitted over to the Oldsmobile again. Not only did it look like the car outside the boarding house but it looked much like the car with the dent in the fender I had seen when I went to the café to meet my father. But from where we were, I couldn't see the right fender to be certain.

The feeling of unease seized my gut—with a vengeance. I was definitely being followed. It had to be in relation to my father, Madeleine, and the egg. But then again, the first time I'd seen the green car, I hadn't yet met with my father. Could these henchmen who'd taken Madeleine have somehow known my father would reach out to me? I swallowed down the paranoia threatening to strangle me.

We got into the car, and Max swung the automobile around, making a U-turn in the street.

"Could you just have him drive around a little before taking me home?" I asked Valentina. I wanted to see if the car would follow us, if my paranoid thoughts were well-founded. I was also now even more concerned for Valentina.

She looked at me as if I'd lost my marbles. "I thought you said you needed to get home to your children."

I sighed, debating whether or not to share my suspicions with her. But of course I should. She needed to be cautious, to stay on alert.

"I do need to get home, but—" I turned around in my seat to see if we were being followed. There was no sign of the green car. Still, I needed to be sure. "I think someone might have followed us here," I whispered. I wasn't sure why I whispered, but with Max up front, it felt appropriate.

Valentina scoffed. "I am followed all the time. Reporters, fans, men who desire to be my lover."

"I know," I said, coming to terms with a bitter, more likely reality. "It might be me who is being followed. I think it has something to do with my father and Madeleine, which means it most likely has something to do with what happened to your aunt. We can't be too careful. This is the third time I've seen the same green car. You'll have to keep an eye out for it."

The driver leaned back and tilted his head to hear us. "What is this?" he asked.

I looked at Valentina for permission to share the information with Max. She nodded. I leaned forward in my seat so he could better hear me. "Max, have you ever noticed a green Oldsmobile touring car with a dent in the right fender when you have been driving Valentina around?"

He shook his head. "Can't say as I have, miss. But then again, I wasn't looking for it."

I leaned back in my seat, realizing I didn't have to be sitting quite so forward. "Well, if you wouldn't mind, you might want to keep a lookout for it. I suspect someone might be following me. And if I'm right, they've seen me with you and Valentina. You'll have to be on alert to make sure she isn't being followed, as well."

"Oh, I will," he said. "I'm used to losing people when I'm with Miss Baklanova. We get followed all the time."

"Well, this person might not be a fan," I said. I wasn't sure how much information Valentina wanted to share with her driver.

"Noted," he said.

I exhaled, settling farther into the seat, satisfied there would be another set of eyes watching out for Valentina but also discomforted at the notion that I was the one being pursued.

AFTER MAX HAD ASSURED me we weren't being followed, I had him take me to the studio. Just to be safe, I didn't want such a conspicuous car driving into the ranch.

I said my goodbyes to Valentina and Max, and hustled into the warehouse that accommodated wardrobe and my office. Once in my office, I rang the house. Rose answered.

"Is Chet there?" I asked.

"He's in the barn, I think," she said.

"Could you ask him to pick me up at the studio?"

"I've got to take a pie out of the oven in a minute, but then I can."

"That's fine," I agreed. Thoughts of the green Oldsmobile resurfaced. "And Rose, ask him to come around the back of the studio to pick me up."

"The back of the studio?" She sounded perplexed by the strange request.

"I have some boxes I need help with," I lied. I didn't want to alarm her.

"All right," she said. I sensed she was about to hang up.

"Wait. How is Stevie today?"

"Seems okay." The sound of a bell chiming came through the

phone. "That's my pie. Gotta go." She hung up before I could say more.

I set the receiver back on the phone stand, hoping "okay" was a good thing. I'd be home soon, I reasoned, and could see for myself.

Next I called Felicity.

"Any luck at the hotels?" I asked.

"Unfortunately, not so far," she said. "I've got a few more to visit. I've been juggling it with meeting with tradesmen at the mansion for the remodel. But don't worry. I'm on it."

I thanked her, appreciative of her efforts, and hung up the phone.

Ambassador Films, with its large outdoor sets covering an expanse of ten acres, was a bit out in the middle of nowhere beneath the hills of the new housing development called Hollywoodland. A dirt road circled the area, and I made my way out toward the back of the warehouse where the interior sets and tons of equipment used to create and maintain them was located.

After about fifteen minutes of waiting, I spotted Chet's truck coming around the bend, a flurry of dust behind it.

"Why did you want me to pick you up here?" he asked through the open window.

I hopped in the passenger's side and shut the door with a loud clang. "I think I'm being followed."

His brow knit with concern. "You're serious?"

"I keep seeing a dark-green car, an Oldsmobile."

"You're sure it's the same car?"

"Pretty sure."

"That's not good." He ran a hand through his hair. There were bits of hay in it, and a layer of grime coated his face. He'd been stacking hay.

"I know. This is getting scary, Chet."

He let out a breath through pursed lips. "I hate that we are trying to chase down stolen property. Marcel obviously tried to sell it on the black market, which is never a wise move. The men who are after it have gone to great lengths to get it back."

"So now we are in way over our heads." My heart thumped in my chest at speaking the words out loud. "My father is right. If we get the police involved, Madeleine will surely be killed."

Chet took in a deep breath, then exhaled. "I hate to admit it, but you're probably right."

CHAPTER THIRTEEN

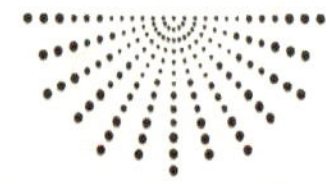

*S*ophia *walks through a dense forest. The trees are immense, their naked branches clawing into one another. Snow cascades softly from the sky. She tilts her head back, and sticking out her tongue, she catches snowflakes on it like we did when we were children. She then rights her head and gazes directly at me. Her mouth is moving as if she is speaking, but I can't hear the words.*

A battle rages around us. Men in dark-green uniforms and helmets run through the trees or crawl on their bellies, slithering like snakes under barbed wire fences. Their faces are dirty, their clothes caked with mud. Gunshots zing through the air, and explosions thunder all around us, but Sophia continues walking.

"Harold," she says. "Cantigny."

The words echo in my head. She stops, standing on a pile of dead leaves. I try to move closer to her, but with every step I take, she retreats. I can't reach her. Panic rises in my chest.

"Sophia!" I call out. I don't want her to abandon me. I need her.

She slowly shakes her head, refusing to heed my plea. Her image fades, leaving me alone and terrified.

A tremendous boom shakes the ground beneath my feet. Dirt, mud, and trees fly through the air all around me. I call out to her again, desperate to reach her. I hold out my hand and—

My eyes popped open, and I bolted upright, blinking into the darkness. A hint of gray dawn was beginning to fill the room.

"Grace?" Chet rolled onto his back and took hold of my hand.

"Sorry," I said.

"You all right?" His voice was thick with sleep.

I squeezed his hand. "I think I need to see Lenora Lange."

"What for?" He raised himself up on an elbow.

"I think Sophia is trying to tell me something."

"Did you have another dream about her?"

I nodded. "I also feel her presence during the day. She speaks to me, but it's only one or two words at a time. Words that don't seem to have any connection. I can't seem to get to her—get close to her."

I suddenly realized how crazy this all sounded, and if I had been speaking to anyone else, they would have thought I needed to go to the loony bin. But Chet was familiar with my visitations from Sophia and knew she often guided me when I was in trouble or in danger.

"What words?"

I told him what she had just spoken to me.

"Cantigny?" he repeated, sitting up. "That's in France. The Battle of Cantigny was the first major battle the Americans fought in the war."

My eyes opened wide. "How strange. I thought she might be trying to tell me something related to the case."

Chet rubbed his eyes. "Maybe she is."

"Were you there? At Cantigny?"

"No, I was stationed at Nancy." He lowered himself onto his back again.

The room slowly filled with more light.

"Do you know what 'Harold' means? Who that might be?" I thought perhaps it was a general or some important person related to the battle.

"No idea." He yawned loudly and stretched. "I should get up. I need to check on Blixa."

Blixa was one of the mares Chet and Joe were rehabilitating. She had sliced open her knee while trying to jump a barbed wire fence.

Chet got out of bed and ran his hands through his hair. I watched him pull on his pants and then pad into the bathroom, my mind still full of the dream, almost as if I were lost in it. I swung my feet to the ground and shoved them into my slippers at the side of the bed. I wrapped myself in Sophia's dressing gown and pulled it tight around me, my heart heavy with sorrow at her loss. I thought of my dad and wondered if he felt the same longing for her.

I got out of bed and headed downstairs. The aroma of fresh coffee greeted me as I entered the kitchen. Rose stood at the wooden butcher's block in the center of the room kneading bread dough.

"How was dinner last night?" I asked.

Realizing we were not going to make it home for dinner, Chet and I had gone to a café in Burbank. When we had finally gotten home, the kids were all tucked away in their rooms doing homework, and Ned and my father had retreated to the bunkhouse. I hadn't wanted to disturb him, hoping he'd gone to bed early. He had looked so tired.

"It was fine."

"How was my father?"

Rose stopped kneading. "A bit fidgety. Quiet. Stevie seems to have taken a shine to him, though. Sat next to him at the table. Kind of doted on him."

I blinked. "Really?"

"Yes. He was late, though. From his paper route. Came in

just as we were sitting down."

I sighed. I didn't like the idea of Stevie being gone from the farm any longer than absolutely necessary, given what we were facing with the case and the possibility that I was being followed.

The door to the outside opened, and Ned came into the kitchen. "Morning." His tanned and handsome face broke into a bright smile. He took a cup from the cabinet and headed toward the coffeepot.

"Morning," Rose and I echoed in unison.

"How was my father last night?" I asked. "Did you talk at all when you went to the bunkhouse?"

Ned shook his head. "No. He didn't say much. Didn't sleep much, either. I could hear him rattling around from time to time during the night, poor guy."

My heart sank. Although, I shouldn't be surprised. He was probably totally consumed with worry for Madeleine. It was an awful situation.

"Do you think he's asleep now?"

"Nah. He's on the porch smoking like a train."

"I'll go check on him," I said.

I stepped outside into the cool of the morning. The air was thick with the moisture of early dawn and the sweet fragrance of alfalfa. My slippers crunched through the gravel as I made my way to the bunkhouse. My father was pacing the front porch. When he saw me approach, he stopped and waited for me.

A momentary flash of disquiet arced through me. It still felt odd that my father was back in my life again, and in such strange circumstances. I couldn't help but wish he'd reached out to me before. Had it not been for this Fabergé egg, would he have continued to let me live in the dark about his existence? I wondered what Sophia would think if she was alive. The uneasy disquiet morphed into the bitterness of resentment. As I neared him, I tried my best to set it aside.

"Hello," I greeted him.

He gave me a brief nod.

"Sleep well?"

"I'm fine," he said, avoiding the question.

Thinking of Sophia, I remembered my dream. "Dad, in the war, did you fight at Cantigny, in France?"

He met my gaze and stiffened. His mouth twitched. My question had made him uncomfortable. Speaking of the war must bring back a torrent of emotions. I almost wished I hadn't asked. He didn't look well.

"No, I was at . . . Aisne. Why do you ask?"

Did I dare tell him that Sophia had spoken of it in my dreams—when asleep and awake? I shrugged. "It's nothing."

When I got closer to him, I noticed a sheen of perspiration on his face. His complexion was gray, and his shirt was drenched with sweat. I could smell the distinct odor of sick on his person. He raised the cigarette to his mouth, his hand violently shaking.

"Dad?" Concerned, I placed my hand on his shoulder, and he shook it off. I recoiled but wasn't offended. He was in a bad way.

"Dad, you should sit down." I indicated to the rocking chair next to the door.

"Can't," he said and resumed pacing.

"Do you want your medicine?" I asked. I didn't like the fact that he was so dependent upon it, and broke the law to acquire it, but I hated seeing him like this.

"Didn't bring it." He flicked the butt of his cigarette onto the dirt and then pulled the red-and-white pack of Lucky Strikes from his front pocket.

I was surprised at his response. In his anxiety over Madeleine, he must have forgotten it.

"Do you want me to go to the boarding house to get it?"

He shook his head. "I flushed it down the commode. Need to kick this." His voice suddenly sounded strangled, and he clutched at his stomach. "Need to be sharp." He grunted. "For

Madeleine's sake." He doubled over, then hurried to the end of the porch and vomited.

"Dad!" I rushed over to him.

He straightened and wiped his mouth with the back of his trembling hand. He waved me away. "I've been through this before." His eyes watered, and his face was crimson with pain. "Worse, even."

He gulped in air and then released it. He reached into his pants pocket and took out a box of matches. He placed the cigarette in his mouth and tried to light it, but his hands were shaking so badly he couldn't manage it.

"Let me?" I offered.

He held the box of matches out to me, and I lit the cigarette for him.

"Dad, maybe this isn't the time . . ." As much as I wanted him to be rid of this vile habit, I was concerned that with the emotional turmoil of the situation, the stress he was putting on his body would be far too much to handle.

"I have to," he said, his eyes filling with sorrow.

"Okay." I was impressed at his resolve. He really was trying —for Madeleine's sake.

I looked up to see Stevie striding toward us. He carried a glass of orange juice in one hand and a plate of food in the other.

"I brought you some breakfast, Mr. Michelle," he said. "Rose made yours special, since you don't like pancakes and all."

My dad's face blanched at the sight of the food. "Thank you, son," he said. "You can set it on the table inside, if you would please."

Touched at his thoughtfulness, I smiled at the boy. "That was kind of you, Stevie."

I also felt a pang of sadness. I had no idea my father didn't like pancakes. It was silly to feel hurt at something so trivial, but it made me feel the gulf between us widen even more.

"It's no problem." He took the plate into the house.

"Dad." I stepped closer to him. "I'm worried about you."

He sucked on the cigarette like it was his lifeline and stepped away from my approach. "I'll be all right. It's going to be rough for a couple of days, but I'll get through it."

"What can I do to help?" I asked.

"Find that egg and get my wife back," he said, his voice hard and flat.

I sighed, wishing I could assure him I had the situation in hand. But, in truth, I was more confounded than ever, so I said nothing

I LEFT my father sitting in the rocking chair on the porch of the bunkhouse. The morning was crisp, and the sounds of activity in the barn lulled me out of my obsessive worry over my father's state of being.

I veered from my intention to go to the house and went into the barn instead. Ned was busy dumping oats and grain into the horses' stall buckets, and Daniel occupied himself with the chore of mucking. He happened to be working in Goldie's stall.

Goldie was my horse, gifted to me by a man named Frank Deerhunter, who had lived in New Mexico. I had met Frank and Goldie when I was on tour with the Ziegfeld Follies, back when I was a showgirl. The horse and I had bonded, and at his death, Mr. Deerhunter had bequeathed her to me.

When she saw me enter the barn, she nickered.

"Hello, girl." I went to her stall door. She lowered her head, and I stroked the area between her eyes.

"Hey, Grace," Daniel said. "Seen Stevie?"

"He took my father some breakfast. I think he's still at the bunkhouse." I curled my hand around one of Goldie's ears, relishing the warmth and softness of it. She closed her eyes contentedly.

"Daniel, how do you think Stevie is doing? I mean, with the chores and school."

Daniel shrugged. "Okay, I guess. He doesn't say much. He has trouble with his schoolwork. Doesn't pay attention in class. He's a right good hand here in the barn and with the horses when he's not sittin' on a hay bale daydreaming. Seems to have hit it off with your dad, though."

"Yes," I said absently, stroking Goldie's jowl. I was glad the two troubled souls had seemed to make a connection, so why did it leave me feeling so hollow? I had been reunited with my father after nearly thirteen years, and yet, he still felt so removed.

The thought sent an ache into my heart. I leaned my forehead against Goldie's and closed my eyes.

Harold. The name crept into my ears, and I opened my eyes.

"What's that?" I asked Daniel. He was now at the back of the stall, still using the muck rake.

He stopped what he was doing and looked up at me. "I didn't say anything."

"Oh." I gave my head a little shake. This was the second time I'd heard that name. Who was it, and what did it mean? I resolved I would ring up Miss Lange right after breakfast.

Goldie swung her head away from me to look at something. It was Stevie approaching, muck rake in hand.

Daniel leaned on his rake. "About time."

"Where do you want me to start?" Stevie asked, seemingly not disturbed by Daniel's irritation.

"Apollo's stall and then move on down. I'm almost done with this side of the barn."

Stevie gave a brief nod and then turned his attention to me. "I almost forgot." He reached into his pocket and pulled out a crumpled envelope and handed it to me. My name was scrawled across the front of it in a rather erratic hand. There was no address and no postmark on it.

"Where'd you get this?" I asked.

"It was stuck in the fence at the gate. I saw it when I came home from my paper route. I was going to give it to you last night, but you weren't home."

I turned the envelope over in my hand. There was nothing written on the back.

"Thank you, Stevie. You'd better get to work. I'm sure Rose has those pancakes almost ready, and she doesn't like it when people are late to the table." I raised my eyebrows at him and hoped he got the hint about arriving late for dinner.

"Yes, ma'am." His face flushed pink, and he stepped around me to go to Apollo's stall.

I slipped my finger into a gap in the seal of the envelope and opened it. I pulled out the note inside. In printed block letters, it read, *Find it yet? The clock is ticking . . .*

My heart sank to the pit of my stomach, threatening to make it come up. This person, or these people—"professionals" as my dad had called them—knew where we lived! And despite Ned and Joe keeping a closer eye out, they'd managed to get this to the gate? It had only been a day since we'd received the first note, and it said to await instructions. But there were no instructions here. Perhaps there was yet another note at the boarding house? If these people were trying to create a pressure cooker of tension, they were succeeding.

Panic sent a jolt of adrenaline through me, causing a tingling sensation in my hands and feet. They knew my dad was here. Would they attempt to take him? I thought about moving him into the house, but then I would be putting the children at even more risk.

Why did I bring him here? I chided myself. But what other option had I had? He couldn't be alone, and I couldn't ask my friends to take care of him. I wrestled with the questions in my head.

"Daniel." I set my hands on top of Goldie's stall door, trying to ground myself. "Where is Chet?"

He stopped shoveling, resting his weight on the rake again. "I think he's out in the field."

"Thanks." I tucked the note inside my dressing gown pocket. I left the barn, scanning the fields looking for Chet. The morning dew sparkled like diamonds on the grass. I spotted him bent over the water trough in the north alfalfa field and made my way to the gate.

"Morning, Grace!" Susie called out from inside the chicken coop as I passed by. She waved at me enthusiastically.

I gave a quick wave in return and picked up my pace, breaking into a jog. When I reached the metal gate, I slid open the latch, slipped through, and closed it again. I broke into a run, my anxiety rising to a crescendo, my mind and heart filled with fear.

Finally, I reached him. "Chet. They know where we are," I said, out of breath.

"Grace, what are you doing out here?" He looked up from his task, eyeing my state of dress, or rather, undress.

I pulled the note from my pocket. "Stevie said he found this tucked into the fence at the entrance gate." I handed it to Chet, and he opened it.

"Damn." He met my gaze. "Did he say if he saw someone on the lane?"

I shook my head. "No. He was late coming back from his paper route and said he saw this in the fence." I ran a hand through my hair. "What have we done, Chet?" I couldn't keep the panic out of my voice. "The kids. Your mother. My dad. We aren't safe here."

He gently took hold of my arms. "Listen," he said, looking into my eyes. "If they had wanted to come through that gate to get your dad or harm anyone, they would have done so. But they didn't."

"That's true." He had a point, and the hysteria I felt bubbling inside subsided a little. "But—"

"They are just putting on a little more pressure," he said.

"We have to find that thing, Chet. But we have nothing to go on."

He squeezed my arms. "Felicity is still questioning people at the hotels. I'm going to head over to the neighborhood of the boarding house again to talk to more of the neighbors there. It might take a little time, but—"

"We don't have time!" I shouted, the panic returning. Hearing the frantic tone of my voice, I took in a deep breath and then released it. "I'm sorry," I said, shaking my head. "It just feels like they are everywhere."

Chet pulled me to him in an embrace. "It's okay. We need to keep focused, keep everyone safe, and move forward."

"I'm going to call Felicity. To tell her about his note."

"Good," he said, releasing me. "I'll talk to Joe and tell him to stay vigilant, and perhaps even armed. Same with Ned."

The thought that we had to consider armed guards, even though they were just the neighbor and our ranch hand, made my stomach roil.

"Do you think we should tell the kids at least something, so that they are more careful?"

"Probably not a bad idea. Let's talk to them at breakfast."

Suddenly, there was a commotion and shouting coming from the barn. Goldie, in a flurry, came running out through the large, open double doors, her eyes wide with fear. She turned the corner and headed for the field. In one large bound, she soared over the fence and landed on the other side, running toward the hills.

"What the—" Chet said.

More shouting came from the interior of the barn. We quickly made our way over, and in the center aisleway, Stevie and Daniel were rolling around on the ground, engaged in battle.

"Hey, hey, hey!" Chet ran toward them. "Break it up, you two."

They remained locked together, fists flying.

Ned came out from the feed room, a startled look on his face. "What's going on?" He quickly surmised the situation and lunged for the boys. He took hold of Stevie by the shirt collar while Chet grabbed Daniel's arm, and they broke the two apart. Ned hoisted Stevie to his feet. The boy's nose was bloodied. Daniel, his shirt ripped, got up of his own accord.

"What in the hell are you doing?" Chet asked him. "I thought you'd be more mature than this."

Winded, Daniel bent over to catch his breath. "I know," he said, holding up a hand in apology. "I'm sorry. He came at me like a lunatic."

"Don't call me that!" Stevie's face contorted in rage and lunged toward Daniel again, but Ned grabbed hold of his arms from behind.

"Don't," Ned said calmly. "Simmer down, Stevie."

"What happened here?" Chet asked.

"He called me crazy," Stevie said, his cheeks turning crimson.

"I was just making a joke." Daniel wiped the dirt away from his shirt and pants.

What had seemed like a joke to Daniel probably hit home all too hard for Stevie. I could understand the boy's sensitivity. Having a parent with mental problems, like his dad and my mom, always led to some scary but inevitable questions: Will this happen to me? Will I go crazy, too? Am I insane? Will they lock me away?

We hadn't told the children about Stevie's father because one just didn't talk about these things, but now I saw how it might have garnered a little more sensitivity and sympathy in the other kids.

"What happened with the horse?" Chet asked.

"We were finishing up in her stall when he came at me," Daniel explained. "You know how she doesn't like anyone

behind her. She tried to jump over the stall door but just crashed
into it instead. She ripped it off its hinges. It's all broken up."

"I'll check it out," Ned said, finally letting go of Stevie. The
boy shook his shoulders and straightened his shirt.

"Daniel, go out and get the horse," Chet said. "We better
check to see if she's injured."

Daniel brushed past us and grabbed one of the halters
hanging on a hook on the wall. He headed out of the barn.

Stevie's face fell, and his eyes welled with tears. "I'm real
sorry. I didn't mean for the horse to get hurt."

I went over to him and wrapped my arm around his shoulder.
"I know you're having a hard time, Stevie, but the fighting has to
stop. You can't deal with your feelings through violence. Daniel
has been more than patient with you."

"The guy just pushes my buttons!" Stevie said, wiping his
nose.

"Come on. Let's get you in the house." I started to pull him
with me, but he stood his ground.

"I want to finish my chores."

I exchanged a look with Chet, and he indicated with a nod
that the boy should continue with his work.

I hadn't known him for very long, but I was beginning to see
that Stevie always wanted to do the right thing. His emotions just
got in the way. And his profound grief at what had happened
with his father just made things worse. A stone lodged at the
base of my throat thinking about what he must being going
through.

"All right," I said. "But breakfast will be ready soon. You'll
want to eat it while it's hot." I smiled at him and tousled his hair,
trying to disguise my own feelings of grief and pity.

CHAPTER FOURTEEN

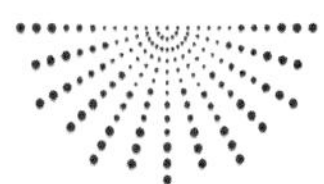

When I got back to the kitchen, Rose handed me a piece of paper. In her other hand was a plate with some toast, freshly buttered and slathered in jam. She knew I preferred a light breakfast.

"Miss Baklanova just rang. Said her aunt is conscious. She wants you to come to the hospital. Here's the address." She then handed me the plate. "Better get dressed."

I looked down at my dressing gown, completely forgetting that I hadn't yet dressed for the day. I took the plate and headed upstairs to make myself presentable.

I arrived at St. Vincent's Hospital an hour and fifteen minutes later. Valentina met me in the hallway outside of her aunt's hospital room. She wore a simple lavender pantsuit, and her hair was tied up in a scarf. She wore no makeup. I wondered how long she'd been there.

"How is she?" I asked.

Valentina shrugged. "She is in and out of consciousness. When she was awake, she recognized me, though." Tears filled her eyes.

I took hold of her hand. "Well, this is progress," I said, trying to sound upbeat.

A nurse came out of the room. "She's asking for you."

Still holding my hand, Valentina pulled me into the room after her. My stomach clenched at seeing Miss Ivanova's face. Yellow and green bruises covered her left cheek and right eye, and her head was wrapped in a bandage.

Valentina dropped my hand and went to sit next to Miss Ivanova. "I'm here," she said.

The battered woman rolled her head on the pillow toward Valentina and opened her eyes, looking at her. The hint of a smile twitched at her lips.

"*Moya tetushka*, this is my friend Grace." Valentina pointed to me, and Miss Ivanova turned her head toward me. She blinked her eyes in greeting.

"Hello, Miss Ivanova." I stayed at the foot of the bed. My eyes strayed to Valentina in a silent inquiry to ask if I should proceed. She nodded her head.

"I won't keep you," I said to Miss Ivanova. "I know you must be tired, but I have some questions for you. It's a very important matter." I refrained from saying it was a life-and-death matter because she most likely already realized that based on her condition. "Do you remember receiving a package from France?"

She closed her eyes and nodded her head. She opened them again. "They were looking for—" she said, her voice raspy from lack of use.

"The people who did this to you?"

She nodded again.

"Do you know how many people there were?"

She held up two fingers.

"Did you hear them speak? Were they French?"

She shook her head. "Russian."

"Can you describe them?"

She looked over at Valentina, her eyes large and sad, and then back at me. "One large, tall. The other—a scar." She ran a finger over the bridge of her nose.

"Thank you. That's wonderful, Miss Ivanova. You are being so helpful. Did they call each other by name?"

She shook her head, and her mouth started to tremble.

I gave her a small smile. "I just have one more question. What did you do with the package?"

She squinted, and her face contorted as if she was in pain. She put her fingertips to her temples.

"I think she is getting tired," Valentina said, her eyes imploring mine. "It's too much."

"Sister Mag-Magdalena," Miss Ivanova croaked. Her face relaxed, and then she fell into the heavy breathing of slumber.

I looked over at Valentina. "Does that mean anything to you? Is that someone at the Mission San Gabriel?"

She ran the back of her hand down her aunt's cheek. I wasn't sure she'd heard my question but gave her this tender moment before asking her again.

"You sleep now," she said to her. She stood up and pointed to the door. "Let's go out."

We stepped into the hallway. Valentina crossed her arms at her waist, and she pressed her lips together.

"Are you all right?" I gently laid my hand between her shoulder blades.

Her eyes filled with tears again, and she sniffed. "She looks so frail. She used to be such a strong woman . . .before."

"She still is, Valentina. She's fighting, which is a good thing. Don't give up hope."

She sniffed again and wiped her nose with the back of her hand, and then swept her fingers under her eyes to wipe away the tears.

"Valentina, do you know who this Sister Magdalena is?"

"Yes." She continued trying to collect herself. "I have not met her, but she is at the Mission. My aunt helps her with work."

"What kind of work?"

She shook her head. "Office work. I'm not sure." She looked at me apologetically.

"This is good, Valentina," I said, my spirits lifting. "This is the best lead we've had so far. Maybe your aunt left the package with Sister Magdalena."

Her lips twitched in an attempted smile. "I hope you find it."

I smiled back at her. "Me too, Valentina. Me too."

I LEFT the hospital and drove to Ambassador Films feeling hopeful. After I finished my work, I planned to head over to the church to speak with Sister Magdalena.

I breezed through the warehouse into wardrobe and was satisfied to see all three seamstresses busy sewing or fitting costumes onto the dress forms. Clara had been doing a good job of keeping things running while I had been, and still was, preoccupied with getting Madeleine back. I made a mental note to put in a good word with her aunt and uncle, the Steinbergs, and tell them what a help she had been.

I entered my office and sat down to look at the continuity call sheets Clara had set neatly in the middle of my desk. I smiled with amazement. It was like she knew exactly what I needed to work on at exactly the right time.

I started to go through them when the phone on my desk rang. It was Chet.

"I have some news," he said, his voice sounding grim.

"I do, too." I smiled into the phone even though his tone made me a bit wary. I told him about my visit with Miss Ivanova.

"That's encouraging." His voice had an edge of warning to it.

"What's wrong, Chet?"

He took in a breath and let it go. "I went back to your father's rooms at the boarding house. There was another note."

"Another one? What did it say? Did it give any kind of instructions?" The sound of my heartbeat thumped in my ears.

"It says they are withholding food from Madeleine. Next will be water."

My stomach clenched. "Oh no. We're running out of time, Chet."

"They are just putting more pressure on us."

"But withholding food? Poor Madeleine." I knew all too well what an empty belly felt like, especially when you didn't know when the next meal would come. The thought struck terror deep into my heart.

"She can probably go without food for a while," he said. "But without water, she could die in a matter of days."

The thought sickened me. "Do you really think they would kill her? They need her to motivate us to find the Fabergé egg."

"They want to show us how serious they are. If you, or we, are being followed, they know things about us. If they kill her, they will just—"

I immediately got his meaning and a stone settled in my stomach. "They'll go for someone else."

"They will."

The gravity in his voice paralyzed me with fear. We'd received a note at the ranch so whoever this was knew where we lived. Probably knew about the children. They'd be the perfect leverage.

"I'm going to the Mission church in a few minutes. See what I can find out from Sister Magdalena," I said, itching to get off the phone.

We hung up and I put the continuity sheets back into the folder. This would have to wait. I'd have to lean on Clara now even more.

I got up from my desk and went to the doorway to look for her.

"Oh!" I jumped when I saw her standing just outside the door holding a bolt of green satin fabric. I placed a hand at my throat. "There you are. I was just coming to get you. I need you for a moment."

"Certainly." She looked up at me with her large blinking eyes and a barely perceptible upturn of her lips.

I showed her into my office. "Listen, I'm going to need your help. I can't be at work today," I said, my words rushed.

"Oh dear." Her eyes widened behind her spectacles. "Does this have something to do with your father's wife?"

"Yes."

"Oh, I see." A frown line appeared in her forehead.

Torn between not wanting to divulge any more information than necessary and feeling like I needed to explain my absence, I went with the latter. I didn't want her to think I was frivolously neglecting my duties or taking advantage of her.

"I've since learned Madeleine did not leave of her own free will," I explained.

"Do you mean she was kidnapped?"

I pulled my bottom lip between my teeth and nodded.

"Oh gosh," she said, concern in her voice. "Have you contacted the police?"

I hesitated. "It's complicated. But according to Valentina, they have been working on the case of the assault on her aunt, but they haven't come up with anything conclusive."

Her eyebrows shot up. "So the two are connected?"

I swallowed, realizing I might have said too much, but I was frazzled and a bit panicky at the idea that these monsters could be coming after someone else if we didn't find the treasured egg.

"Maybe," I said, trying to cover. "We aren't exactly sure," I lied.

"Kidnapped. How awful." Her pert lips pressed together in a frown of dismay.

"Clara, you must promise to keep this to yourself."

"Promise." She ran a finger down and across her heart. "What can I do to help?"

I took a deep breath, feeling confident she would keep her word. "I need you to make sure things around here are running smoothly. How is casting going?" As I asked the question, guilt shot through my belly and made its way into my chest. Never before had I been so out of touch with the happenings of a project I was working on.

"Well, I think Timothy is down to two candidates for the Pierre role. Things are going slower for the Collette role."

"All right. So I have some time. I'm sorry to dump all this on you." I frowned.

"It's no problem, Grace. I'm happy to help. It's great experience. Who knows? Maybe I'll get the lead designer job on a film." She tilted her head and smiled.

I swallowed again, her words giving me pause. Had she just threatened to take over my job? Her aunt and uncle owned the studio, after all. The thought had me completely rattled. I loved my job, excelled at my job. Yet, I was also putting it in jeopardy.

My guilt played at the corners of my mind, making me feel defensive and raw. I bit the corner of my mouth, studying her face, trying to see if there was indeed a threat there. Her eyes blinked up at me with her usual friendliness, easing my feelings of paranoia.

I returned the smile. "Maybe," I said. "Someday."

"Miss Michelle?" One of the seamstresses came into my office pulling my attention away from Clara for a moment. "I'm having a problem with one of these garments. Can you look at it?"

I glanced at Clara again, who was looking at me expectantly, waiting for me to turn it over to her. I needed to get to the church, but my guilty conscience took over.

"Of course. I'll be right there," I said, hoping it wasn't something that would require a lot of time.

"Will you go over these continuity sheets and check them against the script?" I asked Clara.

"Of course," she said, smiling sweetly.

Careful, a voice from somewhere said in my ears. Probably Sophia, but again, what was the message referring to? Clara?

I inwardly scoffed. I realized my anxiety over the Fabergé egg brought out all my insecurities. I really needed to speak with Lenora Lange to find out what these messages were all about.

I took in a sharp breath, suddenly overwhelmed with all the things I needed to accomplish to keep my job and keep Madeleine alive, and maybe even someone else.

"You all right?" Clara asked, touching my elbow.

I managed a tight smile. "Yes, fine. Just fine. Would you go tell Marie I'll be right there? I need to make a phone call."

"Yes, ma'am. And, oh, I almost forgot." She rushed over to her handbag, which sat on one of the club chairs. She pulled something from it and brought it over to me. "Western Union brought this for you. It came last night. I was here, working late." She handed me a yellow telegram envelope.

I was here working late.

The ugly sensation of shame oozed through me like a vile, black ink, and that insecurity raised its ugly head again. The statement reminded me once again that Clara was carrying a lot of the workload. I felt so torn, like I needed to be everywhere and everything to everyone at once: at the ranch for the kids and my husband, and at work to do what I loved. People were relying on me, and vast amounts of money were being spent on this film. And then there was the matter of Madeleine. Her very life hung in the balance, and I needed to find her.

Her very life.

The words repeated in my head in Sophia's voice. I took in a deep breath, realizing that very second what the priority needed to be, and it wasn't my job. I had to save Madeleine.

"I hope it isn't bad news." Clara blinked up at me.

"Me too." With a sinking feeling in my stomach, I tore open the envelope and pulled out the telegram. It read, *Bring package to far northeast corner of your ranch. Place it in the oil drum. No police. I will be waiting.*

I stared at the words, trying to comprehend them through the feelings of utter dread and fear pounding through me. The person, or people, who had sent this telegram knew where I worked as well as where I lived. I swallowed hard and refocused on the words in front of me.

The tone of this note was a little bit different from the others. I wondered at the use of the word *I.* As far as we knew, there were two people working to find the egg. Yet, one of the previous notes had mentioned instructions, and here they were. That sinking feeling returned. I had nothing to deliver yet.

I closed my eyes to better organize my thoughts. An image of Sophia standing in front of a mansion appeared in the darkness behind my eyelids. The mansion was familiar, but I couldn't quite make it out. Sophia was shaking her head.

"Grace?" Clara's voice broke my train of thought. I opened my eyes. "Is it . . . bad news?"

Still distracted by the image of Sophia, I hesitated before saying, "I'm not sure. I need to make that call. Do you mind?" I indicated the doorway, signaling to her that I wanted some privacy.

"Not at all," she said, concern written in her eyes.

I waited for her to leave and then grabbed my handbag, which was sitting on the desk, and rummaged through it until my fingers found the calling card. I pulled it from the bag and flipped it over to find Lenora Lange's phone number and dialed.

CHAPTER FIFTEEN

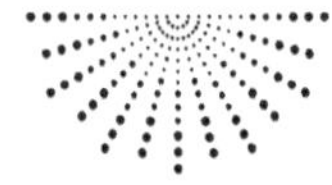

To my disappointment, Miss Lange could not meet with me 'til the following day. I reconciled the minor setback with the surety of the more concrete lead I'd received from Miss Ivanova.

Twenty five minutes later, after checking my side-view mirror at least one hundred times, I pulled up to the Mission San Gabriel, fairly confident I had not been followed.

It was an austere building and looked ancient. The front was comprised of yellowed plaster and an arched wooden door with no adornment. Two niches, placed high on either side of the door, contained statues of religious figures, and between them, a smaller rectangular door was set into the wall. A lantern hung from a wrought iron rod above the arched doorway. A few smaller, newer buildings with the familiar Spanish tile roofs stood in close proximity to the church. I got out of the car, contemplating which building to enter.

I chose the church. Cool and damp, the interior smelled of wood and frankincense. Two rows of wooden pews led up to an altar. Colorful frescos were set behind an archway, adorning the church wall at the back. To the left of the altar sat a bank of small votive candles burning brightly.

I walked slowly down the aisle, my heels clicking on the brick floor, worn and warped with age. A palpable stillness hung heavy in the air, wrapping me in a cloak of serenity. I breathed in the rich fragrances, the tension in my body and the whirling thoughts in my mind melting. The immediate and utter relief was astounding.

I slid into one of the pews to bask in the peacefulness of the church, if just for a minute. I closed my eyes, and immediately, a vision of Sophia came to me. She sat on a stone bench under two palm trees that had bent themselves into an arch over her. She was in a garden surrounded by a profusion of flowers. She motioned for me to come to her.

The sound of footsteps startled me. I opened my eyes to see a plump, middle-aged Hispanic woman with a feather duster in her hand, running it over some items in the sacristy. She then came around the front of the altar, bowed her head, and crossed herself, then went to the other side.

I rose from the pew and approached her. "Excuse me," I whispered.

She turned and smiled at me. Dimples sank deep into her full cheeks. *"Sí?"*

"I'm looking for Sister Magdalena."

"Ah, *sí*. She is in the office." The singsong quality of her Spanish accent was thick. "Go through there—" she pointed to a side door "—and walk this way—" she indicated behind her "—to the first building on the right."

"Thank you."

I went through the door that led to an arched corridor. Soon I reached the correct building and pushed open the door.

A nun sat behind a desk strewn with papers. The neatness of her black habit and veil, offset with the white wimple that covered her head and cascaded down over her shoulders, stood in stark contrast with the mess on the desk. She looked up from the chaos in front of her and, at seeing me, raised her eyebrows.

"Are you Sister Magdalena?" I asked timidly, daunted by her formidable attire and the serious expression on her face.

"I am," she said.

I introduced myself. "I'm here to ask you about Anna Ivanova."

She reached into her habit and pulled out a small pocket watch and looked at the time. "I was just about to go into the courtyard for my midday prayers. Walk with me." She stood up from the desk, folded her hands under her habit, and led me from the room.

We went back to the side door of the church. When we passed the altar, she stopped, faced it, bowed, and crossed herself, and then continued to a door on the opposite side. From there, we entered a large, beautiful, paved courtyard surrounded by beds of flowering bushes. Terra-cotta pots were positioned around a gurgling stone fountain, the base of which was decorated with colorful Mexican tiles.

She walked toward a wooden bench at one end of the courtyard, which was placed in front of a domed grotto fashioned from lava rock. A statue of the Virgin Mary nestled within the curved walls of the enclave. Small pots with clusters of red roses springing out of them surrounded the base of the structure.

"Come sit," she said, motioning to the bench. I lowered myself down next to her.

"I pray for Anna every day." She fixed her eyes on the statue of Mary. "It's a terrible thing that happened to her."

"It is," I agreed. We sat in silence for a few moments. "Miss Ivanova works here?" I asked, breaking the stillness.

"Yes. She is so giving of her time. A truly devout woman. She was of the Russian Orthodox Church before she converted to Catholicism," she said, answering my previous curiosity about her faith.

"I see." I wanted to get to the point. "Sister, I'm looking for something Miss Ivanova had in her possession. It is now lost. When I asked her about it, she mentioned your name."

The nun turned to face me, her wise, gray eyes open wide. "She has regained consciousness? Praise God!"

I held up a cautionary hand. "She is in and out of consciousness. Not out of the woods, as I understand it."

She crossed herself and mumbled a quick prayer. When she finished, I proceeded.

"It was a package. I'm not sure, but I believe it was about this big." I roughly indicated the size with my hands. "Do you know anything about it? It's very important that I find it."

She shook her head. "I know nothing of this package."

"She didn't leave it in your care?"

"No, child."

I slumped against the back of the bench, unable to hide my disappointment.

"Miss?" she inquired.

I looked at her in earnest. "Finding this item is extremely important, Sister." I lowered my voice. "Someone's life depends on it. Are you sure you don't remember Miss Ivanova mentioning it? Do you remember seeing it?"

"Dear Lord." She squinted against the notion. "No, I'm sorry, I don't."

I sighed and thought back to Anna Ivanova lying in the hospital bed. She had been unconscious mere moments before we had spoken. Had she even heard my question about the package properly? Could she have remembered what she'd done with it so soon after regaining awareness? If Sister Magdalena knew nothing of this, why had Miss Ivanova mentioned her name?

A small, older man with dark hair shot through with gray passed by carrying some gardening tools. He lifted a hand in greeting to the Sister. She smiled and nodded a greeting back.

"What did Miss Ivanova do for you here at the church?" I asked, wondering if there was a place she might have hidden the egg.

The nun pressed her lips into a pensive frown. "A number of things. Anything I asked of her. She worked in the office, she often helped Rosalita clean, she even helped José." She tilted her head in the direction of the man who'd just walked by. "She loved being here."

"I understand she helped a Father Michael with some land-scaping?" I inquired.

"Oh yes." Sister Magdalena beamed. "She made all of this possible." She raised her hand aloft, indicating the courtyard. "It had not been touched in twenty years. But she and Father Michael, God rest his soul, brought it back to its original beauty. They found plans from when the Mission was first built. When he died, she had that bench over there—" she nodded to a white stone bench on the other side of the courtyard, surrounded by a circle of rosebushes "—dedicated to him. He loved to sit there and pray."

"How lovely," I said. "Thank you."

The information did not seem to provide much help, but I was grateful just the same. I dug into my purse and pulled out the small notepad I kept in there and a pencil. I scrawled my name and telephone number on it, then ripped off the page and handed it to her.

"This is my telephone number. If you should find this pack-age, or remember anything about it, would you please call me?"

"Certainly," she said.

"Thank you again for your time." I stood to leave her to her prayers.

I turned and scanned the courtyard, looking for José. I figured I might as well speak to him, too, while I was here. He was bent over a potted rosebush that stood next to the trunk of a palm tree, snipping off the dead blossoms.

I walked over and introduced myself. "I'm a friend of Miss Ivanova's."

"Ah . . . Anna." He nodded. "How is she?"

"She's hanging on."

I then asked him about the package.

"I don't know nothing about it." He raised his hands in the air apologetically.

"All right," I said with resignation. *"Gracias."*

"De nada." He smiled, revealing a mishmash of chipped and yellow teeth.

I left him to his pruning and went back into the church. The Hispanic woman stood next to the altar, dusting the two large standing candlesticks and the candles perched on top of them with her feather duster. I asked her about the treasured package. She answered with a simple shake of her head.

I left the church confused. I had the marked impression I had missed something, but I couldn't figure out what it could be.

CHAPTER SIXTEEN

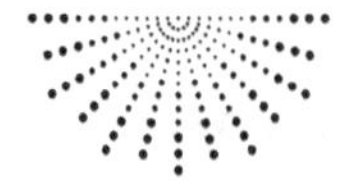

The following day, after spending some time at Ambassador, I met Felicity at the Hotel Miramar in Santa Monica where Miss Lange lived in one of the luxurious, newly built beachside bungalows. We met in the garden oasis courtyard next to the swimming pool.

"Thanks for coming," I said.

Felicity looked fresh, as always, wearing wide-legged trousers and a feminine, crepe blouse. It had become her signature look. A bicorn hat graced her dark, wavy bob. "Certainly, dear. Anything I can do to help. I wish I'd had luck at the hotels. I just checked at the front desk here as to our two goons, but no one has encountered anyone of Russian heritage." She appraised me with her dark-blue eyes. "How are you holding up?"

I took in a sharp breath. "Okay. Frustrated. Worried. There was another note left at the boarding house informing us they were withholding food from Madeleine."

"Oh dear. How awful."

"And I received one at work—this time a telegram, which was odd. It mentioned time was running out. I'm worried what these people will do next, who they will hurt next." I then repeated what the telegram said. "They are following me. Keeping tabs on me. It's creepy."

"Creepy is right," she said with understanding. "Do you think you were followed here?"

I shook my head. "I don't think so, but I can't be absolutely sure. Whoever this is, is really good at it. It seems that if I let my guard down for one second—"

"But if they wanted to hurt you, they would have by now, don't you think?"

"That's what Chet said." I took comfort in the fact that Felicity had thought of this independently from him.

"They know you are actively looking for this Fabergé egg. They are just waiting for you to lead them to it."

A terrifying thought overshadowed my momentary reprieve. "So they can get it themselves . . . which means they will kill Madeleine, or already have."

Felicity took me by the arms. "Let's not go there. Just keep moving forward. We have no other choice."

I took in a deep breath and let it out. "You're right," I conceded.

She released my arms. "How's your father?"

I pressed my lips together in a half smile, remembering him vomiting off the side of the bunkhouse porch.

"He's a mess."

"I'm sure," she said, obviously talking about the fact that his wife had been kidnapped, not that he was physically and emotionally ill from his time in the war and his morphine addiction.

"So, are you ready?" she asked with a note of concern. She knew Miss Lange made me nervous.

Although I believed the medium had the gift of speaking with the dead, and also knew her to be the genuine article, the whole idea spooked me. Perhaps it was because I'd lost the people who were dearest to me in the world. I'd struggled so much with accepting their deaths that to risk hearing from them again made me fearful of slipping back into that mind-numbing grief that had been so paralyzing. I had made a valiant effort to move on with my life after the loss and was succeeding. I had a wonderful husband and a new family. I was happy. I feared that to fully encounter those lost to me might set me back. Sophia's brief visits and messages I could handle. Barely. They often left me feeling disconnected and confused. But the idea of summoning her for a full-blown conversation scared the heck out of me.

I straightened my shoulders, shaking off the disquietude. "Yes, I'm ready."

"Don't worry, Grace. You've done this before. And Lenora is a sweet woman," she added.

I smiled, a little surprised at her description of the medium. *Sweet* was not a word I'd ever associated with her. *Larger-than-life, ethereal, intimidating,* and *strange* were words that came to my mind.

We walked down the meticulously manicured pathway lined with azaleas and neat rows of palm trees. We passed a few of the bungalows before Felicity stopped.

"Here we go," she said. "Number seventeen."

We stepped up onto the stoop, and Felicity knocked.

Miss Lange answered immediately, as if she had known we were there. The sensation of cold water drifted down my spine.

"Felicity." She took my friend's hands and planted an air kiss at each of her cheeks. Miss Lange then turned her ice-blue gaze to me. "Miss Michelle."

"Hello, Miss Lange." My voice sounded small and childlike. I cleared my throat.

"Do come in." She swept her arm toward the interior of the bungalow.

It was a sunny, open space with a living room, dining room, and modest kitchen. I assumed the bedroom or bedrooms were at the back of the bungalow. A crystal vase, profuse with white roses and Casa Blanca lilies, sat on an elegant entry table, and a sweet, intoxicating fragrance filled the room.

Lenora led us through to the living room. "May I offer you something to drink?" she asked. "Coffee, water, something stronger?" She pointed her gaze at me, obviously feeling my unease.

"No, thank you," I whispered.

"Nothing for me," Felicity said.

Lenora asked me to sit in one of the armchairs that stood angled toward each other in a corner. I obeyed, and she sat in the other chair. Felicity lowered herself on the sofa.

"Then let's begin," she said and closed her eyes.

"Uh, Miss Lange?" I inquired, wanting to tell her of the cryptic words I'd heard and the visions of Sophia at the battlefield and in the garden.

"Shh," she uttered, her eyelids still closed.

Realizing I had a death grip on my handbag, I set it on the floor next to the chair. I looked over at Felicity for reassurance, but she had leaned back on the sofa and was flipping through a magazine.

The salty breeze mixed with the fragrance of the flowers and the sound of the waves and the seagulls coming through the open windows swept away my discomfort, and I felt myself start to relax. I turned back to Miss Lange and studied her face. Her brow pressed downward, and the corner of her mouth twisted upward.

She opened her eyes and gazed into mine. "You must open your mind." She leaned forward and took both my hands in hers. "Close your eyes and breathe."

I did as she said and took in a deep breath, trying to clear the thoughts racing through my head.

"Yes, yes," she whispered.

I resisted the temptation to open my eyes again.

"Ah . . . A woman is coming through, but I can't see her clearly. She is telling me she is lost."

I squeezed my eye lids tighter together.

"She stands with her back to an open window. She is frightened. Terrified."

"Who is the woman? Is it Sophia?" I asked.

As Sophia's name came out of my mouth, a vision of her appeared.

She stands on a grassy bluff surrounded by red roses, overlooking a battlefield. Is it Cantigny? A soldier lies facedown on the ground. Sophia stands over him. She reaches down to turn him over. His face is unrecognizable, covered in blood. His ear is missing, the side of his face pulpy and raw. She shakes her head, tears streaming down her face. She mouths words I cannot hear.

"She is falling," Miss Lange says, her voice strangled.

"Is it Sophia?" I repeated, opening my eyes.

Miss Lange's face contorted in fear. "I can't— I can't see clearly now. What?" The muscles around her eyes relaxed, and an expression of serenity returned to her face. "I can see them now."

"See whom?" My heart pounded with exasperation. These readings were always so cryptic, disjointed, and infuriating.

"There are two women. One, a dark-haired woman, is taking the other, a light-haired woman—by the hand. Leading her to safety. They sit under kissing palm trees."

I gasped, remembering the vision of Sophia sitting on a bench under two palm trees bent toward each other, their umbrella tops fluttering in the breeze.

"What does it mean?" I asked.

Miss Lange opened her eyes. They were glassy and unfocused, as if she'd just come out of a deep, dream-filled slumber. "I believe your sister has helped someone cross over."

Immediately, Madeleine came to mind.

"Oh no," I choked out. "Who was it? Do you know?"

She pressed her fingertips to her temples and blinked rapidly as if her head pained her. "She's well-dressed. Bejeweled." She released her hands, and her features took on their usual placid expression.

I pulled my lower lip between my teeth. Whomever she was describing did not sound like Madeleine—at least not by the clothing. Madeleine had come from money, but according to my father, the two of them were now destitute. The thought sent a pang of pity straight to my stomach.

"Miss Lange, I don't understand this reading." I had wanted to speak with Sophia. Find out what she had been trying to tell me. "I know my sister is trying to send me a message, but I've learned no more from this encounter than I have on my own— except for this mystery woman who has crossed over. I've seen the palm trees, a mansion, and a battlefield."

"Cantigny," she said flatly.

"Yes!" My heart fluttered with excitement.

"I've seen it, too." She pressed her hands together as if in prayer.

"But what does it mean?"

She sighed and opened her hands in question. "Joshua is sending me many messages, but I can't make sense of them. I need time to confer with them and sort it out."

By "them" I knew she meant her collective of spirits that she called Joshua.

Utterly frustrated, I exhaled loudly. Time was running out, and we were getting nowhere. I needed to get home to do some of my own sorting out.

"I will be in touch," she said, pushing herself up from the chair and suddenly looking very tired.

"Yes. Thank you." I rose, my head swirling like a tornado with these messages and a multitude of possible scenarios all presenting themselves like nothing but fragments on the air.

The previous serenity and peacefulness of the room now felt

cloying and claustrophobic. The smell of the flowers had turned sickeningly sweet, like something in decay.

I almost ran for the door. Once outside, I took a deep breath and turned my face to the sun. I focused on the sounds of the breeze swaying through the palms and the seagulls soaring over the ocean.

I heard the door click behind me. Felicity joined me at the bottom of the two steps leading into the bungalow.

"What happened in there?" she asked, placing her hand gently on my shoulder.

I shook my head and scoffed. "I get so confused when I talk with Miss Lange. It's like when we're done with the reading, I don't know up from down."

"I know it seems that way, Grace. But you'll make sense of it. Like you did with Lizzy. You just need to give it some time."

"Ugh!" I grabbed the sides of my head in frustration. "But that is the one thing we don't have! And we are no closer to finding this Fabergé egg than we were in the beginning."

"Come on." She slipped her arm through mine. "Let's go to the hotel restaurant."

I pulled away from her. "The restaurant? How can you eat at a time like this?"

"We don't have to eat, but let's get coffee or tea. Grace, you are wound tight as a clock. Let's just take thirty minutes to breathe and relax. Let's talk about what to do next."

"But I need to get home," I protested.

"What's thirty more minutes?" She set her hands on her slim hips.

I bit my lip, considering her proposal. "All right," I relented. "Thirty minutes and not a second longer."

She smiled and slipped her arm through mine again. "You drive a tough bargain, lady."

～

WE WENT to the main building of the hotel. Once a mansion, it was constructed with red brick in the modernist style with two opposing turrets on each side. Built in the eighteen hundreds, it had a long history in Santa Monica, serving once as a home to former United States Senator John Percival Jones and later to King C. Gillette of the Gillette razor empire. It then served as a military academy, and finally, it was opened as a hotel three years ago.

The restaurant, situated at the back of the manse, opened onto a wide veranda that looked out at the beach. We sat at a table near the open French doors. Felicity ordered coffee, and I ordered tea. A large party of mostly men sat at a table on the other side of the veranda. The tinny sound of music came from that direction, and I spotted a cathedral radio sitting atop a table against the wall. I thought it a nice touch to provide music for the patrons, and the soft melody with the sounds of the waves in the distance provided a relaxing ambiance. I wasn't quite sure, but I thought the song playing was Gershwin's "Rhapsody in Blue."

"I'm so stuck, Felicity," I said, staring into my teacup. I hadn't yet taken a sip. "I don't know what to do next."

"You said this latest note, the telegram, gave instructions on where to bring the egg." She twirled her coffee cup on its saucer.

"Yes. And that's another thing. The telegram didn't actually mention the egg." I pulled it out of my handbag. "See here." I held it out to her. "It says 'bring the package.'"

Felicity shrugged. "Why does that matter?"

I rested against the back of the chair, my thoughts jumbled. "I don't know. It just feels different."

The music suddenly stopped, and the voice of a broadcaster cut in. I glanced toward the radio. One of the men from the group at the other end of the veranda got up from the table and leaned over the radio to hear it better. His companions, now being served their meal by the waiter, sat silent, transfixed to it as well.

"How awful!" a red-haired woman exclaimed.

"Such a pity," came the man at the radio. "She was a real looker."

"Felicity." I turned to her. She was sipping her coffee. "Can you hear what's going on over there?" I tilted my head toward the large group.

She craned her neck to see over my head. "I can't really tell."

The waiter, who had finished serving their food, strode over to our table. "May I bring you anything else?" He directed his gaze toward me. Young and handsome with dark, meticulously pomaded hair and warm, brown eyes, he exuded efficiency with his tray tucked under his arm.

"I'm fine," I said.

"Me too." Felicity raised her cup to him.

"Can you tell me what's got everyone over there so upset?" I asked him.

He frowned. "The Russian actress, Valentina Baklanova, just died. Suicide."

"What?!" Felicity and I shouted at the same time. I nearly choked on my tea.

"Jumped from a second-story window, I guess."

Lenora Lange's words slammed into me with a force that took my breath away. *She stands with her back to an open window.* She had seen Valentina's death!

The blood drained from my head, and the space around me whirled like a cyclone. I grabbed on to the sides of the table to steady myself.

"Miss? Are you all right?" The waiter lightly touched my shoulder.

I took a deep breath, gathering myself together, but I couldn't speak.

I met Felicity's sapphire gaze, and then she addressed the waiter. "She was a friend of ours." She tipped her cup and drained the rest of her coffee. She tapped the rim of it, signaling she wanted another.

"Yes, yes, of course," he said. "I'm sorry for your loss."

He turned to me. "More tea, miss?"

Still unable to speak, I just shook my head.

He left us, and we sat in stunned silence.

My mind slowly broke through the wall of shock. Suicide? It made absolutely no sense. Aside from the fact that she was engaged to be married and her career in the United States was taking off at a meteoric rate, if nothing else, Valentina wanted to see her aunt well again. The woman had finally made some progress on the road back to health.

"It wasn't suicide," I said, suddenly feeling guilty for telling her about the egg. Did her knowledge of it lead to her death?

My eyes met Felicity's, and a trembling in my stomach made the partially consumed tea turn suddenly bitter. My insides felt as if they were caving in on themselves. I pushed the half-empty teacup away from me, a deep sense of foreboding weighing heavily on my chest.

"The poor soul was murdered," Felicity said, reading my mind. Her dark, silky skin had dappled with light splotches, and her eyes brimmed with tears. She quickly set down her coffee cup, sloshing some of it onto the saucer.

My elbows on the table, I rested my head between my fingertips, my mind whirring with this dreadful news. Where had this happened? At her house? Had someone followed us there after all? Max, her driver, had been so certain no one had tailed us, said he could lose anyone following her.

The jittery feeling in my stomach rose to my chest. What of Madeleine? Was she still alive? Who would be next? My mind raced with all the possibilities: my father, my husband, the children, Rose, Miss Meyers, Ned, Felicity. Me . . . if I failed.

The waiter reappeared, jerking me out of the vortex of

thoughts spinning in my head. He poured Felicity another cup. "The coffee and tea are on me."

Both of us still numb, we nodded our thanks. Felicity pulled a handkerchief from her purse and dabbed at her eyes.

"I'm so sorry," I said. "I know you were friends." Felicity was normally not one to give in to her emotions, at least not in front of others.

"She didn't deserve this," she said through clenched teeth. Her tears gone, her face took on the hardened expression I had seen so many times back when we were in New York City, when she was with Marciano. She knew how to shield herself from sorrow and fear, and I saw that wall go up now.

Somehow it gave me strength. I had to push aside my own fears. I had to find that egg.

I leaned back in my chair, trying to settle and organize my thoughts. "During my reading, Miss Lange said she saw a woman with her back to a window."

"Yes, I remember." Felicity's eyes snapped up from her cup. She had been lost in her own contemplation.

"She saw this murder, Felicity. She said she believed Sophia had helped someone cross over to the other side. The way she described this woman . . . It was Valentina." Goose bumps rose on my arms and legs. I shuddered at the sudden chill, amazed by Miss Lange's abilities.

The deep, rich color of Felicity's skin returned to its normal chocolaty tone, and her eyes sharpened into focus. "Did she see her fall from the window?"

I shook my head, trying to remember what she'd said. "I don't think so, but she said the woman's *back* was to the window."

"That could mean she was pushed," Felicity said.

"Exactly."

"Did she see anyone else with this woman—er, Valentina?"

"I don't think so. We could go back and ask her." My eyes

traveled to the interior of the restaurant and settled on a clock positioned over a grand fireplace, taking note of the time. "But I have to go. Come with me to the ranch?"

I didn't want Felicity to be alone. Even though she had put up her shields against her pain, I knew she was suffering. To my relief, she agreed and then drained the rest of her coffee.

I threw a couple of coins on the table for the tip. More than necessary. It was kind of the young man to buy our coffee and tea.

We got up, and Felicity led the way to the path leading to the beach. A man standing on the sand quickly turned away from us as we passed. He had his hat pulled down low over his face, and his suit was rumpled, as though he'd slept in it. A shudder ran through me as I remembered the man at the train station, and the one at the bank. Had I been followed to the hotel? We continued down the path, an eerie sensation coursing through me. Who was this person? Was he one of the Russians?

A surge of anger swept through me. I was sick of this game. Sick of being sick with worry every waking minute of the day. Sick of the feeling of dread at who might be next. I was suddenly consumed with a primal need to know who this man was.

"Felicity, wait," I called out. "I'll be right back."

I turned and jogged down the pathway back toward the beach. I would confront this person, demand to know who he was and where he was keeping Madeleine. He wouldn't dare try to harm me in public. At the least he would know that I knew he was following me and that I wouldn't be intimidated.

The place where he'd been standing on the beach came into view, but he wasn't there. I scanned the veranda and then walked to the seawall and scanned the oceanfront. He was gone.

"Grace?" Felicity took hold of my elbow. "What are you doing?"

"Darn it." I sighed in exasperation. "I thought I saw somebody."

"Who?"

"The man who's been following me. Someone is tracking me in my search for the egg, and they knew the egg was sent to the home Anna Ivanova and Valentina shared."

"Do you think this person killed her?"

"I do," I said, certainty washing over me.

"Maybe she found the egg? These people got what they wanted and then they killed her—"

"So she wouldn't identify them," I finished. "It's a definite possibility. And if they did finally get their hands on it, Madeleine doesn't have a chance."

"And if Valentina didn't find the egg?"

"We can't possibly know if she did or didn't. We need to keep looking." I said the words with resoluteness, trying to disguise the abject terror that had settled in my belly. Because if and when I found this egg, the people following me would want to see me dead, too.

CHAPTER SEVENTEEN

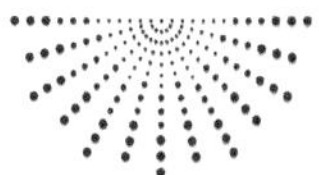

ithin the hour we had gathered in my living room with Chet, Ned, and my father. Felicity and I told them the news of Valentina and about the man on the beach at the hotel.

My father sat next to me, his elbow on the arm of the sofa and his hand resting onto the side of his head, and he looked horrible. The pallor of his skin was pasty and gray, and his shirt was soaked with sweat at the collar and under his arms. His despair at the news was palpable, and I sensed he was losing hope. He occasionally buckled at the waist, wincing in pain. His emotional distress mingling with the physical duress of his withdrawal symptoms made a violently bitter cocktail.

My heart went out to him at his suffering, but I had to admire his determination and fortitude. I reached over, took his hand and gave it a squeeze. He didn't respond.

"Sounds like murder to me," Chet said.

"Yes," I agreed. I thought about Anna Ivanova and Anton Belsky. They would be devastated. "This will be difficult for her loved ones."

Chet nodded. "We'll need to speak with her fiancé, Belsky."

"I have his telephone number," I said. "Valentina gave it to me in case I needed to reach her at his home."

I went to my purse, which was sitting on the gossip table, and pulled out the piece of paper. I picked up the receiver and dialed. I waited for about a minute, but there was no answer. I thought about going to his home, but it was late and I didn't relish the idea of driving around in the dark with someone following me. It'd have to wait 'til morning.

My father rose from the sofa, and with his hands against the sides of his head, he started his customary pacing. My eyes followed him as he ping-ponged back and forth in his anguished state. A lump formed in my throat. Then a warmth, like the touch of a hand, spread over my right shoulder and a tingling sensation, like someone's breath, passed over my ear.

It's gone too far, a voice whispered to me. *You are in too deep.*

I knew it was Sophia.

But I have no choice, I answered back. The voices and people in the room blurred, and all I could see was my father pacing like a caged animal.

Cantigny . . .

That word again.

What is Cantigny? I asked her. *What does the battlefield have to do with any of this?*

Deception.

Deception of what? Of whom?

The warm sensation evaporated, leaving a vacancy in the room. Everything and everyone came back into focus.

Deception. I think I knew what Sophia might be trying to tell me. In fact, as much as I tried, I couldn't ignore the niggling feeling of certainty in my gut. My father was lying about something. I didn't know about what and I didn't know why, but somehow, I knew. I watched him in his agitation, pacing the floor and holding his hands up to his head. The certainty of my conviction grew, but I needed evidence to be sure.

"Gracie," Sophia calls to me. Her voice is soft and sweet, like it was when she was a child, before the harshness of our life on the streets and the cold realities of show business had hardened it, draining the spirit from it.

She stands in a mist, an effervescent white cloud surrounding her, rolling across the pine needle carpet of the forest. She is surrounded by rosebushes, oddly out of place and flaming red in their brilliance. The dampness in the air sinks into my bones, its icy chill raking down my back like hooked fingers. Sounds of gunfire and explosions fill the air.

I join her, and she holds my hand. I marvel at the solidness of it, the warmth, as if she is really here. As if she's alive once again. With her other hand, she points into the distance.

Two men sit at a wooden table. One has his back turned to us, and one sits facing us. The table is old and worn and stained. The man with his back to us tips a whiskey bottle, filling two glasses, and cigarette smoke curls upward from an ashtray. They are playing cards. Something glints in the dim light. It hovers over the chest of the man facing us—a military identification tag. The dog tag's brilliance increases in intensity, filling the room with light.

I opened my eyes and blinked into the darkness of the room, the image of the two men still burning in my mind. In the dream, I hadn't been able to make out their faces. Feeling muddled from the depths of slumber, I closed my eyes and willed myself back to sleep. Sophia was speaking to me, and I needed to let the message unfold.

IN THE MORNING I made my way to the bunkhouse to check on my father. I knocked at the door, but there was no answer. I knocked again to no avail. He was either asleep or—

I turned the knob and pushed open the door.

"Hello?" I stepped into the modest living area.

We had furnished it with old, hand-me-down furniture. The sofa and armchair were still in good condition, if not a little worn, and mismatched. An old trunk served as a coffee table nestled within the crook of the chairs, and it all sat atop a multi-colored hooked rug Rose had made from old tablecloths and dresses. It livened up the dusty, masculine air of the room. There were three bedrooms, one right off the living area and two others off the long, narrow hallway.

Ned occupied the front room. The door was open. His bed was neatly made, the room tidy, but he wasn't there, which didn't surprise me. He'd been long awake, I was sure, to tend to his chores.

I made my way down the hall to the first bedroom. The door was ajar so I peered in. My father lay in the bed, tossing and turning in his sleep, and I was surprised to see Stevie slumped in an armchair next to the bed, snoozing. My heart warmed at his presence.

My father moaned and kicked off the covers. His underwear, a white cotton union suit, was yellowed with perspiration, and the room smelled of body odor.

Stevie must have sensed my presence because he woke up and straightened in the chair.

I beckoned for him to meet me in the hallway. "Stevie, have you been out here all night?"

He nodded, rubbing the sleep from his eyes. "Yeah. After I went to bed, I remembered I'd left my newspaper tote bag in the barn. I was late from my paper route for my evening chores. So I went out to get it, and I found your dad in Chet's truck. He was in an awful state. Said he needed to find the keys. Said he had to get his medicine. I got him back to the bunkhouse and into bed. I was worried he'd go outside again so I stayed."

I smiled at him. "That was very brave of you. And it was a very grown-up thing to do. Thank you for watching out for him."

Uncomfortable with the praise, he averted his gaze and his cheeks colored.

"I feel sorry for him," he said quietly. "My dad—" He stopped short and looked up into my eyes. "My dad was a hophead, too. Until he kicked it. Tried a few times before it stuck. When he'd try to quit, Mom and I used to have to take turns staying awake to make sure he wouldn't leave the house. Mom had special locks put on the doors, and we kept the keys hidden. I learned how to talk to him to settle him down."

I marveled at the maturity and strength of this young boy-man. "You must be tired," was all I managed to say, choked up at his declaration. What a heavy burden for a child. Having faced inconceivable burdens way too young myself, I felt a deep kinship with Stevie. What a blessing it was that he'd been sent to us.

"I'll be all right," he said with a yawn. "Better get to my chores." He moved past me, and I watched him walk down the hall, pinpricks stinging the back of my eyes.

Creaking sounds came from the bedroom. I peered back in to find my father sitting on the edge of the mattress, his arms braced next to his sides to support his bent-over frame.

"Dad?"

He looked up at me with a ravaged expression. "I can't do this. I need my medicine." His voice was weak, fragile. "I know a guy—"

"You can." I knelt down next to him. "Think of Madeleine."

"I can think of nothing else," he croaked, clearly on the verge of a sob. "I need to do something. I need to help."

It was a sound idea, but the thought of him setting foot off the ranch and making an escape to somehow get to this "guy" to get his drugs tarnished it.

"It's best you stay here," I said firmly. "If you need to do something—to keep your mind off things—you can help Ned around the ranch." I figured the physical exertion would also be good for him, help purge the toxins from his body and get him out of the confinement and all-consuming anguish of his withdrawal.

He looked up at me with the expression of a surly teenager. Having lived with teenagers for the last year and a half, I was used to attitude and I knew this was my cue to be absolutely resolute in my conviction.

"Get dressed," I commanded. "Take a shower. Then come to the house and eat some breakfast. Fifteen minutes."

He shook his head, muttering to himself, and then ran his hands through his spiky, greasy hair.

"Come on," I urged.

His gaze shifted away from mine. He loosed a sigh and then nodded. He stood up, his body stiff, looking like a man much older than his years. I watched him shuffle out of the room and down the other end of the hallway to the bathroom. The door clicked shut, and the shower turned on.

I stripped the sweat-stained sheets from the bed and rolled them into a ball. I'd take them into the house for Rose to launder. I went to the closet and found a fresh pair of trousers and a clean shirt, and I laid them on the bed. I then went to the dresser in search of clean underwear and opened a drawer. Nothing. I opened the one next to it and found some undergarments. I pulled out an undershirt and some boxers when I heard a clink from within the drawer.

I moved some rolled-up socks to the side and then lifted them out. Lying beneath them was a silver chain with three silver disks attached to it. Stamped into the upper arc of one disk was the name *Peter Michelle*. Below it was *Pvt.* and below that was *B. Co.* The last line read, *4th Inf. U.S.A.* I picked it up, the chain trailing below it, and I turned it over. There was a series of numbers punched into the back of it. Dog tags.

I scanned another of the tags. It was identical. The third was almost the same, but the name stamped into the upper arc was Harold Huxley.

Harold.

A noise at the door startled me. It was my father, a towel wrapped around his waist and another over his shoulders, his wet hair dripping onto it, and his dirty underwear in hands.

"What are you doing?" he asked, his eyes narrowed to slits.

"I, um, I was getting some fresh clothes for you," I stammered, still holding the dog tags.

"I can get myself dressed," he snarled.

"I know, I'm sorry." I felt like a child again, caught with my hand in the cookie jar.

"Put that back," he said, pointing to the chain in my hand.

I laid it in the drawer. "Who is Harold Huxley?"

He tossed his underwear on the bed. "Buddy of mine. Killed in the war. Stepped on a buried artillery shell right in front of me."

"Was that at Aisne?" I asked.

"What?" He met my gaze, his brow pulled down in confusion.

"Did your friend die at Aisne?" I repeated.

He blinked as if finally understanding the question. "Yes, yes. Terrible battle."

"I see." I wondered why he had this Harold's dog tag. "Does he not have family?" It seemed like it would be appropriate for them to have the tag.

"He doesn't." He looked at me directly. I almost had the sense he was challenging me.

Suddenly aware he was standing there nearly naked, I pushed

the drawer closed. "I'll see you in a few minutes," I reminded him.

The only way he was going to get better was to just push through, not wallow away in bed. Besides, he seemed a bit stronger, not so racked with pain and nausea.

"Fine," he said flatly, as if annoyed with me. He probably was annoyed with me.

I left and went back to the house, a deeply uneasy feeling settling into my bones.

MY HEART HEAVY with mixed emotions concerning my father, this whole situation with the Fabergé egg, and now Valentina's death, I fought to keep a positive perspective.

I walked into the kitchen to hear the phone ringing. Chet, who was closest to the door that led into the living room, left the kitchen to answer it. I poured myself a cup of coffee and nibbled on a generously buttered toast point.

He came back a few minutes later. "Timothy. On the phone for you."

Coffee cup in hand, I swept past him and went to the phone.

"I can't believe it, lass," Timothy said. "Suicide. Never saw that coming."

"I know," I said, afraid to divulge more.

He sighed. "I'll have to find a replacement for her."

I knew the idea pained him. Valentina had been perfect for the role. He wasn't proving to have much luck getting this film off the ground. He'd had to halt production of his last film a few times surrounding the murder of Edward Travis, and then it had never happened. I felt for him. He was a gifted director, trying so hard to make his mark in Hollywood.

"I've already spoken to Marion Mayfield," he said.

That was fast. Marion was a young, up-and-coming actress

who had worked for Paramount. Rumors abounded that she'd been unhappy there, had severed her contract, and was looking for new work. Truth be told, she'd be perfect for the part.

"How's Valentina's aunt faring? Do you know?" he asked.

"No."

But I knew what I had to do next, and the thought filled me with dread. I needed to go see Anna Ivanova. Was she still in and out of consciousness? Had she even been told of Valentina's death? Or had the nurses and doctors kept it from her, afraid it would impact her recovery? What about Anton Belsky? Had he told her? Were they close? How was he doing?

I shook my head to rid it of all the extraneous questions. I needed to find this egg, and I needed to find it fast. I longed to go to the authorities and tell them that Valentina had been murdered, but they would never believe me. I needed concrete evidence first.

"I'm going to the hospital this morning," I told him.

"Good lass. I'll be in touch."

I hung up the phone and went back to the kitchen where Rose was preparing her usual hearty breakfast. The kids were still out doing their chores.

"I'm going to the police station today," Chet said. "To see what I can find out about Miss Baklanova's death."

I told him of my plans to go to the hospital.

Just then my father walked into the kitchen. His face sagged and his eyes were red rimmed, but he was freshly showered and was wearing clean clothes for the first time in days.

"Dad is going to help Ned today," I announced, giving no room for protest from anyone, namely my father.

"That's great," Chet said, giving a nod of approval.

"I want to help find the egg," he grumbled.

"You'll be safer here," I said, sliding my gaze over to Chet for backup.

His eyes shone with understanding. "Grace is right, Peter. Especially given what happened with Miss Baklanova."

My father clenched his fists at his sides. "I feel so helpless."

"I know," I sympathized with him.

He went over to one of the chairs at the kitchen table and slumped into it.

"Work will take your mind off things for a bit," Rose said, coming over and setting some eggs in front of him. His face soured. Perhaps the nausea was still making him feel green.

With a tilt of my head, I bade Chet to follow me into the living room. "Something's not right with him," I said, thinking about my earlier encounter with him, and also about Sophia's voice in my head with the word *deception* ringing loud and clear.

"Well, no," Chet agreed. "He's a junk head, and his wife is missing."

"I don't mean that. I think he's withholding something." I couldn't quite bring myself to say the word *lying* out loud. It hurt too much. "But, I can't figure out what it is."

I told him about the dog tags and Harold Huxley. "Well, actually, there is only one for Harold Huxley."

Chet frowned. "When a soldier is killed, one tag is kept with the body, and the other one is sent home. If this Harold had no one, no family, it makes sense that your dad would keep the dog tag if they were close."

"I see."

I still felt something about this was off. "I'm going back to the boarding house to search the apartment again. And to see if another note has been left there. Oh, can I see the note you found yesterday?" I asked.

"Yes. It's in the pocket of my coat." He went to the hallway closet and pulled out his coat. He produced the note. It was type-written like the first one my father had received. The unevenness of the letters with the dipped *a* made the words somehow more ominous, more threatening.

I heaved a sigh. "I pray she's all right."

An image of Valentina falling out of the window sent a shudder through me.

Chet placed his hands on my shoulders. "I'll go with you. Let's go to the police station together, and then we'll head over to the boarding house."

"No." I shook my head. "We'll make better use of the time if we split up. And I want to go to the hospital, too."

Chet pressed his lips together, concern in his eyes.

"I'll be fine." I wrapped my arms around his middle and pressed my head to his chest. He squeezed me tighter to him and kissed the top of my head.

Folded into his arms, I breathed in his scent—an earthy, woodsy smell that made me feel grounded and safe—and in that moment, I wanted to stay there forever.

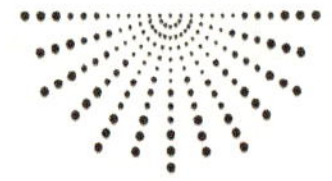

CHAPTER EIGHTEEN

When I reached the hallway leading to Anna Ivanova's room, I took in a deep breath, readying myself for what I might encounter when I saw her.

A blood-curdling scream came from down the hallway, and I had a feeling I knew where it was coming from. I picked up my pace. A nurse burst from a room across the hall and ran into Miss Ivanova's room.

"Out! Out!" Miss Ivanova screamed.

As I reached her door, Anton Belsky backed out of her doorway. His eyes were wide with alarm, his movements jerky. He pressed a shaking hand to his forehead.

"Mr. Belsky? What happened?" I asked.

"Uh, she . . . she woke up. Saw me there. Started screaming like madwoman."

"Did you tell her about Valentina?"

He ran a hand through his hair. "Yes. Yes, I thought she should know. But someone already—"

"Did the staff tell her?"

"I don't know." He backed away from me, turned, and fled down the hall.

"Mr. Belsky, wait!" I hurried after him.

Still walking, he raised his arm, signaling he didn't want to be bothered. I stopped, respecting his silent request. He was grieving and probably needed time alone. The last thing he'd want is me pelting him with questions. I'd do that later.

I made my way back to Miss Ivanova's room. The nurse was leaning over the bed, ministering to her.

"Is she all right?" I asked.

The nurse nodded. "I think so, but she's unconscious again."

A pillow had fallen from the bed and onto the floor. I picked it up and set it at Miss Ivanova's feet, not wanting to disturb her or the nurse who was taking her pulse. She gently laid the prostrate woman's wrist back down on the bed.

"She must be distraught at the news of her niece. How did she find out?" I asked.

The nurse nodded toward a radio on the table in the corner. "She likes to listen to music. I think it helps her. She heard the broadcast."

"How awful," I said. What a horrible way to receive such news.

"Yes. It's set back her recovery, I'm afraid."

"But she will recover?"

The nurse pressed her lips together. "Not fully. She seems to have partial loss of language. Only time will tell if she will be able to speak properly again."

My heart sank. Aside from the fact that I wanted her to get better, to have a full recovery and go on living, she was also the key to finding the egg.

"May I sit with her for a while?" I asked. "I'm . . . I'm a friend . . . was a friend . . . of Valentina's."

The nurse tucked the sheet tighter under the mattress. She gave me the once-over, considering my request. "Yes, I suppose that would be all right." She checked Miss Ivanova's pulse one more time. Satisfied, she slipped by me, her soft-soled shoes squeaking on the linoleum floor.

I placed one of the two chairs in the room next to the bed and settled in. I told myself I would stay an hour, hoping upon hope that Miss Ivanova would wake again.

I took a deep breath, studying her face. Her mouth was slack, hanging open a bit, her head tilted toward me. It seemed the poor woman had aged since I was here just a few days ago. I was no doctor, but she didn't look good to me at all.

To my astonishment, she opened her eyes. She blinked, trying to register me sitting there. "Who?" she croaked.

"I'm Grace Michelle. I was here the other day with—"

She closed her eyes and shook her head, her face crumpling with emotion. A tear slipped out from the side of her eye and cascaded down her temple to the pillow.

"I'm so, so sorry for your loss." I reached out and touched her hand.

She took in a deep breath and let it out in an anguished sigh. "He . . . he . . ." she stuttered. Her brows knit together in confusion. "He . . . he said— Going to . . . He's the . . ."

I pressed my brows together, trying to figure out what she was trying to say. Her speech certainly had deteriorated since the last time I'd seen her. I wondered if her condition had truly worsened or if it was due to her state of utter distress.

"Who?" I asked.

She pointed to the door.

"Mr. Belsky?"

She nodded. "He . . . It not— It not suic—" She couldn't finish. Garbled noises came from her mouth, but I knew what she was trying to say.

I leaned closer to her. "I don't believe Valentina committed suicide, either, Miss Ivanova. I believe she was murdered. And I believe it had to do with this package that was sent to you. Do you remember what you did with it?"

She squeezed her eyes shut, as if trying to pry the information from her mind. "Saint . . . court," she said, opening her eyes.

I pinched my brows together, trying to understand.

"Saint," she uttered again.

"What saint? What do you mean?" I pressed.

"Ro-roses."

Roses. Then I remembered the intoxicating aroma of roses at her house. The images of roses surrounding Sophia in my dreams and visions.

"Do you mean the rose garden at your house?"

She shook her head. She opened her mouth to say more, but nothing came out. She wrinkled her nose, screwing up her lips. She tried to speak again but only emitted obscure noises. She sighed, the life draining from her face. She released my hand and placed hers at her chest. She tapped at a chain around her neck.

"What is it? What are you trying to say?"

She pinched at the chain with her fingers.

"I don't understand."

She tapped at the chain again.

Gingerly, I put out my hand. "May I?"

She let her hand fall away from her chest. Carefully, I lifted the chain and pulled it out from under the cotton hospital gown. An oblong medal hung from the end of it. I turned it over in my fingers. Engraved in it was an image of a bearded man standing in what looked like water or waves. He was holding a staff in one hand, and a child sat on his left shoulder. The inscription surrounding the image said, *Behold St. Christopher and go your way in safety.*

"St. Christopher," I whispered out loud, trying to make some kind of connection. I raised my eyes to Miss Ivanova's face. It had gone slack again.

"Miss Ivanova?"

There was no response. She'd fallen back into unconsciousness.

"Oh dear." I sighed, my mind trying to make sense of what she'd been trying to tell me.

The nurse appeared at the door again. "All okay in here?"

"She was conscious for a few minutes, but now . . ."

"It doesn't last long, I'm afraid. Consciousness, I mean. We thought it would get better, but it hasn't, the poor woman."

I took hold of Miss Ivanova's hand again, fighting the lump forming in my throat and fighting the desperation threatening to overtake me. I had to find this egg to put a stop to all this madness.

"I'm afraid it's time to go." The nurse's voice pulled me out of my reverie.

"Yes," I said. "Thank you for letting me stay."

She gave me a smile. I squeezed Anna Ivanova's hand in a silent gesture of goodbye and then left with a dark cloud hanging over my head.

I LEFT THE HOSPITAL, my mind whirling, trying to figure out what Anna Ivanova had been trying to tell me. What roses, and what did St. Christopher have to do with them?

My thoughts drifted to Mr. Belsky and how Miss Ivanova had been so upset at his presence, at what he'd said to her. Or possibly how he'd said it? He couldn't have known she'd already heard the news.

I felt for Mr. Belsky at Miss Ivanova's outburst. He, too, had suffered a terrible loss and was most likely not in his right mind, either.

I knocked at the front door of the boarding house. Mrs. Wilkins, the plump, rosy-cheeked owner of the place, answered.

"Ah, you again," she said, placing stout hands on her hips. "How can I help you?"

"My father asked me to pick up a few things, and to bring

you this." I didn't want to go into any of the details of my true mission. I pulled an envelope full of cash from my purse and handed her the week's rent payment.

She ushered me into the house. "Where have those two been?" she asked, closing the door. "Seems silly to pay for rooms and then not occupy them."

"I know," I conceded, trying to come up with an explanation. I couldn't very well tell her we were paying for the rooms because we were waiting for a note from kidnappers. "My father is ill, and we've taken him to my house for a few days to recover."

"Hmm." She looked at me skeptically. "Guess it don't matter to me. As long as I get payment." She held the bills I had given her up in the air.

"Mrs. Wilkins, have you seen anyone or anything out of the ordinary around here lately?"

She shrugged. "No. That handsome husband of yours asked me the same thing the other day. What's going on?"

"Oh . . . well," I fumbled, trying to come up with a reason for my question. "I, well, we've heard there's been some suspicious activity in this neighborhood, that a house on the next block was burglarized." Guilt stabbed at my stomach with the lie.

"Where did you hear that? I didn't hear anything about any burglary." She lowered her brows, making the hooded lids of her eyes appear even heavier.

"Really? Um—" Gosh, how I hated lying. "We have a friend living nearby. He told us about it."

"Oh my. " She pressed a hand to her mouth with concern.

"But you probably have nothing to worry about," I said lamely, feeling bad for scaring her and not wanting to further embellish my already embellished deception. "Well, I'd better get going. Busy day and all. I'll just get what I came for and be on my way."

I sidestepped past her and made my way down the hallway,

the heels of my shoes clicking rapidly on the wooden floor. Slipping the key into the lock, I let myself in. I closed the door and leaned my back against it, letting out a breath. It had been hovering at the top of my chest throughout my encounter with the landlady.

Eager to see if a message had been left, I went to the kitchen. A few items of mail were scattered on the linoleum underneath the mail slot in the door. I bent down to pick them up when I noticed something odd. The door hung open, and the wood on the doorjamb had been fractured.

As I picked up the letters, a jolt of adrenaline zapped me, sending tingles into my hands and up my arms. Someone had broken in.

I scanned the kitchen and then went into the living room. Nothing had been moved. My heart in my throat, I peered into the bedroom. The bed was unmade—a rumpled mess and not how we'd left it. I swallowed. Somebody had slept here. Had Mrs. Wilkins let someone spend the night here in my father's absence? But then why had the kitchen door been forced?

I backed away from the bedroom, my senses on high alert. I quickly shuffled through the letters until my eyes rested on a blank envelope. I tore it open and pulled out the contents. There was another picture of Madeleine—her hands and feet bound, a gag pressed between her lips and tied around her head. She lay on a tattered mattress on the floor, her head cocked at a strange angle and her eyes closed.

I read the typewritten message: *We're watching you. Time is running out. Your friend is hungry and thirsty. When you have found the egg, leave a light on in this kitchen. We will contact you at your home with further instructions.*

At your home. I hated the reality that these people were watching our every move. I read the message again. My eyes stuttered on the familiar letter *a* that hung below the rest of the letters.

I looked at the photograph again, and my heart sank.

But wait . . . The earlier message, the telegram delivered to Ambassador, instructed us to leave the egg in an oil drum at the northeast corner of our alfalfa field. Why the change?

A creaking noise came from the kitchen, sending my heart into spasms. Then footsteps. I dashed for the door leading into the hallway of the house.

"Hello, Grace." A male voice froze me to the spot.

I slowly turned to see James Johnson.

I blinked, unable to believe my eyes. "But, you're—" I couldn't finish the sentence, my mouth had gone dry as sawdust.

"Dead?" he said, a grin oozing over his face. "As you can see, I'm not."

The blood drained from my head, and my lungs seemed to refuse to work. I couldn't breathe. I stumbled backward, my knees giving way as if I'd been punched in the stomach. I grabbed hold of the arm of the sofa.

His already-wiry physique had become even more wizened with hard labor and, I'm sure, a lack of decent food in prison. His hands rested casually in his pockets, and that Cheshire grin mocked me.

"But how did you—" And then it dawned on me. The body that had been burned in the car had been unrecognizable. "You set it up. You planted evidence to make them think the body was yours—the insulin kit, the hat." His diabolicalness knew no bounds. He was ruthless.

"Who did you kill this time?" I asked with the sickening feeling that I would surely be next.

"No one of importance." He shrugged. "A vagrant living on the beach. But let's not speak of that. I was hoping to run into you."

With a sudden surge of energy, I turned to make my escape out the door, but he was on me in a flash. He grabbed my arm, squeezing hard.

"Let go of me or I'll scream," I rasped.

"I wouldn't do that—for Madeleine's sake."

My eyes widened. "You?"

He shook his head with a chuckle. "No. I don't have *her*." He put a strange emphasis on the word that I couldn't quite comprehend. "But I want to help you get her back."

"You do?" What kind of game was he playing? "But how did you—"

"Clara told me all about it."

"Clara?" I blinked, trying to make sense of this. He clutched my arm harder, and it started to throb. I tried to pull away, but he produced a gun from his pocket with his other hand and shoved the barrel in front of my face.

"No, no, no," he said, his tone like that of a father scolding a child. "Have a seat." He motioned toward the sofa and, still gripping my arm, led me over to it, then shoved me down onto the cushions.

"What did Clara . . . ." I was still reeling from the mention of her name in connection with him.

He towered over me. "Sweet girl. We go way back. Well, not *way* back. I met her a couple of years ago at one of the Steinbergs' famous parties. She was completely infatuated with me."

My stomach turned at the thought. How anyone could be infatuated with this bug-eyed snake was beyond me.

"I took her out a few times, but I don't know. I like my women a bit saucier, a bit more . . . fiery."

Florence Thomas came to mind, Edward Travis's widow. I had wondered at the time of Edward's death if she and James Johnson had been having an affair.

"When I was in prison—thanks to you," he ground out, "Clara and I struck up a correspondence."

I shook my head in disbelief. How could she have aligned herself with a murderer?

"And she just recently told me about this amazing treasure

you're after—a jewel-encrusted egg. Worth a fortune." That oily grin returned, sending a shiver down my spine.

My mind reeled at Clara's betrayal, and my thoughts drifted back to the few times I'd seen her lurking in the doorway of my office, once when I had told Valentina about the egg. She'd been eavesdropping.

"So you've seen her?" I asked, still spinning at the idea that she had deceived me, that she'd plotted with him.

He didn't answer with anything but a continuation of that blood-freezing, sinister smile.

"What do you want?" I balled my fists at my thighs.

"I want in. I want this egg worth a fortune. And you're going to find it for me."

I swallowed. "But Madeleine's life—"

He laughed. "Do you think I care about Madeleine, your father's concubine?"

I gritted my teeth at his disgusting comment. "And if I don't help you?"

He sighed. "I'd hate to see that poor orphan, Stevie, die. He has such a bright future ahead of him."

My stomach caved in. "Stevie . . . "

Then I remembered his earlier comment about Madeleine's captivity, the strange emphasis on the word *her*.

"You have Stevie." I could barely utter the words because my throat had closed up.

"I do," he said with glee. "Seemed like a good idea. You've been pretty motivated to find this treasure and save this Madeleine person so I thought I'd give you a little inspiration, too."

I felt the blood drain from my face. He must have noticed because he raised his hand in assurance. "He's all right . . . for now. But I guess you'd better get busy. And don't even think of alerting the police. They'll never find him, and if I'm sent back to prison, he will surely perish."

"But how did you . . . ?" My eyes drifted to the arm of the sofa. I hadn't noticed it before, but a canvas shoulder bag lay crumpled on the sofa. A rolled-up newspaper stuck out of it. My lungs collapsed, and I fought for breath. He'd seized Stevie on his paper route.

I wanted to scream, to run, to dash into the house yelling at the top of my lungs that the escaped murderer James Johnson was on the premises. But I had a gun pointed in my face, and if I died, both Stevie and Madeleine would die, too.

A watery sensation flooded my body. Had I been standing, I probably would have collapsed.

"Did you kill Valentina?" I asked.

He hesitated. "What? Who? Oh, the actress. No. Pity, though." He grinned again. "So here's what's going to happen."

He stepped a few inches closer to me. My neck ached from the strain of looking up at him.

"I'm going to leave here," he continued, "and you are going to stay for at least ten minutes. You will not follow me. Did you know I am an expert shot?" He waved the barrel of the gun back and forth in my face. "Every day, at four o'clock, you will be at your ranch, waiting for my phone call. If you don't answer—you personally—I'll break that boy's fingers, one by one. Understand?"

My stomach clenched. Poor Stevie. He must be so frightened. I hoped he wasn't hurt.

My fear was quickly replaced with surge of anger pulsing through me. If that boy had been harmed in any way . . .

"When you find it, you will do as I said in the telegram. You will leave the egg in the oil drum at the northeast corner of your alfalfa field. Understand?"

So he'd sent the telegram. I thought of all the notes we'd received. I had been right that some of them had been inconsistent—in tone and in how they conveyed the messages.

"And Stevie?"

"He'll be there. Don't worry, dear." His expression morphed from the hideous grin to a look of mock concern. "I'm a man of my word."

I gritted my teeth. "And why should I trust you?"

He narrowed his eyes at me. "Do not underestimate me, Grace. You know what I am capable of."

I swallowed, knowing all too well.

"I'm going to leave now. Don't you move." He backed away from me.

I held my breath, my whole body frozen as he backed into the kitchen, disappearing from view. I heard his footsteps on the linoleum and listened for the opening and closing of the door, but all was quiet. What was he doing? Had he left?

I bit my bottom lip, trying to decide if I should get up or not. I waited a few more minutes and then rose from the couch. I tiptoed to the kitchen and peered in. It was empty.

I ran to the door, looking out its paned windows. I pressed myself closer to the glass to peer around the corner. He was nowhere in sight. I pulled the door open and ran out into the alleyway. He had vanished.

Dashing back through the apartment, I went directly to the phone in the hallway.

"Hello, Rose? Is Stevie there?" I asked in the desperate, yet ridiculous, hope that James Johnson had lied, that he had made it all up.

"I'm glad you called," she said, interrupting me, her voice heavy with concern. "We haven't seen him since he left for his paper route. Ned and your father are scouring the fields on horseback."

The idea of my dad riding a horse jarred me for a moment, but it was quickly replaced with a sinking feeling in my stomach. James Johnson had been telling the truth.

"Is Chet there?" Anxiety coursing through me raised my voice an octave. "Does he know Stevie is missing?"

"No. He left before we realized Stevie hadn't come back. Said he was going to the police station to inquire about that woman's death."

In my heightened state of emotion, I had completely forgotten. Yes, the police station. I bit my lip, considering James Johnson's warning. No police.

"Grace? Do you know something? Do you know where Stevie is?"

"No," I said. "I'll explain later. I have to go."

I hung up the phone, my hand still gripping the receiver so hard my knuckles were white. Nausea collapsed my stomach. Why had my father gotten me involved in something so dangerous? All because he wanted this stolen egg, for god's sake— stolen from the country of *Russia*. What was he thinking?

And how had I become so sucked in? I was ready to punish myself for this when I remembered how. *Madeleine.* Hopefully, she was still alive. If I'd put Stevie at risk for nothing, I'd never forgive myself.

I took a deep breath. I couldn't think about that. Not now.

I went back into the apartment to grab my handbag. Realizing I still had the letters and the note from the kidnappers clutched in my hand, I picked up my purse and stuffed them inside. I would give them to my father later. But, for now, I had to find Chet. I had to give him the horrifying news that a murderer was holding an innocent boy in his grasp.

CHAPTER NINETEEN

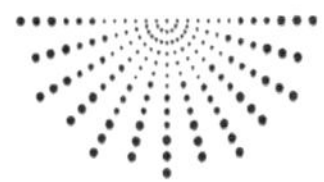

I pulled up in front of the police station just as Chet was coming down the stairs onto the street. He didn't notice me and headed in the opposite direction toward his truck parked on the other side of the road. I tooted my horn.

I stepped out of the car and jogged over to him.

His face registered surprise. "Grace, what are you doing here?"

"James Johnson has Stevie," I blurted.

He blinked in astonishment. "What?"

"He faked his death! He was there, at the boarding house. He wants the egg."

I explained what had happened, and he gently took hold of me by the arms. "My god, Grace. Are you all right? I should have never let you go there alone."

"I'm fine, Chet. But Stevie . . . You know how ruthless James Johnson is. This is over our heads. And we still have no idea where the damn egg is!"

He let go a breath and ran hand down the sides of his mouth. "We need to tell the police he's alive."

"But he said no police. He threatened to harm Stevie if we told the police."

"They have more resources than we do, Grace. More manpower."

True. They did. Things had escalated to the point that we couldn't handle it on our own anymore. At least not all of it. Now not only was Madeleine in danger but Stevie, as well. We needed to pull out all the stops.

"So we tell them about James Johnson—that he has Stevie," I agreed. "But I don't want to tell them about the egg."

"Why not? Because of your father's drug habit? It's not an issue anymore. He's getting off the stuff."

"No. Because if the police find it first, they're not going to hand it over to Johnson. They can't. We will have lost our leverage. With the Russians, too. They'll kill Madeleine for sure. This way, we are covering all the bases. The police will be looking for Johnson, and we will be looking for the egg. When we find it, and we *will*," I said with all the conviction I could muster, "then *we* decide what to do with it, not the police."

Chet nodded. "Good thinking."

I let out a breath with an audible exhale, satisfied with the plan for now. "What did you find out about Valentina?" I asked.

"The police are investigating, but for the time being they still consider it a suicide. Valentina apparently left a note, but they are looking at everything, which is good."

"A note?" I shook my head. She couldn't have wanted to kill herself. It just wasn't true. "Someone must have forced her to write it."

"Perhaps," he said. "I think we need to go see her fiancé. He knew her better than anyone, I imagine. Aside from her aunt."

"I agree. But right now we need to tell the police about that hoodlum James Johnson."

"Come on," he said, taking me by the elbow.

A few minutes later, we were standing at a tall reception desk talking to a pimply-faced junior officer. The place smelled of wood and typewriter ink. The clack-clacking and occasional dings of carriage returns hummed in the background as policemen pecked away at their desks, typing their reports.

"I've seen James Johnson," I said to him. He looked to be about nineteen years old and was tall and scrawny—all angles.

He scoffed, looking at me like I was some crazy woman off the streets. "James Johnson is dead, miss."

I set my jaw and fixed him with a glare to convey the seriousness of the matter. "He's not. I just saw him, in the flesh. Alive and well."

He narrowed his eyes and then, resting his elbow on the counter, pointed a finger at me, recognition in his gaze. "I know who you are. You're the one who helped put him behind bars."

"Yes. He's out for revenge. He's kidnapped one of the children who is living at our ranch. He's after—" I stopped myself.

"Miss?" the officer inquired.

I cleared my throat. "Like I said, he's after revenge. He wants to make me pay for putting him in jail."

Just then a portly man in a dark suit appeared at the officer's elbow. I immediately recognized the heavy brows. He was the detective who'd come to Felicity's to inquire if James Johnson had visited the mansion after his escape.

"Mr. Riker?" he addressed Chet. "Was there something else?"

"Detective Baptiste, this is my wife, Grace. We have something to report."

"Ah, yes. Mrs. Riker—or you go by your maiden name, am I correct? Miss Michelle, is it? From the Edward Travis case. I saw you at his estate the other day. Thought you looked familiar at the time. Now it's all coming together."

"Yes," I said.

With a tilt of his head, he bade us to come around the reception desk. "Let's go to my office."

We followed him past more desks and stepped into a windowed office with DETECTIVE JONATHAN BAPTISTE painted on the glass in black letters rimmed with gold.

He gestured for us to sit in the chairs opposite his desk. "What's this you want to talk about?"

I told him about James Johnson.

"What were you doing at the boarding house?" he asked.

"My father is renting some rooms there," I said. "But he's ill so we've taken him to the ranch to recover. I was there to . . . to pick up some mail for him." It was harder than I thought not to tell him about the egg and Madeleine, but I knew I had to stick to the plan.

"And you are certain the boy is missing?"

"Yes. I called the house. Rose, Chet's mother, said Stevie hadn't come back from his paper route, which is unusual in the morning. He's always back before school." And to think I had been worried about his occasionally returning late from his evening route. The irony stung.

"Any chance he's playing hooky?" The detective leaned back in his chair, folding his hands over his belly.

"No!" I almost shouted. Why wasn't he taking this more seriously? "James Johnson admitted he has Stevie. I saw his newspaper tote in the apartment. I also think Johnson's been following me for days. In a green Oldsmobile with a dent on one of the fenders."

The detective scribbled a note on his pad.

"He knows where we live—" I continued.

"All right," the detective interrupted. "Is there anything else you can tell me? Do you know where James Johnson might be staying? Do you think he's working with someone else?"

"Clara!" I blurted. "Clara Stapleton. She works with me. James Johnson told me they had a relationship, that they've been in contact."

"Do you know where I might find this woman?"

I wanted to bite back my words. Had I just made a huge mistake in telling him about Clara? If he interrogated her, she might tell him about the egg, and if she did, there went any power I had left. I had to find the egg before they did. If the police were successful in finding James Johnson and Stevie first, then I'd hand it over to the Russians for Madeleine, and do everything in my power to help the police track them down. But not now. I swallowed down the bile rising in my throat.

"I . . . I don't know where she lives, but she's the niece of Barney and Alice Steinberg, the owners of Ambassador Films."

"Okay," he said, scribbling their names on the pad of paper. "Anything else?"

I looked over at Chet, and our eyes locked. He lifted a shoulder as if to tell me that revealing more was at my discretion.

"Please find Stevie," I implored.

The detective tapped the pencil on the pad of paper. "We'll do everything we can, Mrs.—er, Miss Michelle."

I DROVE AS FAST as I could to Hotel Miramar, my body humming with adrenaline and my heart shattered by the reality that Stevie had come to harm while in our care. It was inconceivable and too much to bear. I had to get him back—and in one piece.

What had I been missing in my messages from Sophia? Why were they so disjointed and fragmented? Had I been subconsciously blocking them? Lenora Lange would help me break through. I had to believe that.

I parked the car and made my way down the little dirt pathway leading to the bungalows. A breeze had picked up, and the palm trees scattered about the grassy grounds rustled above me. The marine air tickled my nostrils, and I breathed deeply, trying to steady myself.

When I reached her cottage, I rapped on the door, expecting her to immediately fling it open as she had before, but the door remained closed. I knocked again. She had to be here. I had to have a session with her—or at least speak with her to see if she could help me put together the pieces of the puzzle that had scattered to the wind.

Finally, she opened the door. She was in a bathrobe, and her silver hair was wrapped in a towel. "Miss Michelle." She greeted me with a warm smile.

"Miss Lange, I'm sorry to interrupt." I was mortified that I had caught her in such a state of undress.

"It's no problem. Please, come in." She pulled the door open wide and gestured for me to go in. I gave an embarrassed chuckle and stepped inside.

The floral arrangement on the table had been changed. Today there were long-stemmed, vibrant red roses set within the enormous crystal vase. There must have been five dozen of them. Their heady fragrance filled the room.

Roses. Sophia surrounded by roses. Miss Ivanova mentioning roses. There had to be some significance there. But what was it?

"I'll be just a moment." Miss Lange glided toward the back of the cottage.

I went to the sofa and sat down, my handbag clutched in my fingers in a death grip. My legs tingled with electricity. I sprang from the cushions and paced the length of the sofa. Back and forth, unable to calm my anxiety at the thought that James Johnson, a man completely unhinged by all accounts, had Stevie in his grasp.

I'd never forgive myself if something happened to him. He'd already been dealt some pretty tough blows for a kid. Knowing firsthand the pain he'd already suffered made me feel connected to Stevie in a way that was different from the other children.

Both of us had been orphaned at twelve. Even though my father was alive, I had lived in the belief that he was gone for half of my life. And his return did nothing to alter what Sophia and I had lived through. Both Stevie and I had suffered the pain, turmoil, and confusion of living with a mentally unstable parent, someone we felt responsible for, a person we wanted to fix but had no power to fix.

I pivoted on my heel for the fiftieth time to find that Lenora Lange had returned to the room. She wore a simple white cotton dress, and her hair was perfectly coiffed in her customary waved bob. I marveled at how quickly she had put herself together.

"To what do I owe this pleasure, Miss Michelle?"

"I'm so sorry to barge in on you like this, but I really need your help. You see, Stevie, one of our wards, has been . . ." The words tumbled out of my mouth in a torrent.

Miss Lange put her hands on mine. I still clutched my handbag as if it were the only thing keeping me from falling into a pit of utter despair.

"Breathe." Her voice came out in a whisper, and she looked deep into my eyes with her crystal blue gaze.

The power emanating from her stunned me into silence. I inhaled deeply through my nose. My lungs expanded, and the oxygen soothed them like water spilling into a parched desert valley. I exhaled, and my body began to shed the armor of my stress.

"There." She took my handbag and set it on the coffee table next to us. "Sit and tell me what you need from me."

I sat down and took in another breath. The torrent of thoughts and emotions holding me captive loosened, and I breathed them out. "I can't give you all the details, but believe me when I tell you this is a matter of life and death."

"Does it have to do with Valentina Baklanova's murder and this item—this package—you are searching for?" She folded her hands in her lap.

Stunned at her powers of perception, I sank back into the

cushion of the chair like I'd been delivered a blow. "You don't believe she committed suicide, either," I said.

She shook her head.

"Do you know who killed her? Did you see who killed her?"

"No." A wistful expression crossed her face. "Her spirit came through so strongly, I could see nothing, feel nothing but her shock, her fear. Joshua embraced her and called to someone who I believe was your sister, to help her make the transition. I did not know it was Valentina until I saw the story in the newspaper."

I stared at her in amazement.

"But this is not why you came here today." Her statement pulled me out of my awe and wonder.

"No. It's this item. The package. I need to find it. I'm afraid the situation has become much more dire, and now two lives are at stake." I told her about Madeleine and Stevie.

"You are in danger," she warned.

"Maybe," I said, not wanting to think about it. "But it doesn't matter. I *have* to find it. I believe Sophia is trying to tell me something about this item. Perhaps where it was hidden. She's been trying to tell me a number of things I can't make sense of, but this . . . this is the most important thing right now. Can you get to her? Can you help translate what she is trying to say? Can you ask her what she knows about this package?"

"You can ask her." She smiled, making the corners of her eyes crinkle. "Are you ready?"

I swallowed down my trepidation. "Yes. Yes, I'm ready."

She took hold of my hands and closed her eyes. I did the same. I searched my mind, straining to see, to hear something, anything.

She squeezed my fingers. "Let your mind go," she whispered.

I took a shaky breath and envisioned a blackboard with thousands of words, drawings, and scribbles all over it. And then a felt eraser levitated in the air, pressed itself against the board, and wiped it clean. My shoulders released. My forehead melted. The area around my eyes relaxed.

"She's here," Lenora whispered.

I scanned my mind for her but couldn't find her.

"Gracie?"

I opened my eyes and looked at Lenora. Her eyes were still closed, and her face exuded a serenity that could only be described as unearthly.

"Sophia?" I peered closer at her.

Lenora smiled. "Hello, darling."

I gasped, my breath hitching in my throat. This was so different from what I'd experienced before. No fragmented visions, no cryptic words. Could I actually be communicating—truly speaking—with her?

"I miss you so much," I croaked.

"I'm here now."

Doubt—or was it my own practicality and pragmatism?—crept in, clouding the moment with shadows. "How do I know it's you?"

"Bramblebug."

My throat tightened, and the sensation of pinpricks stung the back of my eyes. It was the name she and I had come up with for the imaginary friend we'd created when we were very young children. I smiled, my heart bursting with joy, love, and hope.

"I need your help, Sophia. I need to find the egg. Anna Ivanova said something about Sister Magdalena, roses, and St. Christopher. What does it mean?"

"You know."

I stared at Miss Lange's face. Her eyes were closed and her expression blank. I couldn't decipher anything from her countenance. How could I know?

"The kissing palms."

I blinked. She'd mentioned this—or had shown me this —before.

"But where are the palms?" I asked.

"You know," she repeated.

"But I don't!" I raised my voice, frustrated with these riddles. Miss Lange flinched but didn't come out of her trance. She sat there, silent, unmoving.

I shook my head, tears of frustration threatening to surface. I let out a sigh, my eyes scanning the room. They settled on the abundant roses in the vase in the foyer. *Sister Magdalena. Roses. St. Christopher.*

Suddenly, I gasped, finally understanding. Miss Ivanova obviously loved roses. Why else would she have such an expansive rose garden? And she had paid for the landscaping of the courtyard at the church. I thought back to the roses surrounding the statue of Mary in the grotto. It had to be at the church. Somewhere among the roses. But I couldn't figure out where the kissing palms came into play.

"Trust. Seek from a different perspective," Lenora said, drawing my attention back to her. She slumped in the chair, her hands growing slack in mine.

"Miss Lange?" My heart stuttered. Her face had gone as white as her dress. "Miss Lange," I repeated, worried she'd keel over like a fallen toy soldier.

She opened her eyes, and releasing my hands, she pressed her fingers to her temples.

"Are you okay?"

The color started to come back to her face, and the serenity returned. "Yes. I'm quite well," she said, even though her voice sounded weak.

"Can I get you something? Some water perhaps?"

"No. But you must go. You know now."

I stared at her, unblinking. Was she confirming my theory of the roses?

"Yes. But I am still confused. Where are the kissing palms?"

She smiled. "I don't know. But you'll see."

I scoffed. "I don't see."

"You will. Trust yourself." She smiled at me, her eyes crinkling in the corners. A wave of certainty suddenly enveloped my whole being. I needed to go back to the church.

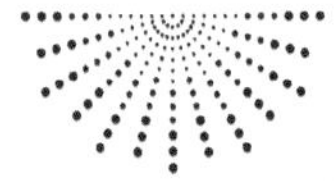

When I pulled into the parking lot of Mission San Gabriel, I was surprised to see the entrance to the church had been blocked off. Mounds of dirt surrounded the steps that led up to the door, and several men, with their backs bent and their shirts drenched in sweat, shoveled the earth out of a large hole. Another man stood nearby, watching them intently. I wondered if he was their supervisor.

"What's happened here?" I asked him.

"Water main broke." He scratched the side of his nose.

Less concerned with the pipes beneath the church, I gave an exasperated sigh. "How do I get in?"

He twisted from the waist and pointed behind him. "There's a gate round the corner. You can get in that way."

"Thank you," I said, hurrying off.

I went around the corner to view an expanse of stucco wall. Farther down I spied a wrought iron gate. I picked up my pace, breaking into a jog. When I reached it, I laid my hand on the latch to open it, but the latch was stuck. I jiggled the handle, but the gate remained impenetrable. I let out a frustrated burst of air. Thoughts of Stevie, scared, hungry, thirsty, and maybe hurt, weighted my mind. My heart thumped an erratic staccato, tapping against my ribs.

Wrapping my fingers around the swirls of black metal, I squeezed my eyes shut.

Sophia, help me.

I opened my eyes and looked beyond the gate into the expanse of the courtyard, lush with flowering shrubberies. Graveled paths led to wooden benches with wrought iron fixtures. My eyes swept to the left and rested on the little domed grotto that protected the statue of the Virgin Mary and the roses surrounding it.

I scanned the area to the right when my eyes locked on something that took my breath away. Soaring above the walled garden courtyard were two palm trees, their trunks curved toward each other, the palms of their leafy tops intertwined. Why hadn't I noticed them before?

Seek from a different perspective.

Of course. I was looking at the courtyard from a different perspective now. This was the sign! The package had to be here.

My heart raced with the desire to get in. My fingers still clasping onto the swirls of metal, I shook the gate. A satisfying click came from the handle. I reached down, turned it, and pushed. To my surprise and utter relief, the gate swung open.

I made my way over to the little grotto. I stood in front of the statue of the Virgin Mary, taking in everything. The roses were of the miniature variety, planted in small pots. I approached the statue and reached out to touch the base. It was fixed solidly into the concrete, immovable. I leaned in and looked toward the back of the grotto. Nothing but votive candles in glass jars.

"Miss Michelle?"

I turned to see Sister Magdalena, her hands tucked under her habit, watching me intently. I felt like a criminal trespasser. Well, technically, I was trespassing . . .

"Sister. I'm sorry for the intrusion—"

"How did you get in? We keep the gate to the courtyard locked. The only way in is through the church, and I was there praying. I did not see you come through," she said with some concern.

"Oh, well, the entrance to the church was blocked by the men working on the pipes. One of them mentioned I should come around to the back. When I pushed, the gate just opened." It wasn't exactly a lie.

"Oh dear," she said. "I must have José take a look at that. What brings you here, my child? Did you wish to pray?"

"Not exactly." I smiled at her sheepishly, relieved she did not seem to be angry at my presence. "I think I know what Miss Ivanova was trying to tell me. She's hidden the package somewhere here in the courtyard."

She regarded me with downturned brows. "But we've seen nothing like that here."

"I know. But I have to see this through. Do you mind if I look?"

She gave me a small nod. "Of course. I will be in my office if you should need assistance."

"Thank you."

I turned my attention to the little potted rosebushes. I searched each one for some kind of clue, but found nothing.

I stood up and scanned the courtyard. There was another array of vibrant red roses—the ones encircling the bench that Anna Ivanova had dedicated to Father Michael.

I walked down one of the graveled pathways toward the palm trees. Beyond the hedges, I could now see a backless stone bench surrounded by rosebushes, all the blooms a deep crimson red. I approached the bench, surveying the area when a small metal placard fixed to the stone caught my eye. It read, IN MEMORY OF FATHER MICHAEL DAMIEN MILTON. BEHOLD ST. CHRISTOPHER. GO YOUR WAY IN SAFETY.

Sister Magdalena, the roses, St. Christopher. This is what

Anna Ivanova and Sophia had been trying to tell me. But where was the egg?

I pulled my upper lip between my teeth. I then remembered my father had said Marcel had buried the egg in his parents' Parisian garden. My gaze drifted toward the back wall and landed on a wheelbarrow. I went over to it, and on the ground beside it was a leather garden tote. José's tools. I picked up a spade and went back to the bench. After flinging my handbag on top of it, I knelt and started to dig.

After several minutes, I realized this task would be much easier with a larger shovel, but I didn't see one. This would have to do. Dirt caked under my fingernails as I struggled to loosen the earth. A single-minded determination took hold of me, and all I could see, hear, think, and focus on was the will to find the egg. It had to be here.

After about twenty minutes, perspiration bloomed on my arms and legs. I had made a complete mess of my dress, and my right hand ached from grasping the handle of the spade, but I dug on, refusing to be discouraged.

Suddenly, the spade hit something hard, and I froze.

"Miss Michelle, what are you doing?" Sister Magdalena appeared to my left.

I looked up at her, my heart hammering in my chest. "I'm sorry. I'm so sorry. I will pay for any damage. I'll make this right. I think I may have found it, Sister."

The shocked expression on her face relaxed. She took a hand out from under her habit and gestured with it for me to continue. I gave a smile of relief and set the spade into the earth again.

Worried about damaging the precious object, I dug more slowly, more carefully. Soon, my efforts revealed the top of a burlap sack. I tried to pull it away but it was stuck, and whatever it contained was wedged into the ground.

"Oh my goodness," the nun gasped. She had come closer to watch my progress.

I sank the spade into the dirt on one side of the sack, removing the earth, and then proceeded to do the same on all sides so I could pry the article from its grave.

Finally, it was free. I lifted the bag, curious at its substantial weight. I loosened the ties that were gathered at the top, then pulled the bag open and withdrew a heavy, jewel-encrusted wooden box. I sucked in a breath as I rotated the box in my soil-stained hands. Rubies, emeralds, and sapphires surrounded by neat metal flourishes dotted the box.

I looked over at the nun, whose mouth had fallen open. I turned my attention back to the treasure. A shining silver clasp held the lid closed. Carefully, I flipped it open. Nestled within a pool of navy velvet lay a gold-and-white-enameled egg, glittering with jewels and resting upon a gold pedestal. The Fabergé egg.

My eyes widened with wonder, and I removed the treasure from its velvety casing and held it up before me. I marveled at the swags of gold encircling the egg. They were offset with diamonds that glinted in the sunlight, nearly blinding me with their brilliance. Crowning the top of the egg was a bejeweled elephant. The pedestal consisted of three golden lions standing on their hind legs, supporting the bottom of the egg with their broad, round paws.

"It's beautiful," Sister Magdalena whispered.

I estimated the egg and pedestal together measured roughly nine inches in height. I let out a whistle of amazement, admiring the intricate design and the jewels twinkling in the sun like stars in the night sky.

"That it is, Sister."

Rotating it in my hands, I noticed a tiny hinge on the back of the egg. I gently pried the top of the egg open to reveal another treasure inside. I lifted out a miniature, ornately designed, diamond studded picture frame, itself on a tiny pedestal. Within the glittering frame was a photograph of a man in royal regalia—

a king. I turned the tiny pedestal in my fingers, and on the other side of the frame was a photograph of a stately-looking, elegantly dressed woman. I had never seen anything more magnificent in my life.

"And this belongs to Anna Ivanova?" the nun asked. "Why did she bury it?"

I placed the egg back into the box, and the box back into the bag. "It's a long story," I said. "And I will tell you all about it, I promise. But it's important that I get this home as soon as possible."

I started to fill the scar I had carved into the ground, alternately tamping the loose earth down with my foot.

Sister Magdalena reached out and gently took hold of my forearm. "You go. I'll have José do this."

"Thank you, Sister." I gave her an appreciative smile.

Picking up the bag, I hefted it under my arm, then grabbed my handbag and fled from the courtyard like a fugitive being hunted by the law.

LATER, Chet, my father, Felicity, Rose, Ned and I sat around the dining room table in silence, all of us gazing at the nine-inch wonder before us. I glanced at my watch. It was a little after three o'clock. James Johnson had said he would call at 4:00 p.m.

I glanced over at my father who, still inhumanly pale and so thin he looked like he was disappearing before my eyes, stared unblinking, transfixed by the treasure.

"Marcel said it's the Royal Danish Egg," he said in a gravelly whisper. "He told us he'd done some research on the egg while he was waiting for the appropriate time to sell it."

"Danish?" Felicity remarked. "I thought it was made for the Russian royal family."

"The tsar had the piece commissioned for his mother, the

Dowager Empress Maria Feodorovna," he answered. "She was born of royal Danish blood, the daughter of King Christian IX. The elephant represents Denmark's ancient Order of the Elephant.

"The Romanovs have been commissioning these eggs since 1885," he added. "First by Emperor Alexander III, and then by his son Nicholas II, who had two created each year, one for his mother, the dowager, and the second for his wife."

Rose held a hand over her mouth. "I can scarcely stop looking at it."

"Who is in the photograph?" I asked my father.

"The dowager's parents, the former King and Queen of Denmark."

Felicity picked up the tiny jeweled, pedestaled frame and twirled it in her fingers.

"James Johnson will be calling soon," I said.

Rose looked at her watch. "Three fifteen. I'd better start preparing for supper. I want to make sure those children keep up their strength. They are so worried about Stevie."

It was hard for me to think of food when Stevie's and Madeleine's lives were at stake. I shuddered at the thought of them scared or hurt or worse.

"Let's put it back in the box," I said, swiping the egg off the table. "I don't want the kids to see it."

My father grabbed me by the wrist. "You aren't really going to let that conman and murderer take this, are you?"

"And what about Madeleine?" Felicity asked.

My father's gaze drifted to the window. "I doubt she's survived." The coldness with which he said the words made me flinch.

"Don't say that," I implored.

Was he steeling himself against the possible reality? Or had he given up on Madeleine? Or—A chill escaped down my spine.

Did he just want the egg for himself, disregarding his wife and the life of an innocent boy?

"We aren't giving up on either one of them," I stated with complete absolution. I didn't want to give the idea, or his insensitivity, any further energy. We had a bigger problem to address. "Two separate parties want the egg," I confirmed.

"How do we give it to both of them?" Chet asked.

I took in a deep breath and let it out. "I have an idea."

Felicity set the pedestal frame gently back on the table. "What do you propose we do?"

The weight of all eyes on me threatened to close my throat. I pushed through. "For James Johnson, we create a ruse. When he calls, I will tell him we've found it."

"And?" Chet asked, his eyes clouded with confusion.

"We arrange to meet where he suggested. At the northeast end of the alfalfa fields. I will ride Goldie out there. It should take about twenty minutes or so at a slow walk."

"Will you have the egg with you?" Felicity asked.

"No. But I will have the box it came in. When I leave the barn, one of you will call the police and tell them he's here at the ranch—at the drop-off site."

"You aren't going to tell them about the egg, are you?" my father interjected, his eyes filled with fear. Or was it anger? I couldn't tell.

"Not yet. We still need it for Madeleine."

He backed off, slumping in his chair. He put his elbows on the table, raised his trembling hands to his head, and pressed his forehead to his palms, resting it there. He didn't look well.

I could tell he was emotionally overwhelmed by all of this. As were we all, but we weren't dealing with drug withdrawal, too. I probably should have sought medical treatment for him, but it was too risky to have him in public with the kidnappers holding all the cards. And as far as a house visit was concerned, we were trying to keep any visitor to the ranch at bay. Knowing what I knew of him so far, he probably would have refused anyway.

"We tell the police that James Johnson has made a financial demand for the boy, and that we have agreed to make an exchange. We tell them to bring all the reinforcements they can. But we need to make sure they don't arrive until Johnson's on the property and I'm out there. I don't want him to get wind that they are on their way."

Ned spoke up. "I can tell Joe to keep a lookout for Johnson. As soon as he sees him, he can let us know, and then we'll call the police. I'll wait for them down the road near Joe's," he added. "I'll take some binoculars so we can see when you and Johnson meet up, and then I'll send them out there."

"Good idea," I agreed.

"What if when you're out there near the oil drum, Johnson sees the police?" Felicity asked.

"Good point. Tell them to split up," I said. "Have some of them come up the lane, and others take the back road, over the foothills. It ends right at the back fence line. That way, Johnson will be hemmed in."

Chet rubbed a hand across his chin. "I don't want you going out there alone. I'm riding with you."

"Fine," I said.

"I'll wait by the phone for Joe's call, and then I'll call the police," Felicity said. "Tell them what you've just told us."

My father raised his head. "What about me? What do I do?"

"Sit tight," I said. "Rest—but not in the bunkhouse. Rest here." I turned to Rose. "Please keep the kids in the house. They can do their afternoon chores tomorrow."

"Will do," she said with a confident nod. "Miss Meyers and I will keep them occupied."

I let out a breath. "I think that's all. Now we wait for Johnson's call."

CHAPTER TWENTY-ONE

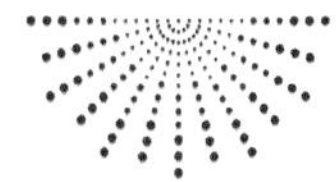

As he'd promised, James Johnson called at exactly four o'clock.

"Do you have good news for me?" he asked.

"I have the egg." I kept my voice steady, even though my hand shook so hard I could barely hold the receiver.

"You wouldn't lie to me now, would you, Grace?"

I didn't answer the question. "Let me talk to Stevie," I demanded.

"In due time. Leave the egg in the oil drum."

"No." I bit my lip.

There was a momentary silence on the other end of the line. "I don't think you understand, Grace. The boy—"

"I'll meet you out there. I'll bring the egg. You bring Stevie."

He heaved an impatient sigh. "Very well. But no funny business, understand?"

"I want the boy back," I said.

"I'll be there in an hour." A click sounded and the line went dead.

Forty minutes later, I was in the saddle. Goldie pawed at the ground, sensing my anxiety as we waited for Chet to finish saddling Copper, one of the ranch horses. I reached down and stroked her neck for reassurance. Ned stood by, holding the burlap sack with the jeweled box inside.

My heart leaped at the prospect of getting Stevie back. I hoped and prayed he was unharmed.

Chet checked his cinch one more time, threw the reins over Copper's neck, and mounted up. Ned handed him the sack, and Chet tied the strings around his saddle horn.

"One sec." Ned held up a finger and trotted over to the tack room. He came out carrying the Winchester shotgun we kept there. "I loaded it earlier this morning."

My stomach roiled at the prospect of having to use it. Especially with Stevie present. "Do we really have to?"

Ned handed the shotgun to Chet, who grasped it firmly in his hand. "It's just a precaution," he said. "I'm hoping it will intimidate Johnson, convey to him that we expect him to keep his word."

"I don't know, Chet," I protested.

"What if *he's* armed?" Ned pointed out.

I remembered staring down the barrel of Johnson's gun when he'd pointed it in my face.

"You're right," I said. "He has a pistol." The mere idea of using weapons made me uneasy, but we had to be prepared for the worst. I nodded my acquiescence.

I squeezed Goldie's middle with my legs, and together with Chet and Copper we walked out of the barn. I forced myself to take in a deep gulp of air. I needed to stay calm—for Goldie and for Stevie.

We passed by the kitchen window where Felicity stood watching us ride by.

"Let's go slow," I said, wanting to give the police as much time as possible to arrive.

"We will," Chet assured me.

"I feel like I'm going to jump out of my skin." My voice felt tight in my throat, as if it would strangle me.

Chet stopped his horse, and Goldie stopped, too. "It's going to be okay, Grace." Chet laid the reins on Copper's neck, and with his free hand, he reached over and squeezed my shoulder. "We'll get him back."

Biting the inside of my lip to keep from tearing up, I raised my chin, hoping to exude confidence. "I know." I swallowed, forcing myself to believe this would work.

We reached the gate that led to the alfalfa field. The field ran perpendicular to the lane that went to Joe's ranch and to ours. The far corner of the field, where the oil drum was placed, was near the back fence line at the base of the foothills. Johnson would access the field through another gate that sat at the lower end of our property, near Joe's house.

I reached down and pulled the latch open. Holding on to the gate, I pressed my leg against Goldie's side, urging her to sidestep, allowing me to open it farther to let Chet through. After Goldie and I passed through, I latched the gate behind us and caught up with Chet.

We walked in silence, and I tried to calm myself by surveying the land around us, searching for the beauty. But in my state of nervousness, it was hard to see. Where once the San Gabriel Mountains looked majestic and beautiful, with their neat, undulating folds of blue and purple, they were now black, craggy, and foreboding. The sun, instead of warming us with its radiance, burned through my clothes, making the fabric itchy and cloying. I gulped in air in a desperate attempt to settle myself. Goldie pranced, sensing my uneasiness.

"It's okay, girl." I scratched at her withers, and a sense of calm washed over me. She blew out, and the reverberation of her breath hummed through me.

After about fifteen minutes, the green Oldsmobile bounced over the alfalfa fields to our left, heading toward the northeast corner of the field. My stomach was awhirl with butterflies. I hoped things went according to plan and that no one got hurt. Goldie felt my apprehension and started to jig, an uncomfortable, nervous gait that was somewhere between a walk and a jog. I tried to relax my seat to calm her.

It wasn't long before I spotted the oil drum in the distance. The pulse of my heartbeat traveled up into my ears, its thready rhythm growing louder by the second. The car reached the fence line at the back of the property and stopped.

I scanned the area looking for the police, but there were no other vehicles in the distance yet. Goldie started to dance again, reminding me to get ahold of myself. I took in a deep breath and let it out, patting her on the neck. She blew out again and came back to a walk.

"Slow down, Chet," I said, looking at my watch. "We need to stall, to give the police a little more time."

He gently pulled up on Copper's reins and checked his watch. "Shouldn't be much longer," he assured me, but already, the seconds seemed like hours as the oil drum loomed closer with each step.

Movement in the car caught my attention. James Johnson got out, walked around the car, and casually leaned against the dented fender, his arms crossed over his chest in a relaxed manner, as if he were waiting for good friends to join him at a picnic.

White-hot rage coursed through me. This poor excuse for a human being had caused so much pain and suffering to his victims, and to those they'd left behind. I strained to see Stevie in the car, but we were still too far away. I fought the urge to squeeze Goldie with my legs and urge her into an all-out run.

Finally, we reached the oil drum and brought our horses to a halt.

A hideous grin oozed across Johnson's face. "Afternoon."

"Where's the boy?" Chet asked, his voice hard.

Johnson tilted his head toward the Oldsmobile. "Hey, kid. Sit up and show yourself, but don't get out of the car."

Stevie sprang up from the backseat. My heart surged with relief at seeing his tousled, red-haired head, but the joy was quickly replaced with dread as James Johnson unfolded his arms, revealing the pistol in his hand. He aimed it at the back seat of the car.

In a swift and graceful movement, Chet raised the shotgun and trained it on him.

The killer's grin faded. "Well, this is interesting."

"Let him go," Chet said.

"Put the egg in the oil drum."

"Grace." Chet nodded at me. "Untie the bag. Take it to the oil drum."

I sidled Goldie up next to Copper and leaned over to release the sack from Chet's saddle horn. The strings had been pulled taut from gravity, and my shaking fingers fumbled with the knot.

"It's too tight," I whispered, adrenaline shooting through my body.

"Take your time. I've got this under control," Chet said.

The even and assured quality of his voice eased my anxiety, if only a little, but it was enough for me to finally get purchase on one of the loops. Slowly, it loosened beneath the effort of my fingers, and I managed to untie it.

Grasping the top of the sack, I rested the bulk in front of me on the saddle.

"Take it to the oil drum, and place it in there," Chet said.

I backed up Goldie, and we went around behind Copper toward the drum. I kept my eyes fixed on Stevie's silhouette in the back window of the Oldsmobile, wanting to reach in, pluck him out, and hold him in the safety of my arms.

When we reached the drum, I bent down and gently placed the sack inside. I straightened and looked back over the field onto the road, and to my utter joy, three police cars were speeding up the lane in the distance, dust rolling in billowing clouds behind them. Hopefully, those coming over the back road would hang back a little until we had Stevie safely with us.

"Okay, Johnson," Chet called out. "Get the boy out of the car."

James Johnson, his gaze still fixed on Chet, waved the gun, motioning for Stevie to get out. He appeared disheveled and rumpled, but unharmed. At the sight of him, my breath caught in my throat.

Johnson took hold of him, wrapping his arm around his neck. He placed the end of the pistol against Stevie's temple.

My blood froze, and I gasped. "Don't—"

"Now," Johnson said. "Here's what we're going to do. I'm going to walk us over to that drum and take the bag. The boy here is going to open it. Make sure you've delivered what we've agreed on."

My throat closed up, and I fought for breath. As soon as he saw that we'd duped him, or if he saw the police, he'd—

I shifted my gaze toward the police cars on the road as subtly as I could, trying desperately not to tip off Johnson to their presence. The cars had parked, and five officers had gotten out of two of the cars and were starting to fan out into the field. One of the drivers remained in his car. I assumed it was in case James Johnson tried to make a getaway.

Johnson sidestepped slowly, pulling Stevie with him toward the oil drum. Chet kept the shotgun trained on him. Chet was an excellent shot, but still, my stomach curdled with fear at the thought of Stevie getting hurt.

"Now, boy, pick up the bag. Move real slow," Johnson said.

He released Stevie but kept the gun pointed at his head. I gnawed at my lip, my breath high and tight in my chest. Stevie bent down to pick up the burlap sack. Johnson shifted his gaze, and a look of shock passed over his features as police cars came into view on the back road.

"You called the police?" he shouted. He grabbed Stevie by the collar and yanked him backward, taking him in a headlock again and setting the muzzle of the gun against his cheek.

Stevie's eyes widened in fear as he struggled to breathe. The burlap sack was clutched in his hand. The air in my lungs froze.

"Let him go," Chet said. "You're surrounded." He kept the shotgun trained on him.

With a growl of anguish, Johnson dragged Stevie back to the car and shoved him into the back seat.

"Stevie!" I called out.

"Damn it!" Chet said.

Keeping the gun pointed at the back seat, Johnson went around the car to get in.

An explosion rang in my ears. Chet had fired the shotgun. Johnson's arm flung backward, and he screamed in agony. Chet cocked the gun again, but Johnson had moved and took cover on the far side of the car. He got in the driver's seat.

The police on foot were running now, their guns leveled. Johnson started the car and turned it around. It jumped and jolted on the uneven ground, and then he floored it, speeding away from us.

I squeezed Goldie's sides with my legs, and she leaped forward. We galloped after the car at breakneck speed. I could hear Chet and his horse thundering behind us, and soon we were neck and neck. He leveled the shotgun again and pulled the trigger. Rubber from the back tire of the car flew into the air, and the car slowed, now limping on three tires. Chet fired again, and the other back tire deflated, slowing the car even more.

The police car that had been waiting at the entrance to the alfalfa field was closing in, as were the police cars from the back road, forming a V that would culminate in front of Johnson's car.

Suddenly the Oldsmobile stopped, and Johnson got out. He pulled Stevie from the back seat with his good arm. Blood soaked the sleeve of his other arm, but he managed to hold the gun to Stevie's head. The boy's face had gone white and stony, but he didn't make a peep.

Johnson's eyes were aflame with rage. "You're going to pay for this!" he yelled.

In a flash, Stevie raised his arm from the elbow, his fist making contact with Johnson's injured arm. Johnson howled in pain, and Stevie then kicked his leg out behind him, knocking Johnson off-balance. He fell to the ground, and the gun flew out of his hand. He growled in rage, scrambling to his feet. Stevie lunged for the gun, and Johnson went after him.

I tapped Goldie's sides with my heels, and we surged forward, heading straight for Johnson. He swiveled around to see us coming at him at a dead run, and he stumbled backward and fell again. Stevie grabbed the pistol and ran toward Chet.

In seconds, Goldie was standing over Johnson, her hooves mere centimeters from his flailing body. I kept the pressure on so he wouldn't have an opportunity to get up. He tried to wriggle away from us, but I kept on him.

"Stop right there!" a voice shouted behind me. Several of the officers had caught up with us, and four squad cars flanked us on all sides. All officers had their weapons trained on Johnson.

"Move away from him, ma'am," one of them said.

Slowly, I backed Goldie away from him, pivoted, and trotted her over to Chet and Stevie. I jumped down from the saddle and pulled the boy into my arms, my heart bursting with joy.

"Thank goodness," I said through tears, squeezing him closer to me. His arms wrapped around me and held me tight. His body shook with sobs. "You were so brave," I muttered into his shock of red hair. "So brave."

I felt a warm hand on my shoulder, and Chet wrapped both of us in his arms, and we stood clutched together like we never wanted to let go.

Someone cleared their throat, breaking us from our embrace. Stevie quickly swiped at his reddened face, clearly embarrassed for displaying his emotions in front of the officers. I smiled affectionately at him and tousled his hair.

Two of the officers escorted James Johnson to one of the squad cars. Another one approached us.

"Everyone all right here?" he asked. He was young, broad-shouldered man and had an air of authority about him. I wondered if he was the senior officer in charge.

"We're fine," Chet said.

"That was quite a risky plan you concocted. Why didn't you contact us the minute Johnson demanded ransom?"

Chet and I exchanged a glance.

"He said he would kill Stevie if we alerted the police," I said. "I've dealt with this man before. I know how ruthless and cunning he is. The risk was actually in contacting you at all."

The officer screwed up his mouth, considering my words.

"What was the ransom?" he asked. "Were you able to meet the demand?"

Chet and I exchanged another glance. He pressed his lips together.

"Cash." He patted the pocket at his left breast. "We were prepared to give him anything to get the boy back."

I held my breath, hoping the officer wouldn't get it into his head to question us further. We needed the egg to get Madeleine back. If she was still alive.

The officer looked from Chet, to me, and then to Stevie. "Well, had I been in your shoes, I probably would have done the same," he said. "I'm glad the boy is back safe and sound." He tipped his hat and then made his way back to the squad cars.

I let out a sigh of relief, my knees threatening to buckle. We watched him walk away in silence.

"Chet." I nodded toward Johnson's car. "The box."

"Right."

He dismounted and got the burlap sack out of the back seat

of the car. I got back up on Goldie and then helped pull Stevie up behind me. Chet handed me the parcel.

"What is that?" Stevie asked.

Chet patted Stevie's leg and then looked up at me and winked. "Insurance. Now let's go home."

WHEN, at last, we got Stevie back in the house, Rose pulled the boy into her arms and gave him one of her rare but warm hugs. His cheeks flushed pink, and his eyes welled with tears.

When Rose finally released him, Felicity wrapped an arm around his shoulder. "Well, you're a sight for sore eyes, sugar."

"Yes, ma'am," he said with a sniff and wiped his nose with the back of his hand.

"You must be starving," Rose said to him. "I'll get you some supper."

She led him into the kitchen as Ned and Joe came in through the front door.

"How's the kid doing?" Joe asked, swiping his cowboy hat off his head.

"He's shaken," I said. "Time will tell. He's had so much to deal with of late. I hope this doesn't set him back too much. We will have to keep an eye on him."

"Well, you know I'm here to help in any way I can," Joe said.

"I've got some projects around the ranch we can work on together," Ned chimed in. "I'll keep him occupied."

"Or give him space if he wants," Chet added.

Ned nodded. "Sure thing."

I heard the familiar creak of one of the planks on the staircase and turned to see Ida making her way down the stairs.

"Is it safe to come down now?" she asked. "Is Stevie back?"

"Yes," I said with a smile.

Her face lit up, and she hollered up toward the bedrooms, "You guys, he's back!"

In seconds, Susie and Daniel came clattering down the stairs.

"He's in the kitchen," I told them.

The kids ran past us and through the swinging door. It lifted my spirits to see their relief at his return, but it was tamped down by the heaviness of the task that lay ahead: getting Madeleine back.

The smell of cigarette smoke drew my attention to the dining room. My father sat at the table staring at the wall in front of him.

I caught Felicity's gaze. "He's been like that since you all left to ride out into the field," she explained.

I gently touched Chet's sleeve and tilted my head toward him, silently signaling to him and the others to join him at the table. We needed to discuss our next move to get Madeleine back.

"Dad?" I sat down next to him.

He extinguished his cigarette in the ashtray in front of him, adding to the half dozen already there. His shaking had subsided, but the pallor of his skin was still gray. "Glad the boy's okay," he said quietly.

"We'll get Madeleine back, too," I said, wanting to reassure him.

The others sat down with us.

"What now?" Ned asked.

"The last note from Madeleine's captors said that when we found the egg, to turn on the light in the boarding house apartment kitchen and then wait for them to contact us—at home," I said, a river of chills escaping down my spine.

"Smart," Felicity said. "They're probably checking the place at night. There's less chance of being seen."

"How do you think they'll contact you?" Ned asked. "Think they'll leave another note?"

I shrugged. "I'm not sure."

"I can go turn on that light," Joe said. "Where's the boarding house?"

I shook my head. "No. Thanks, Joe, but they made it clear they've been watching me. I need to do it. If they are surveilling the place, I want them to see me there. I don't want them to think I'm setting some kind of trap. It's too risky."

"Well you're not going alone," Chet said. "Not after the last time you went there only to be greeted by James Johnson. I'm going with you."

I figured Chet would say as much, and I wasn't going to argue with him. I didn't relish the thought of going there alone, either.

"Joe, we need you and Ned to stick around here and keep an eye on the place and the kids until we get this situation resolved."

The two men nodded their agreement.

"Felicity, since we're going out, we can take you home," Chet said.

She waved a dismissive hand in the air. "Just call me a taxi. I'll be fine."

"No." I shook my head. "I don't want you to be alone."

"Then let me call Bernardo, the groundskeeper at the mansion. He'll pick me up," she said with a smile. Before I could protest, she walked over to the phone.

"We should go," Chet said.

I went to the coat closet in the hall and grabbed my light-weight, plaid, single-breasted coat.

"There," Felicity said, hanging up the phone. "He's on his way."

"You be careful," I advised her.

"Like I said, I'll be fine, sugar." She gave me a peck on the cheek and ushered Chet and me out the door.

We arrived at the boarding house at dusk. Chet parked the Birmingham out front. There were no other cars on the street. He accompanied me to the alleyway to access the kitchen of my father's rooms. Both of us scanned the area, looking for any unusual activity. All seemed quiet.

When we reached the door, I noted it had been repaired. In my haste to meet Chet at the police station, I had neglected to tell Mrs. Wilkins it had been damaged. I pulled the key my father had given me from my purse and tried the lock.

"It's been changed," I said, not surprised.

"We'll have to go in through the front," Chet said.

We went around the corner and knocked on the door.

After a few seconds, Mrs. Wilson opened it. "You're back."

"Yes," I said. "I'm sorry to bother you. We need to get some more of my father's things, and the lock has been changed." Guilt threatened to take hold of me at not being honest with her, but frazzled from the day and eager to get on with my task, I pushed it aside.

"Well I guess you were right about that burglary in the neighborhood," she said, placing her hands on her hips. "Someone busted into the side door. I had to have it fixed."

"Oh my," I said. As much as I wanted to come clean and tell her about what had happened, I didn't really have the time. I made a promise to myself that I would when it came time to pay the rent again and that I would offer to pay for the repair.

"I'm not sure if anything of your father's was taken . . . But it's kind of hard for me to tell."

"We will go see," Chet said. "I'm sorry for your trouble."

She let us in while muttering under her breath about what the world was coming to. She went to a box that was sitting on the small entry table. "Here's the new key. Rent's due on the twelfth."

Using the new key, we entered the apartment and went to the kitchen. Chet turned on the light, and then we left through the kitchen door. I locked the door behind us, securing the place, and we went back to the car. There seemed to be nothing amiss on the street. All was still quiet.

We drove in silence back to the ranch.

Once in the house, Chet and I went into the kitchen. He wanted coffee, and I wanted some chamomile tea to sooth my jangled nerves. I was assured by the sound of footsteps on the ceiling, as it meant the children were upstairs doing their homework and preparing for bed. Rose and Miss Meyers must have retired to their rooms, and I assumed Ned and my father had retreated to the bunkhouse.

We sat down at the table with our beverages and sipped in silence.

I heaved a sigh, my stomach in knots, the anticipation of what would come next overcoming any comfort the tea might have provided. "Now we wait," I said to Chet.

"Yes." He reached out and took my hand. "Are you okay?"

I shook my head, reliving all that had happened that day with James Johnson, Stevie, and the police. The heaviness of the anxiety at having to interface with ruthless Russian mobsters weighed on me, drowning me with dread.

"I honestly don't know," I answered him.

A knock came from the other side of the kitchen wall.

"Is that the front door?" Chet asked, getting up from the table.

"I think so." I followed him through the swinging door and into the foyer.

Chet opened the door, but there was no one there. The sky had turned dark, and the stillness of the night was interrupted only by the sounds of crickets and other night creatures.

My gaze fell to the doormat. A corner of paper peeked out from underneath.

"Chet," I pointed.

He reached down and pulled out the folded piece of paper. He opened it up and read the typewritten note aloud, *"Come to the boarding house at three o'clock in the afternoon tomorrow. Bring the egg."*

"It doesn't say anything about Madeleine?" I asked.

He shook his head and handed it to me. My eyes went immediately to the familiar dropped *a*.

"Three o'clock tomorrow." I sighed. "It seems like a lifetime away."

Chet wrapped his arm around my shoulder. "It's going to be okay, Grace. We will get her back."

I swallowed hard, trying to ignore the doubt bubbling up in my chest.

CHAPTER TWENTY-TWO

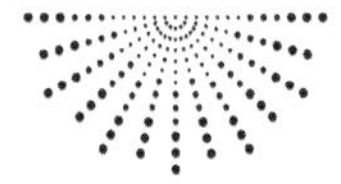

*S*hafts *of sunlight shoot through the trees. The forest is blanketed in leaves cascading from their branches and fluttering to the ground. A spotlight shines on two men seated at a campfire. Sophia stands in the distance, her hair floating around her in a breeze that isn't there.*

The two men are deep in conversation, their breath hovering like icicles in the air. They are cold, holding their arms crossed over their chests to ward off the chill. One of them is my father—exactly how I remembered him. He wears a red scarf. It's a scarf Sophia and I bought him for his birthday once, when we were young. Mother helped us pick it out at the haberdashery. It's pulled tightly around his neck. The other man is also my father—the one who showed up at the café.

The man with the red scarf is showing the other man photographs and telling him about his life, his wife, his children. He shakes his head, and placing a hand over his eyes, he shudders with sobs. He sets the photographs down, spread out like a fan. They are photos of me and Sophia.

The image shifts, and the two men fuse into one. But the scarf remains. He is lying on the ground, his face unrecognizable with blood. His dog tags glint in the icy sunlight.

A shrill, metal ringing echoes in my ears, then stops. Then it starts again. And then there is silence, the only sound the tick-tock of a clock. Then a sharp, rapid knock.

"Grace?" A woman's voice pulled me back to wakefulness. I opened my eyes to see Rose peering into the bedroom.

"Grace," Rose repeated, opening the door farther. "It's the police. They want to see you."

"The police?" I pushed myself to sitting. Next to me, the bed was empty, the covers thrown back. I looked at the clock on my night table. Eight o'clock.

Exhausted from the trauma of yesterday afternoon, and filled with trepidation at our upcoming encounter with the Russians, I'd tossed and turned all night, and as a result, I'd overslept.

I blinked, trying to chase away the grogginess of sleep. My mind was still trapped in the vision of Sophia and the two men sitting at the campfire.

"I've made a fresh pot of coffee." Rose slipped away and closed the door.

After splashing cold water on my face, running a brush through my hair, and throwing on some wide-legged trousers and a short-sleeved silk blouse, I made my way downstairs.

Rose greeted me at the foot of the stairs with a steaming cup. Two men, one in a suit and one in uniform, sat on the sofa in the living room, their backs to me. They both rose when I entered the room.

I recognized both of them. One was Detective Baptiste, and the other was the young uniformed officer who had been here yesterday to apprehend James Johnson.

"Miss Michelle." Detective Baptiste held his porkpie hat in his hands.

I nodded a greeting. "Hello, Detective."

"This is Officer Randall," he said, tilting his head toward the man in uniform.

"Good to see you again, Miss Michelle." The officer tipped his hat to me.

Detective Baptiste cleared his throat. "We'd like to ask you some questions in reference to James Johnson and what happened yesterday."

I swallowed. "I see. How can I help?" I hoped they did not hear the reluctance in my voice. This interruption was not what I needed at the moment.

"We'd like to take you down to the station."

I blinked at him in surprise. "What? Why?"

"It's better that way," he said. "Don't want to disrupt anything going on here—you know, with your family members."

"Oh." I gulped. What was this about?

"How long will I be there?" I asked. I didn't want anything to deter me from going to the boarding house later that day. My eyes darted to Rose, who was looking at me with raised brows.

"Shouldn't take too long." Detective Baptiste gave me a reassuring smile.

"I see. I'll get my coat." This seemed rather extreme and unnecessary, and quite frankly, confusing.

I went to the hall closet and pulled out my plaid coat and my hat. "Rose, please let Chet know where I've gone."

FORTY-FIVE MINUTES later I was sitting alone in an interrogation room with only a cup of coffee for company. But I was unable to drink it, my stomach feeling as though it would heave at any second.

Finally, Detective Baptiste breezed into the room and then shut the door. He sat down opposite me. Resting his elbows on the table, he pressed his fingers together at his lips, as if trying to gather his thoughts. Feeling a little light-headed, I reminded myself to breathe.

"We've had some interesting discussions with James Johnson," he said.

"Oh?"

"He claims you are in possession of a priceless objet d'art that was stolen from the Kremlin."

The blood drained from my head, and my mouth went dry. So this was how James Johnson would do it, how he'd get back at me for sending him to prison—twice. He wanted to return the favor.

"Is this true?" he asked.

I wanted to say something to defend myself, but the words froze in my throat.

"You realize you could be in big trouble. The Russians would deem this an act of aggression—an international offense."

I reached for the porcelain coffee cup with shaking hands and took a sip, trying to collect myself. The coffee had gone cold and was bitter, and the acidity of it soured in my mouth.

"I can explain," I finally managed to say.

Detective Baptiste smiled through the steeple of his hands. "That's what I was hoping."

I swallowed, the vile tang of the coffee still sitting on my tongue. And then I spilled everything, feeling like a traitor, worried I'd just put Madeleine in her grave.

"How long has it been since this Madeleine Michelle went missing?"

I counted the days in my head. "Since early last week. It's been six days, I believe."

"And how long had your father and Mrs. Michelle been in the country?"

"Three weeks. He didn't contact me right away."

"Do you believe his story? That Mrs. Michelle's brother was the one who stole this Fabergé egg?"

I took in a short breath. "Well, yes."

"Do you think your father would lie?"

"I . . . I, uh . . ." I didn't know how to answer because I honestly couldn't say for sure. I had the sense he was lying about something, or withholding something, but what? He was a shell of the man I once knew, the man I had fantasized about in my inner child's longing for him. But he was nothing like I remembered. I realized then that I didn't know him at all.

"How close are you and your father?"

I pulled my lower lip between my teeth, the painful realization sinking into my heart and cleaving it in two.

"Not close," I uttered, feeling the betrayal work the other way around. His betrayal of me. How could he have put me in this position?

The detective leaned back and rested the weight of his upper body on an elbow on the arm of the chair. "So this Fabergé egg was sent to Valentina Baklanova's residence?"

I straightened, finding my voice again. "Yes. Well, it was sent to her aunt. The two live together. Don't you see? This is why I don't believe Valentina committed suicide. She was killed. These people, these black market criminals, killed the Gallois family. They attempted to kill Valentina's aunt, Anna Ivanova, who is lying in a hospital bed fighting for her life. Valentina must have found out something. I'm certain they killed her."

Detective Baptiste lifted a shoulder in a shrug. "We've been looking into that, but she left a suicide note. Her finance said she was distraught over her aunt. Said she couldn't go on living if she died. I understand Miss Ivanova is struggling to live, and it doesn't look good."

"But she's still alive! Why would Valentina kill herself when there was a sliver of hope her aunt would survive?"

"We thought of that, but we also found out that Miss Baklanova was deeply in debt. She'd made some bad investments over the course of several years."

"But she was engaged to be married to Anton Belsky, a wealthy banker." I shook my head in disbelief. What kind of investigation had this detective done?

"His banks are in trouble. He wouldn't be able to help her."

I still wasn't buying it. I sighed in exasperation. "How do you know Valentina wrote the note? Did you compare her handwriting with the handwriting in the note?" I asked, incredulous that I had to inquire if the detective had done his job properly.

"It was typewritten," he said.

My mouth dropped open, and a surge of excitement lit up my senses like a Christmas tree. This could be proof. I remembered back when the police were certain that Sophia had committed suicide, too. The note she'd allegedly left was typewritten, as well, and I had been able to prove that she'd been murdered.

"May I see the note?" I asked.

He pursed his lips, his eyes searching mine. I held his gaze, certain in my conviction.

He then set his hands down on the table and pushed back his chair. "I'll be right back."

He returned in minutes and handed me the folded piece of paper. I opened it, set it on the table, and read:

I CANNOT BEAR *my burdens any longer. Tell* moya tetushka *that I will meet her on the other side.*

I STARED in amazement at the letters, particularly at the letter *a* that was a fraction lower than the rest.

"Don't you see?" I slapped my hand against the desk. "This is proof that she did not kill herself." I told him about the notes we'd received at the boarding house. "Whoever is sending these notes, whoever has Madeleine, typed this note and killed Valentina."

"I'd like to see these notes," the detective said.

"They are at the ranch."

He nodded. "All right. Just as well. We need to go back to retrieve the egg."

"But what about Madeleine?" I implored. "We need the egg in exchange for her return."

I revealed what was written in the note we'd received last night. "The kidnappers told us to go to the boarding house at three o'clock, today. Please let us see this through. You can watch our every move."

He regarded me with steely eyes, sizing me up.

"Believe me," I continued. "I don't want this egg anywhere near us or our family. We just want Madeleine back."

He leaned forward in his chair. "We won't miss a beat," he warned.

"I know. I'm counting on it," I said. "But please be discreet. If they know we've involved the police . . ."

He gave me an indulgent, if not insulted, smile. "I think we know how to do that."

"Yes, of course." I flushed, embarrassed that I had come across so presumptuous.

"All right." He stood up. "I'll get you back home. And I want to set eyes on this Fabergé egg myself."

CHAPTER TWENTY-THREE

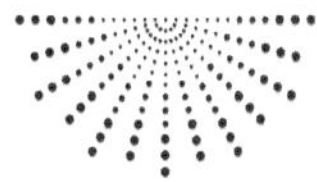

The sounds of the children talking and laughing as they ate their breakfast echoed from the kitchen. The household was up and bustling about with its returned merriness, and it lifted my spirits. Everyone was happy to have Stevie back in the fold.

"Could you give me a moment?" I asked the detective as I laid my coat and handbag on the gossip table. I wanted to retrieve Chet from the kitchen.

"Sure," he said, sinking his hands into his trouser pockets. Officer Randall stood silently next to him.

I peeked my head in through the kitchen door. The kids were so involved in their conversations, they didn't even notice me.

"Morning, Grace." Ned was standing near the coffeepot, pouring himself a cup. All heads swiveled toward me, and Chet got up from the table.

Susie waved, and the others cheerfully greeted me. Stevie beamed with a wide smile. The sight warmed my heart.

"Are you all right?" Chet whispered. "My mother said you were taken to the police station."

"I'm fine." I took hold of his hand and pulled him into the

living room. "I had to tell him everything." I nodded toward Detective Baptiste, who acknowledged Chet with a tip of his hat. Officer Randall stood still as an iceberg. We went over to join them.

"He wants to see the egg," I said.

"And we'd like to speak with Peter Michelle," the detective added.

Guilt washed over me, followed by trepidation at how my father would react to this turn of events.

Chet nodded. "It's in the dining room. I stashed it in the sideboard, out of view."

We stepped into the dining room, and Chet went over to the stately piece of solid walnut furniture. Rose had brought it with her when we'd moved her to the ranch. Chet opened one of its doors and froze. He opened another, then the third.

"It's gone," he said.

"What?" I breathed out.

"I put it back in the box and put the box right here."

The detective regarded him with raised eyebrows.

I dashed to the door that led to the kitchen and pushed it open. "Rose, Ned, could you come in here please?"

They dropped what they were doing and came into the dining room.

"Did you do something with the egg?" I asked.

"No," they said in unison.

"I haven't seen it since yesterday afternoon," Ned added.

Rose scoffed. "I didn't want anything to do with it." She flipped her dishtowel over her shoulder.

"What about the children?" Chet asked. "Do you think one of them has it?"

"They didn't even know of its existence," I said, unable to keep the defensiveness out of my voice.

"Your father was watching it when we were dealing with

James Johnson," Chet said. "When we got back, he saw me put it in the sideboard. He hadn't moved from the table."

"Come on," I said. "Did he come in for breakfast?"

Chet shook his head.

We led the police officers out of the front door instead of going through the kitchen. I didn't want to alarm the children with their presence. We hustled out to the bunkhouse.

"Dad!" I called, stepping through the door. I dashed through the living room, past Ned's room, and then turned left down the hallway. When I reached my father's room, I gasped.

The bed, unmade, was a tangle of sheets. Dresser drawers hung open. The wardrobe door was ajar, revealing only empty hangers. Only the envelopes I'd brought from the boarding house remained on top of the dresser.

"Oh no," I gasped, sensing the others at my back.

The detective pushed past me and stepped into the room. "Gone, too, I suppose?" He removed his hat and scratched at his head.

"I can't believe it," I said, blinking my eyes and willing away the emptiness of the room. "How could he?"

I felt Chet's hands go around my arms. "Maybe he wanted to go it alone. Or got impatient. Now that we'd found the egg, he had what he needed to get Madeleine back."

Worry for him wormed its way into my gut. "But he's not well!"

Chet sighed. "He's probably gone back to the boarding house to wait for the kidnappers. After you went to bed, I went out to the bunkhouse to tell him about the note we got last night. I thought he should know."

I was about to protest because the lock to the kitchen door had been changed, but he could enter through the boarding house front door, as we had.

"Where is this boarding house?" the detective asked, flipping through the envelopes on the dresser. He lifted one of them from the pile and opened it.

"A ransom note," he said, handing it to the other officer. "The type matches Miss Baklanova's suicide note." He met my gaze. "Good work, Miss Michelle."

I nodded, taking no pleasure in the praise.

"The boarding house?" the detective repeated.

"Alvarado Street," I murmured.

"Got an address?" He eyeballed the other officer, who whipped a notepad and pencil from his jacket pocket.

I gave him the house number.

"So you said the plan was to go to the boarding house at three o'clock today?"

"Yes."

"Okay," he said, securing his hat back on his head. "We'll take it from here."

"But—" I protested. What if the kidnappers had gotten to my father, too? What if they'd killed him? What if the police were too late? He was out there all alone. On the other hand, would he have taken the egg for himself? No. He wouldn't abandon Madeleine. He'd been distraught over her kidnapping.

"But I need to find my father," I said, stepping out of Chet's grasp. "He needs me. He's sick. He suffers from battle fatigue, and he's quite fragile." Worry gave rise to panic. He would be defenseless against the ruthless kidnappers.

"It's best if you leave this to us. We'll go to the boarding house right away. We'll set up a stakeout. Don't worry, Miss Michelle. If he's there, we'll get him home."

"But—" I protested.

Chet put an arm around my shoulders. "Leave it to the police, Grace."

I wilted with disappointment and the imposing weight of helplessness. That, mixed with the anxiety of guilt, tied my stomach in knots.

"Let's go, Randall," the detective said to the other officer. He tipped his hat to me, shook Chet's hand, and then the two of them left.

I turned to face Chet and looked up into his eyes. "I'm so worried about him."

He smoothed my hair. "I know, but there's really nothing we can do now."

I leaned my head against his chest, wanting to turn back the clock. If we had gone to the police the minute we'd learned about this Fabergé egg, none of this would have happened. Madeleine might be safe right now, and James Johnson would never have taken Stevie. It was all such a mess.

"Come on." Chet pressed his lips to my forehead. "Let's go back to the house. You haven't had breakfast."

"I'm not hungry." My stomach flipped at the thought of food.

"All right, then."

"I'd like to stay out here for a bit. Alone."

I needed some space—time to process and room to sort out my feelings, which were muddled and in disarray.

Chet lifted my chin so that our eyes met, and he gazed at me with sympathy and compassion. "Take your time." He kissed my forehead again and then left.

I surveyed the room and made my way to the bed and sat down, trying to sort my feelings. I was worried about my father, but there was something else niggling at the edge of my emotions. I squeezed my eyes shut, trying to reconcile it when it sank deep into my heart. Clear and unmistakable. *Abandonment.*

He'd left me again. I raised my hands to my face, covering my eyes, trying to shut out the reality. I may never see him again. He might be lost to me again. This time for good. Fighting back tears, I lowered my hands, and my eyes rested on the dresser, on the envelopes scattered on top.

I got up from the bed and gathered them in my hands, looking over them one by one. There were some bills, but nothing of interest except the last one. It was addressed to Peter Michelle, and the sender was Ralph Huxley from Brighton, Ontario, Canada. *Huxley.* The surname on the dog tag.

I tore it open and stared at the neat handwriting.

Dear Harold,

I'm sorry, Brother. I just can't get used to the idea of addressing you as Peter. Why did you change your name? You must have had your reasons.

Anyway, thanks for the letter. It was good to hear from you after all these years. I thought I'd never hear from you again. I'm glad you contacted me. I have some news, as well. Our mother passed away . . .

The rest of the words blurred on the page, and a wave of dizziness swam through my head. Clutching the letter, I reached for the bed and sat down again.

Images of the forest, the trenches, and the explosions collided in my mind.

Sophia is pointing to the two soldiers. They look very much alike. One is taller, a little more robust, but they share many of the same facial features. The two of them sit at a camp table, their whiskey glasses in front of them, talking and sharing the details of their lives, their joys, their sorrows, their deepest secrets.

Harold. Cantigny. Deception.

One of them leans over the prostrate body of the other. The face of the prone soldier is blown off, unrecognizable. Dog tags glint in the sunlight on his chest. The other soldier reaches down, grasps the tags with his hand, and yanks them from the body of his fallen comrade. He holds them up to the light. The name Peter Michelle *is stamped into the metal. He removes his own dog tags, takes one of them off the chain, and lays it on the chest of his felled friend. Clutching the remaining three tags in his hand, Harold Huxley runs.*

Sophia emerges and stands over the body of Peter Michelle. Her father. Her hero. She sinks to the ground and lies next to him, burying her face in his chest.

Sophia . . .

I sucked in a lungful of air, my eyes wide and blinking. I stared at the letter. Harold Huxley's letter. Not my father's. The edges of my vision blurred, cutting off the corners of the paper. Blackness crept in upon the page like spilled ink. My head swam, and I fought to keep my eyes open. But I was losing the battle. The letter fell from my hand, cascading to the ground with a whisper.

CHAPTER TWENTY-FOUR

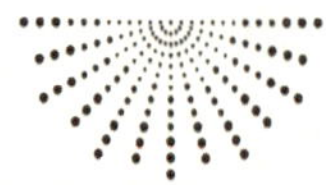

I came to slumped over on my side, my body on the bed and my feet still on the floor. I mustn't have lost consciousness for very long. Groggy, I sat up, and my eyes found the letter on the floor. I picked it up and laid it on the dresser.

Harold Huxley had deceived me. He had deliberately lied to me and used me. He'd put me and my family—the children—at risk. Because of him, Stevie had almost been lost to us. Anna Ivanova lay in the hospital fighting for her life. Valentina had *died*. And what about Madeleine? Had she known he'd assumed the identity of Peter Michelle? Had this all been an elaborate ruse? Or had Harold lied to her, too? Perhaps he'd been using her, as well, to get to the egg her brother had died trying to protect.

I'd like to believe Madeleine knew nothing of his deception. But now that I knew the truth about Harold Huxley, I was free of this mad and dangerous game we'd been playing with the Russians. It was in the hands of the police.

I stood up on leaden legs. I needed to speak with Anton Belsky, to tell him I had failed to find the men who'd harmed Anna Ivanova, but that the police were now involved. I also had to let him know I'd found proof that Valentina had not committed suicide. I hoped it would bring him some comfort.

I SAT in the reception area of Anton Belsky's office at Pacific Savings and Loan. His secretary informed me he was on a telephone call but would be available shortly. So I waited for him, filled with anticipation of delivering both good and bad news on this sobering occasion.

The secretary rose from her desk. She was middle-aged and all contradictions with a softness beneath her air of competence. Her kind eyes contrasted with the severeness of her obsidian hair, combed into a neat bun at the back of her head.

"I'll just check in with Mr. Belsky again. He should be off the phone by now," she said.

She quietly knocked on his door and then opened it just wide enough to peek her head through. She went in for a few moments and then came back out.

"He'll see you now," she said.

I stood, straightened my blouse, and ran a hand over my bobbed waves. The secretary held open the door for me. I thanked her and slipped inside. The click of the door let me know she had gone.

"Miss Michelle." Mr. Belsky rose and offered me his hand. He seemed a little disconcerted at my presence. Or was it annoyance I detected?

I extended my hand and gave his a firm shake, and then he indicated for me to sit down in one of the chairs opposite his desk.

"Mr. Belsky, I am so sorry for your loss."

Taking a seat, he heaved a sigh. "Thank you. What can I do for you today?"

"I need to tell you something. I—"

"You have news?" he asked. "Have you found the egg?"

"Yes." The word caught in my throat. Had Valentina told him about the egg? She'd said she wouldn't.

His eyes brightened. "This is wonderful. How did you find it?"

I thought the reaction strange for a man grieving over his dead fiancée.

"That's rather a long story. I came here to—"

"I'd love to hear it. Please." He gestured with his hand for me to commence. "Can I get you anything? Water? Vodka?" He tilted his head toward a bar cart in the far corner.

"No, I'm fine."

He gazed at me expectantly. He'd been part of this journey, too, so I suppose telling him about it wouldn't hurt. I settled in my chair and took a deep breath.

"After my last visit with Miss Ivanova and through a reading with Lenora Lange, I had obtained enough information to deduce where the egg had been hidden. At the Mission San Gabriel."

"Lenora Lange, you say?" he asked. "That's incredible. I thought the woman a charlatan."

I chuckled. "I did, too—when I first met her. But she's helped me before. It's quite remarkable, really. And I have something else to tell—"

"So where is the egg now?" he asked again, cutting me off.

"Oh, well . . ." I hesitated, biting my lower lip. "It's gone. Again."

"What?" His eyes widened in surprise. "You mean it was stolen?"

I pressed my lips together into a frown. "I'm afraid so. My father—" I couldn't bear to admit the ugly truth about the man who'd deceived me, "took it. But the police are now involved and—"

"The police?" He leaned forward in his chair, gripping the

arms of it. "I thought I said— I thought we agreed, no police. I wanted *you* to find the egg. I didn't want police involved."

I blinked at him, surprised at this remark. He and Valentina had asked for my help because they felt they weren't getting enough help from the police in finding who had ransacked Anna Ivanova's house and had harmed her. He never "told" me not to involve the police.

I sucked in a breath, a realization hitting me in the face. "You asked me to find the men responsible for harming Anna Ivanova on Valentina's behalf, not to find the egg."

His eyes narrowed, and he opened his mouth to say something.

"Mr. Belsky?" The secretary entered the office. "I'm sorry to interrupt, but you are needed on the floor. It shouldn't take but a minute."

He rearranged his face and manufactured a smile.

"Very well," he said and then turned his attention back to me, the tension in his mouth easing. "Please don't go, Miss Michelle. I'd like to finish our conversation. I won't be long."

"Of course," I said. "I'll wait."

"Here is the letter you asked for," the secretary told him. "It just needs your signature, and then I'll pop it in the mail." She laid it on the desk.

"Thank you, Marge. I'll sign it when I return. I need it mailed as soon as possible."

They both left the office and the door clicked shut behind them.

Gripping my handbag, I tapped my fingers against it. Now alone, I was left with nothing but my thoughts, which had been dancing beneath the surface of my mission to take care of business with Mr. Belsky and to tell him of the proof I'd found of Valentina's murder. His remarks about the egg pricked at the forefront of those thoughts.

Then thoughts of Harold Huxley and his deception crept in.

Why had he assumed my father's identity? What would possess him to do that? Was he running from something? Hiding something? Had he so loathed himself and his own life that he found it necessary to assume the life of someone else?

My mind traveled back to the images of the battlefield. My father lying on the ground, his face covered in blood, the eyes staring.

My heart wrenched. He was lost to me again. This time most certainly forever. But the fact remained that he had survived the train crash, yet, he hadn't found me and Sophia. Was what Harold had said true, that he'd thought we were better off thinking he was dead? I shook my head, not knowing what to believe. I hoped to see Harold Huxley again. I had so many questions.

The turmoil in my mind forced me to get up out of the chair. I had to move my body. I paced the area behind the two armchairs.

After a few turns, I looked down at my wrist to see the time, my thoughts turning to the three o'clock meeting at the boarding house, but I'd forgotten to put on my watch. It was late morning, I assured myself. Hours before the meeting time. I wondered if the police had set up their stakeout yet. Or, if they'd found Harold Huxley there.

I didn't know what time Mr. Belsky had left, but it seemed as if he'd been gone fifteen minutes, although I knew he hadn't.

I studied a painting on the wall to distract myself. It depicted a snow scene with a horse-drawn sleigh. The people in the scene all wore heavy coats, the women with colorful scarves wrapped around their heads and the men in fur hats. I assumed the setting was some Russian landscape. Probably a reminder of home.

I circled the desk and came back to the chair I had been sitting in. My eyes glanced the papers on Mr. Belsky's desk. The letter the secretary had brought in lay on top of the pile. I leaned down to peruse it. I didn't mean to be nosy; I just wanted to clear my mind of the tumultuous thoughts surrounding Harold Huxley and my father.

My eyes settled on the salutation in the correspondence: *Dear—*

I gasped, staring at the word. The *a* sat a fraction lower than the rest of the letters. I scanned the rest of the note. Every *a* stood out in awkward unevenness.

The ransom notes. The suicide note.

I hired you to find the egg, Belsky's voice boomed in my head.

It was him! He, or people working for him, had attacked Anna Ivanova, kidnapped Madeleine, and *killed* Valentina! *He* wanted the egg!

I swiped the letter from the desk, folded it, and placed it in my handbag. The police needed to see this. I was just about to open the door to leave when Belsky stepped back into the room.

"Miss Michelle? Were you leaving?" he asked. He closed the door behind him, remaining between me and my escape.

"Um, yes . . . I know you are very busy. We can talk about this another time."

"Another time? Nonsense." He smiled. He gestured toward the chair. "You've come all this way. Please, sit. I want to hear more of this story."

I gulped and sat down, my hands gripping my purse so hard my fingers ached.

"I just need to sign this letter first—" He reached for it, and realizing it was no longer there, he froze. His eyes slid over to mine, and my mouth went dry.

"Did you—" he started.

I looked past him toward the door. I'd never be able to get by him.

"I know you killed Valentina," I blurted out. "Why? Did she find out that you were responsible for hurting Anna Ivanova? That you kidnapped Madeleine?"

His face hardened, and his gaze bore into mine, sending a spike of adrenaline through my body.

I suddenly remembered the scene at the hospital. Anna Ivanova shrieking at him as he backed out of the room. The pillow on the floor.

"You didn't go to the hospital to tell Anna Ivanova about Valentina. You went there to kill her. To finish the job. You tried to smother her."

"Get up," he said.

I raised my chin in defiance. "You won't get away with this. The police will figure it out." I had no idea if they would or not, but I wanted to scare him.

He grabbed hold of my arm. I tried to yank it out of his grip, but his fingers were like a vise. I winced. He hauled me from the chair and pulled me around the desk with him. He opened a drawer and took out a pistol.

"We're going for a walk," he said, squeezing my arm even harder. My fingers were growing numb from lack of circulation. "You make one sound or try to make a run for it, and you're dead. Understand?"

My heart clanging in my chest like a bell in a fire station, I nodded. He placed the hand holding the gun in his coat pocket, aiming it at me. Still clutching my arm, he led me out of the office.

"Mr. Belsky?" Marge looked up. "Do you have the letter?"

"Later," he said. "I have an errand to run. I'm walking Miss Michelle out."

The secretary frowned. "But, Mr. Belsky, you said—"

"I said *later*." His words carried a finality to them.

"Okay," she said with resignation.

"I'll be back soon."

Marge gave me a friendly smile. "Goodbye, Miss Michelle."

"Goodbye," I choked out, wondering with terror if those were the last words I would ever speak.

CHAPTER TWENTY-FIVE

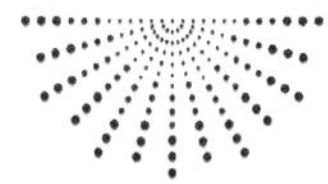

*B*elsky led me to the driver's-side door of his Mercedes-Benz 500K, his grip on my arm merciless.

"You're driving," he growled. He opened the door for me, and I got in. "Don't move."

I set my handbag in my lap and placed both hands on the wheel. He got in on the passenger's side, took the pistol out of his pocket, and pointed it at my ribs.

"Where are you taking me?" I asked, trying to keep the waver out of my voice. Was he taking me somewhere to kill me? Would he fake my suicide, as well?

"Just drive," he said.

I pressed the starter, my heart pounding so hard I was certain he could see it beating through the fabric of my blouse.

"Pull out of here and turn right," he commanded. I swung the big car out of the parking lot and onto Wilshire Boulevard.

"Stay on this road and be quiet."

I cleared my throat to keep it from closing shut. The miles seemed to take hours, but soon we were headed into Beverly Hills. I assumed he was taking me to his house to do away with me in private. We passed the Beverly Wilshire Hotel and then came to Whittier Boulevard.

"Turn here," he said.

I obeyed and drove up the street past the Los Angeles Country Club. He then had me turn right, and I drove up a long and winding private road. Soon, a large mansion loomed in the distance. I gripped the wheel tighter, my brain going a mile a minute trying to figure out a way to escape.

"Drive to the back of the house," he said. I swung the car around the corner, and he had me park in a shaded alcove. I kept my hands on the steering wheel, my eyes fixed straight ahead.

He got out of the car and came around to open my door. I sat, frozen in the seat.

"Get out," he said, wrenching my arm and pulling me from the car. My handbag fell to the ground. "Come on." He led me to a tidy shed some distance from the house. He pulled some keys out from his pocket and held them out to me.

"Open it," he said, the gun now pointed at my head.

My hands shook so violently I had trouble getting the key into the keyhole, but finally I managed. I turned the key and the door opened. He ripped the keys from my hand and then pushed me inside. I almost tripped and fell down a stairway that led underground. Was it a root cellar? I couldn't imagine why he would have one. Living in the lap of luxury, he surely wouldn't need it.

He pressed the barrel of the gun into my back. "Go," he said.

It was dark, and I had trouble seeing in front of me. I placed my hand against the wall for balance, and we descended, the air growing cooler with each step.

At last, we reached the bottom and entered a cavernous room with scalloped shelving lining the brick walls. Wine bottles, hundreds of them, rested within their curves.

My eyes adjusted to the dimness, and I heard a faint mewling —like a kitten. I followed the sound with my eyes and made out a body, a person, lying on a mattress on the floor. I blinked, trying to force my eyes to see.

A blond head took form.

"Madeleine?" A wave of relief passed over me to see she was still alive. Clearly, Harold had not turned over the egg for her release.

Belsky shoved me toward her, and I fell to my knees. She reached out and weakly took hold of my hand.

"I brought you some company," he said.

"Hey, boss," a shout came from above.

Belsky turned and went back up the stairs. The door slammed with a bang, and I heard the key turn in the lock.

My eyes finally came into focus. A faint sliver of light filtered through a narrow, upper window. Madeleine lay on a thin mattress. She wore ill-fitting clothing that was clearly not her own. I remembered the bloody dressing gown thrown in the trash. They had taken her in only her nightdress.

The silhouette of a couple of plates, an empty pitcher, and a glass took form next to her. So they hadn't been starving her. Not exactly. Her hair was in tangles, and parts of it were dark and matted with dried blood. Her right eye was swollen, and her lip was split. She clutched at her ribs.

"Madeleine," I whispered. "Oh, dear Madeleine."

"Grace," she croaked. "I'm so sorry you got dragged into this."

I, too, was sorry but also relieved to see her alive.

She slowly pushed herself up to sitting, groaning as if it took every last bit of energy she had to do so.

"Your father—" she started.

A sudden rage engulfed me. My father. *My father was dead.*

"He's not my father," I cut in.

She stopped short and went silent for a moment. She tilted her head in question. "What? What are you talking about?"

"That man, the one you are married to, is not my father. Did you know?"

"Know what?" She sounded like she was about to cry.

"Harold Huxley?"

"Who is Harold Huxley?"

Could it be she really didn't know? That he had deceived her, too? At this point, why would she lie about it?

"You mean, you didn't know Harold Huxley had assumed my father—Peter Michelle's—identity?"

She shook her head, her eyes wide with alarm. "I don't understand."

"I found a letter addressed to Peter Michelle, but the salutation was to Harold Huxley."

"But . . . it could have been a mistake. Maybe whoever wrote the letter put it in the wrong envelope."

"I also found dog tags among my—*Harold's* things. Two with my father's name, and one with the name Harold Huxley." I frowned, sympathetic to her shock and disbelief at such a huge betrayal. It probably made her question everything about their relationship.

I softened my tone. "It was from his brother. The first thing he said was that he couldn't get used to addressing him as Peter."

Her jaw dropped open. "But why? Why would he pretend to be your father?"

I shook my head with a sigh. "I don't know. But we've been lied to and used—very badly."

She took a sharp inhale. "And your father? I mean, your real father?"

I remembered the dream. My father had been lying on the ground, his face blown off. "He's dead." I raised my shoulders in an acquiescent shrug, strangely feeling nothing. I had mourned my father and my mother years ago.

"I'm sorry."

"Me too. But I can't think about that right now. We have to

figure out a way to get out of here." I stood up, my eyes straining to see. "It's so dark in here."

Madeleine fumbled with something near the mattress and then a whoosh and snap sounded, followed by a warm glow of light that filled the room. She'd lit a match. She held the flame over a candle, and it sputtered to life.

"I found these down here." She had resumed her despondency, probably processing what I had just divulged about the man she loved.

My heart went out to her, but we had bigger problems to address. I didn't know how much longer she would last in her condition, and I knew if Anton Belsky found the egg, we would be of no use to him anymore. He would surely kill us.

I scanned the room. There were no other openings and, obviously, no windows other than the narrow one that was too high to reach. Only the door at the top of the steps, which was locked from the outside.

"How often does he come down here?" I asked.

"Someone comes once a day. But it's usually not him." She coughed and then clutched at her middle.

"Madeleine?" I knelt down next to her.

"I think I have some broken ribs. It hurts to breathe." She had been beaten pretty badly. "There are two other men who work for him. One of them brings me a small glass of water and some crumbs to eat. He's actually rather kind, if you can believe it. I think his name is Dimitry. The other one is a different story. Brought his questions and his fists, but that stopped, thank god. I think they finally believe I don't know where the egg is."

"Well we have to find a way to get out of here," I repeated.

A click sounded at the top of the stairs, and then the stairway filled with light. Anton Belsky closed the door and then came down the steps.

"Well I see you've made it quite cozy down here." He

pointed to the lit candle. "And you two are catching up." A grin spread across his face, and then faded as quickly as it came.

"Let Madeleine go," I said. "She needs a doctor."

"Aww." He pursed his lips into a frown. "Your concern is endearing."

I clenched my teeth. "Let her go."

He sighed, holding his arms out from his sides. "But I need her. I need you both. For leverage."

Another figure came down the steps. "Mr. Belsky, someone is here to see you. They are in the house."

His grin returned. "Ah. Busy, busy. I must leave you ladies— for now."

After they left, I grabbed the candle and made my way over to the stairs.

"What are you doing?" Madeleine whispered.

I held up a finger to silence her and went up the steps. I pressed my ear against it and strained to hear the voices on the other side.

"The *Vaughn* leaves for the Orient at ten o'clock in the morning, tomorrow, sir." I detected a Russian accent.

"You think he'll be on the ship?" Belsky's voice.

"Possibly. Didn't the woman say they planned to take the egg to Europe somewhere?"

"Sweden."

"*Da*, Sweden."

"From here, he'd go via the Orient." Belsky again. "Makes sense. He wouldn't risk taking the train to New York."

"But we have his woman and now his daughter. Do you think he'd leave them?"

Belsky snorted. "I would."

His daughter. If only they knew. If they did, they'd realize I was of no value to them at all. Belsky was right. Harold Huxley could care less if I lived or died. And now he had the egg. If he'd wanted Madeleine back, he'd make it known to Belsky he had what he wanted.

I thought back to when I'd first seen Harold Huxley at the cafe. His interest in the movie stars I worked with, and later, Valentina who was the key to finding the egg. That was all he wanted, all he cared about. I glanced down at Madeleine who was curled up again on the mattress. He'd already let her go. He'd be on that ship. I knew it.

The voices fell silent. I pressed my ear to the door harder, straining to hear something, but there was nothing. They had gone.

I went back down the stairs and sat on the mattress next to Madeleine.

"My fa— Harold told me about your brother, your family, and the Fabergé egg. Did the two of you plan to take the egg to Sweden once you'd obtained it from Anna Ivanova?"

She nodded and sniffed. She'd been crying.

"Yes, my brother told me he'd shipped the egg to Miss Ivanova's. We didn't want to tell you what it was because—"

"It was stolen from the Russian royal family," I finished for her.

She nodded. "We needed you—" she looked up at me with sad eyes "—to introduce us to Valentina Baklanova. Your father —" She squeezed her eyes shut, shaking her head. "I'm so sorry. I didn't know."

"It's okay, Madeleine. I believe you."

"How did you know about Sweden? Did your— Did Harold," she said the name between clenched teeth, "tell you that was our plan?"

"No. I just heard Belsky and his man talking about it. You told them?"

She covered her face with her hands. "I wanted the beating to stop. I had to give them something."

The two of them going to Sweden felt like a betrayal, but

then I reminded myself that Harold Huxley really had no reason to stick around. I placed my hand on her leg in sympathy. "No one would fault you for that."

She sniffed again. "He'll go without me. He was obsessed with that egg. It's obvious now he's a liar. And a thief—a thief of the worst kind, stealing the identity of another human being, someone with family, loved ones. It's despicable."

I patted her leg, commiserating with her, wondering how in the world we would get out of this fix.

"They'll get him at the port," she said. "And if they don't, he'll be on that ship. Either way, they are going to kill us and it's all my fault. We are of no value to them now."

"But they don't know that for sure. I think we have some time," I said, trying to assure her—and also trying to persuade myself.

CHAPTER TWENTY-SIX

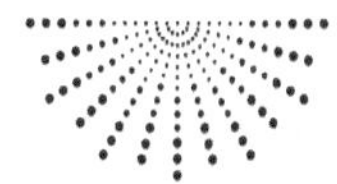

*S*ophia beckons to me. I join her in a field of flowers, and she takes my hand. We walk, the yellow and orange blooms grazing our bare legs. The sun shines bright white in the midst of the sea of gold and warms our backs as we stride toward a gazebo.

A figure stands under the lattice archway. As we get closer, I can see it is a dark-haired man dressed in white.

My breath catches. "Father?"

He holds his arms wide, and I run to him. I throw my arms around him, then pull back and look deep into his eyes. "It's you. It's really you."

"I'm so sorry, Gracie. I'm sorry I abandoned you. It wasn't right."

I press my head against his chest, squeezing him tight. I can feel his heart beating against my cheek.

"I thought I was doing the right thing," he whispers.

Sophia puts one arm around him and one around me. She lays her head on his shoulder.

"I'm so proud of you girls," he murmurs.

Something cool touches my back. I turn to see what it is, and

I am staring into the face of my mother. She is beautiful, her eyes glowing with serenity and warmth. Her skin radiates with light. She smiles and lays her cool hand against my cheek.

"Fight," she says.

I woke with a start. The air was icy, sinking into my flesh. Madeleine shivered next to me, her fragile body racked with cold. I scooted closer to her, pressed my body against hers, and wrapped my arm around her.

I wondered what time it was. Was it morning? The room was so dark it was difficult to tell. When would Belsky or one of his men come back? Would they come back? Or would they go to the port and leave us here to die?

No. They still needed us, I assured myself. I hoped.

The lock on the door clicked, and I sat up. Two figures silhouetted in the light descended the stairs. A rope dangled from one of their hands.

Madeleine stirred. "What the—" She held a hand to her eyes, shielding them from the light.

"Grab her," Belsky said to the other man. He was short, squat, and rotund. A scar snaked across the bridge of his nose. He came over, and taking a viselike grip on my arm, he hauled me to my feet. I tried to wrench away, but he took hold of my other arm and cranked it behind my back. Sharp pain spread throughout my shoulder.

"Get up," Belsky said, looming over Madeleine. He held the rope firmly in his fist.

She turned her head to look up at him and then pressed it back onto the mattress.

"I said, get up!" He grabbed her arm and pulled, but she went limp like dead weight.

"She's too weak," I said. "You've nearly killed her."

He turned to look at me, a hideous grin on his face. "And I'm going to finish the job." He held up the rope. "I don't want blood in my wine cellar. Too messy."

"No! You can't. You need her. Har— My father would do anything to get her back," I lied.

"But we have you."

"He doesn't care about me," I blurted.

He scoffed. "Nice try, dear" His gaze traveled to the man holding me. "Take her out of here."

"No!" I screamed. "Don't you touch her!"

He ignored me and went to take hold of her arm again. I raised my leg and kicked at Belsky. I made contact with his backside, and he lurched forward.

"Hey!" The man holding me wrenched my arm back harder.

Hot coals seared the top of my shoulder. I spun toward the arm he was holding and rammed my other fist into the side of his head, hitting him in the ear. He howled in pain, and I lifted my knee right into his groin. He bellowed again and doubled over.

Belsky roared and flew at me, his hands wrapping around my neck. "You shouldn't have done that!" He squeezed, and I gasped, fighting for air, pain shooting up my throat and into my head. "Perhaps the old man doesn't care about you. Maybe we don't need you after all. Or maybe he doesn't need to know you are a dead woman. That you are *both* dead. You know too much anyway. It's too risky to keep you alive."

I blinked, my eyes feeling like they were bulging from my head. I batted my hands against his, trying to beat him off me. I wasn't able to get any air, and it felt like knives were shooting into my skull. My vision blurred before darkness flooded my periphery, closing in like a dissolve on a movie screen.

Suddenly there was a crash. Liquid splattered against my face. His hands loosened around my neck, and I gasped for air, coughing. He fell to the ground.

Madeleine stood in front of me holding a broken wine bottle in her hand, red wine running down her arm and splattered onto her clothes.

Groaning came from behind me, and I turned to see the other

man stirring. I reached down and fumbled through Belsky's pockets until my fingers found the cool metal of his gun and the splay of keys.

I whipped out the pistol and trained it on the man still writhing on the floor. "Don't move," I warned. "Come on, Madeleine." I reached out to her, still keeping my eyes on both men. She took my hand, and I dragged her up the stairs.

Once outside, I slammed the door shut and locked it. Madeleine sank to the ground.

"I need to get you to the hospital," I said.

She shook her head. "No. We need to go to the port."

I blinked at her. "You are in no condition— Wait." I studied her face, suddenly thinking the worst. "You don't aim to go with him?"

Her brows pressed down, and she opened her mouth in indignation. "No! He needs to be stopped. I want to see him pay for what he's done."

"We'll call the police, then. You are too weak. You need help."

"Grace, please. Do you want him to get away with this? To go on and live a life of luxury? Do you really want that? Does he deserve that? Not in my book."

I took in a breath and winced, my throat still aching. No, I didn't want Harold Huxley to get away with this. I didn't want that at all. "You're right."

"Then let's go. We have to stop him."

"But we still need to call the police."

I wanted some kind of backup. Madeleine was too weak in case we got into a scuffle. Although, she'd rallied when I had been in trouble. And I had a gun. I gripped it firmly in my hand.

"How do we call the police?" she asked. "We can't go into the mansion. We don't know how many people he has working for him in there. And we don't have time. By the angle of the sun, I'd say it's approaching midmorning."

I looked at my wrist and was reminded I'd forgotten my watch.

"All right. But we're stopping at a payphone to call the police."

She looked up at me and twisted her mouth in question. "Do you have any money?"

I remembered my handbag falling to the ground when we'd gotten out of Belsky's Mercedes. "Come on," I said, helping her to her feet and hoping my handbag was still there.

The car was not where we'd left it. I scanned the area, and there was no sign of my purse, either.

"Let's go to the front of the mansion," I said. Maybe the car was there.

I strode down the lane and realized Madeleine wasn't with me. I turned around. She had dropped to her knees.

I ran back to her. "Madeleine!"

"I'm all right," she said through clenched teeth. "Just help me get to the car."

I helped her to her feet and hoisted her arm around my shoulders. Wrapping my arm around her, I supported her at the waist. I walked with her as fast as I could. She was heavy, her body sagging against me.

We rounded the corner of the mansion, and I sighed with relief. The car was sitting out front, gleaming in the sun in all its glory.

"We're almost there," I encouraged her, finding the strength to pick up the pace.

I helped her into the passenger seat, got in on the driver's side, and started the car, and then we were off.

CHAPTER TWENTY-SEVEN

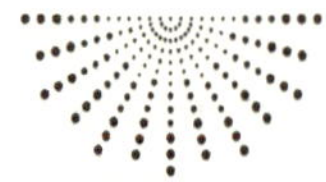

The drive from Beverly Hills to the Port of Los Angeles was about an hour and a half in my car. In this beautiful machine, it took less time. The traffic was light so I knew we'd missed the early-morning rush. I weaved in and out of the other cars, driving like a madwoman.

We finally approached the port. It was a huge affair with a rail yard, warehouses, and stacks of lumber and steel beams that seemed to go on for miles.

I spotted the gigantic steamer, its pinnacles flying in the breeze, still nestled against the dock.

I parked the car, swiped the gun I had set next to me, and stuffed it into the pocket of my trousers. It was heavy and bulky, but if I wanted it for protection, I had to make do with the discomfort.

I helped Madeleine out of the car and supported her weight as we headed toward the ship. There were what seemed like a million cars in the lot, and hordes of people surrounded us. Several of them, seeing the state of my friend, looked at us with concerned faces.

"Is everything all right?" a tall gentleman with a mustache and a John Barrymore–look about him approached us.

"Yes, thanks," I blurted, not wanting to be derailed from our mission. I hoped he didn't see the bulk of the gun in my pocket. "Is that the *Vaughn?*" I asked him.

"Yep," he said. "Headed for Hong Kong. Can I give you a hand?"

"We're fine," Madeleine said. "I just twisted my ankle. It will be right as rain in a minute. We just don't want to be late to see off our friends."

He turned his wrist over to look at his watch. "You've got plenty of time. She doesn't leave port for another thirty minutes."

"Oh, that's good. Thank you." I forced a smile at him.

Thirty minutes might be a long time for someone standing on the docks waving goodbye to friends or loved ones, but to find Harold Huxley in this veritable haystack in that time would be a challenge.

We struggled forward. Madeleine was growing heavier by the second. She could barely walk, even with my help.

"Come on, dear," I encouraged. "You can do this."

She was out of breath. "My legs don't want to work."

I stopped and readjusted my grip around her waist. She went limp, nearly pulling the two of us to the ground. Hefting her up, I leaned her against a Chrysler Phaeton.

"I just need to rest a minute." She supported her weight against the car with her arms.

It had been a bad idea to bring her, but I hadn't had a choice. As it was, we might not be able to find him anyway. I, too, leaned against the car. A wave of hopelessness passed over me as I surveyed the area. There was a sea of people, all surging toward the ship. "We are never going to find him."

My gaze locked on a woman wearing a periwinkle dress. She was not moving with the tide of travelers and well-wishers, but she stood still as a steel pylon about fifty yards away from us. She was staring at us as the wave of bodies streamed passed her. My knees threatened to buckle.

Sophia?

I blinked. Surely I was mistaken. It was just someone who looked like her.

"Do you see that woman?" I pointed in her direction. "Standing over there?"

"Where?" Madeleine asked.

"Right over there." I pointed again. "Wearing a purple dress. She's just standing there looking at us."

"I see lots of women," Madeleine said. "But none of them are standing still. They are all heading toward the ship."

The woman in the periwinkle dress—Sophia, if I could believe my eyes—slowly raised her hand and beckoned to me.

"Stay here," I said to Madeleine.

"What? N-no," she sputtered. "We have to find him!"

"Stay here," I repeated, this time my tone like a mother commanding a child to obey.

She stared at me open-mouthed and then nodded in acquiescence. "You'll be faster without me. I just need to rest. I'll catch up in a minute." She sank to the ground, her body sliding down the car door.

I rushed over to her, taking her by the arms. "Madeleine—"

"I'm okay," she said, her voice barely a whisper. "Just a little weak. Go find him."

"You're sure?" I asked, looking into her eyes. They were glazed, out of focus. Her skin was pale, white and smooth as a lily. Perspiration shone on her forehead and upper lip like dew.

She batted a hand in the air. "Go."

I squeezed her arms and then stood up, turning to search for the woman—Sophia. She was still there, still beckoning me to her. And then she turned and walked away.

I followed, weaving in and out of the cars. I looked toward

the ship, wondering how much time had passed. Maybe ten minutes?

Passengers filed up the boarding ramp at the front of the ship in a steady stream, waving to the well-wishers below on the dock. Had Harold Huxley boarded yet? If so, he'd surely get away.

I turned my gaze back to Sophia. She looked over her shoulder and urged me forward with a tilt of her head. As I got closer, still weaving in and out of the automobiles, I couldn't believe my eyes. She was walking *through* the cars.

She came to a warehouse and rounded the corner, disappearing. I picked up my pace, moving into a jog. Where was she going? Had she left me?

I reached the building, turned the corner, and caught a glimpse of her dress as she skirted around the next corner. I jogged after her and then found myself at the aft of the ship. There was another gangway, heavy with passengers making their way up the ramp. At this point, hundreds of people had gone aboard, I was certain. My heart sank. We had arrived too late.

I placed my hands on my hips, catching my breath.

A sudden wave of pungent cigarette smoke tickled my nostrils. I turned my head to follow the smell. It was coming from the warehouse.

And then I saw him through the open doors. Harold Huxley was sitting on a small crate, a valise next to him, smoking a cigarette. He must have been waiting in here, hoping to go unnoticed before he boarded the ship.

I took in a sharp breath. Not seeing me, he stood, flicked the cigarette to the ground, and bent down to pick up the crate.

"You!" I shouted, running toward him and into the warehouse.

He turned, and his face blanched when he saw me. He picked up the crate, hefted it under his arm, and was about to pick up the valise when I took the pistol out of my pocket and aimed it at him.

"I wouldn't do that," I said.

He raised his free hand in the air. "Grace, darling, I can explain. Put the gun down."

"Darling? You have no right to call me that, *Harold*."

His eyes narrowed. He put down the crate and he slowly walked toward me. I extended the gun farther away from my body.

"Don't come any closer," I commanded. He stopped.

"Why?" I asked. "Why did you steal my father's identity?"

"Gracie." His face softened. "What are you talking about?"

"Don't call me that," I snapped. "I know you're not my father. Answer the question."

He slowly moved toward me again, his hands still raised in the air. I tightened my grip on the butt of the pistol.

"It's quite simple, really," he said, a smile spreading his lips. "I didn't want to be in France. I didn't want to be fighting. My tour had just begun, and his was ending in a matter of weeks." He continued moving toward me.

I moved backward, away from him. "How did you know so much about Sophia and me? About our lives?"

He shrugged a shoulder. "Peter and I had become friends. Quite close. People thought we were brothers because we looked so much alike. He told me all about you and your sister, his crazy wife, the train crash. And how he didn't feel fit to be a father anymore."

I recalled the visions of the two men, their heads close together, their intense conversations. My father had shared his life with Harold Huxley, had told him everything. That's how the deception had been so complete.

"And did he die in battle or did you kill him?" I asked, seething at the idea.

Harold clucked his tongue. "You wound me, Grace. But rest assured. He died valiantly in battle, while we were at Cantigny."

My heart wrenched, and tears pricked at the corners of my eyes. I had seen all this in the dreams, the visions. In that moment, my heart ached for my long-dead father.

"How dare you take advantage of him, of his memory . . . of me."

He smiled again, moving closer. "It worked out quite perfectly," he said. "With my new identity, I figured I should earnestly play the part. I started following your sister's career, and yours, too, of course. News of your sister's fame was all over Europe. The French adored her."

The ease with which he spoke about my family made my blood boil. The violation was palpable, and anger surged through me, tightening my chest and contracting the muscles of my body.

"And then Madeleine got news of the egg. The very valuable Fabergé egg that had been sent to Anna Ivanova, the aunt of the famous Hollywood actress Valentina Baklanova. And imagine my luck! My very own daughter lived in Los Angeles and worked in the motion picture business."

The pistol trembled in my hand. His utter disregard and callousness concerning my lost family made me want to pull the trigger, but I refrained—for now.

"And Madeleine? You were fine just leaving her to die?"

Sadness swept over his features but only for a moment. His gaze shifted from mine and then returned. He set his jaw, his face hardening again. Emboldened, he moved closer to me. Large crates and stacks of railroad ties loomed in my periphery as he moved me toward them.

"It was true, what I told you of our relationship. She nursed me back to health."

I shook my head, appalled at his lack of empathy for her. Chet would have sacrificed himself several times over for me, and I for him. "Did you ever love her?"

He shrugged. "What is love? I told her what she wanted to hear. That I needed her. Women always want to be needed, don't they? Isn't that what Chet tells you—that he needs you, the children need you?"

Anger surged through me. "Don't you ever—"

"I knew the Russians would never return her to me. You were naive enough to think so but not me. So when I was left alone with the egg, I decided to stick to our plan—on my own."

He had inched closer to me, almost close enough to touch me. I backed away, still aiming the gun at his face. Sensing I was about to back into a stack of railroad ties, my gaze shifted from his.

In that second, he rushed at me and took hold of the barrel of the gun. I flailed my other arm toward him, my palm making contact with his chin. He stumbled but still had a viselike grip on the pistol. He swung his other fist toward me, and stars exploded behind my eyes, blinding me. My head throbbed with an intensity that went all the way to my stomach. I stumbled backward, and my heels hit against something. It was the low stack of railroad ties.

Another blow, this time to the other side of my face, sent me sprawling. My back slammed against the pile of ties, waves of pain radiating throughout my body. My head snapped backward, slamming into the stony wood, and then everything went black.

THE SUN'S warmth bathes my cheeks as I raise my face to its radiance. Huge, puffy clouds bloom before my eyes, shining silver and gray and gleaming white.

I sense a presence next to me and know it is Sophia.

"Now, you know the truth," she says.

"I am alone," I say back, my heart heavy with the weight of yet another loss.

She smiles at me and points to a large oak tree. Sitting beneath it amid the long stems of lush grass are our mother and father. Their heads are bent together, their bodies arced toward each other like the kissing palms. They are talking, laughing— young and carefree.

Sophia takes my hand, and we walk toward them. They turn their faces toward us and smile.

"You are never alone," she says.

"But I want to be here. With you."

As we near my mother and father, they each reach a hand toward me. They are standing now, against the trunk of the massive oak, the sunlight flooding around them and wrapping itself around the trunk from behind like a tender embrace. Their images grow faint. They are sinking into the tree trunk, engulfed by the sun. They are fading, transparent, like the wisp of a cloud.

A deep, resonant burst of noise fills my ears. It is loud, inescapable as it blares and vibrates through my body. The sound of joyful, shouting voices surrounds me. A pain starts in my head and radiates down my neck. It's tugging at me, growing more intense, more insistent. My shoulders and back ache. Something hard presses into my body.

"In time," Sophia says.

The sound booms again, overwhelming the shouting and cheering voices. The pain grows sharper, pulling me from the dream.

"Grace!" a voice calls out.

"Grace!"

My eyelids fluttered open. A face came into view, but it was blurred, coming in and out of focus. It was Madeleine.

"Thank God," she said. "What are you doing in here? I've been looking all over for you."

I tried to pull myself to sitting. Pain seared through my skull and darted into my eyes. I reached my hand around to the back of my head. My hair was damp, my fingers warm and sticky.

"Madeleine . . . What are *you* doing here? How did you get here? You're so weak."

"I didn't want you to face him alone. I forced myself up. I was too slow, though." She reached forward toward my hair. "You're bleeding. You've taken a nasty blow to the head." Her voice was shaky, floating on the air. Dark moons beneath her eyes made her skin look even more alabaster than usual. She shouldn't have come after me. I marveled at her fortitude.

I struggled again to get up, but I couldn't make my arms work. I turned my head from side to side to see why my body felt so awkward. I was sprawled against a pile of railroad ties. Madeleine sat on the ground, her legs curled to one side, supporting herself with her hand.

A man walked by, and I shouted out to him. He stopped and looked in, and then rushed over to us.

"Are you ladies okay?" He was a tower of a man who looked to be in his midtwenties. He wrapped his hand around my arm and helped me sit up.

"You've taken a fall," he said, examining my head. His soft brown eyes looked into mine.

The blare of the ship's horn boomed in the air, reverberating through the ground and into my limbs. The cheering voices were like the consistent buzz of static through a radio.

"The ship!" I said.

Energy coursed through me, and I struggled to get up. The man pulled me to my feet as if I were as light as a kitten. My head throbbed, and blackness crept in around my periphery, threatening to snuff out my senses again. I blinked it away.

"We have to get on that ship," I said, pulling away from him.

The man, with one arm wrapped around my shoulder and the other enveloping my bicep, held on to me tightly, supporting my flagging body. "I'm afraid you're too late. It's leaving."

I shook him off and staggered toward the entrance of the warehouse, toward the steamer that was slowly inching away from the dock. Masses of people crowded the deck, throwing colorful streamers and confetti down to the cheering throng below. I pushed my way through the crowd, through the slivered-paper rainbow, my eyes raised toward the passengers on the ship. Men, women, and children, their faces lit with joy, clung to the railing, waving to their friends and loved ones.

Scanning the masses, my gaze stopped on a man standing at the aft of the ship, separated from the crowd. He was focused intently on me. He held a small packing crate under his arm. With the other, he raised his hand in the air, bidding me farewell.

"No!" I shouted.

The young man's arm went around my shoulder again.

"I have to get on that ship!" I cried.

"It's too late, miss," he said, his voice soft and soothing. "You're hurt, and your friend isn't doing too well, either. You both need a doctor."

I watched the ship pulling away from the dock, and my heart sank to the pit of my stomach. He was getting away. That liar and cheat and thief was getting away with the Fabergé egg.

"That man . . ." I pointed, but he was growing smaller by the second. "That man is a thief. He's stolen something very valuable. We have to alert the police."

The young man chuckled. "I am the police."

I looked at him aghast. "But why didn't you stop him?"

"Stop whom?"

"Harold Huxley! Er, Peter Michelle. He's an imposter, a thief. Do you know Detective Baptiste?"

"By reputation only. I don't work in his precinct. I'm a deputy for the Orange County Sheriff's Office. Dan Harrison." He smiled.

"That man has to be stopped," I said. "He's taken something very valuable—something belonging to the Kremlin."

His eyebrows pressed downward, and he looked at me as if I'd fallen from outer space.

"You have to believe me! Call Detective Baptiste."

"All right, all right," he said in that buttery voice again. "Let's get your friend, and we'll find a telephone. We'll call the detective and then an ambulance. You two need medical care."

I wilted in his arms, my legs shaking with weakness.

"You!" he hollered at a man standing nearby. He was an older gentleman with graying hair and stiffly squared shoulders. "I need some help here."

The man, seeing the state of my head, rushed over to us. Deputy Harrison pointed to Madeleine, who sat listlessly with her back against the railroad ties. "Help her to her feet. Let's take them into the terminal."

The man jogged over to Madeleine and pulled her up, but her legs were unable to support her and she crumpled to the ground. With a surprising strength for a man his age, he swept her up into his arms and carried her.

Inside the terminal, a high-ceilinged building with gleaming, faux marble linoleum floors, we searched for a payphone. On the opposite side of the vast space, there was a bank of five wooden phone booths. Four of them were occupied. We made our way over to them, and the older man set Madeleine down on a wooden bench.

Deputy Harrison led me over to the bench, but I stiffened. "No. I have to speak with Detective Baptiste."

He nodded and led me to the available booth. I lowered myself into the chair, and he reached into his pocket and produced some coins. He placed them in the slots.

"Operator," a voice echoed through the receiver. "How may I direct your call?"

"Burbank Police Department," I said. A wave of pain rolled through my head, and I squeezed my eyes shut against it. The world tilted, and my stomach flipped, reminding me of the sensation of riding on the Race Thru the Clouds roller coaster in Venice Beach.

"I'll connect you."

After I spoke with another officer, Detective Baptiste got on the phone. "Miss Michelle, we've been looking for you. Your husband said you didn't come home last night."

I told him everything that had happened. I told him about Anton Belsky and that he and one of his henchmen were locked in the wine cellar at his estate, and that Harold Huxley, posing as my father, was sailing away with the Fabergé egg.

"Damn," he breathed into the phone. "All right. I'll get someone out to the Belsky residence. You say you have a deputy there with you?"

"Yes, Deputy Harrison."

"Put him on the phone."

I rose to my feet and handed the deputy the receiver. I scooted out of the booth and made my way over to Madeleine and the man who'd helped her. She was slumped on the bench, her head leaning against the back of it.

One of the other telephone booths freed up, and the older gentleman pushed to his feet. "I'll call an ambulance," he said.

"Thank you." I pushed a lock of Madeleine's hair away from her eyes.

She rolled her head to look over at me. "He's getting away," she whispered. "He's getting away with it."

"No, he's not," I said, trying to reassure her but not so certain myself. The thought of him selling the egg and living in comfort off the proceeds—as my father, no less—made my stomach roil again. Another wave of pain stabbed down my neck, and I winced.

Deputy Harrison hung up the phone and came over to us. "I'm going to alert the authorities here. Detective Baptiste is contacting the officials in Hong Kong. They'll be waiting for this Harold Huxley, or Peter Michelle, at the port."

I sighed with relief, taking hold of Madeleine's hand.

The older man hung up the phone and joined us. "Ambulance is on its way."

"Good," Officer Harrison said. "Can I impose upon you further to stay with these ladies until it arrives while I report to the authorities here?"

The man nodded. "Certainly."

"Thanks. And Miss Michelle?" Deputy Harrison addressed me. "Detective Baptiste told me to tell you you've done good work here."

I offered a polite smile, my gut wrenching, thinking anything but. I'd found the egg for Harold Huxley and played right into his hands. And now he was getting away.

CHAPTER TWENTY-EIGHT

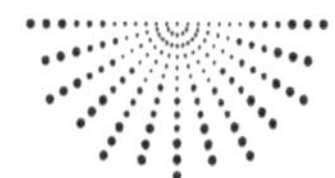

I sat in the visitor's room of the Los Angeles County Jail, where we'd learned Clara Stapleton had been sent. My head still pounded with the mild concussion the doctor had diagnosed me with. Thankfully, they had discharged me fairly quickly, though Madeleine would be kept under observation for a while longer, possibly a couple of days. Chet had urged me to go home and rest, but I needed to see Clara first.

So, here I was, waiting to speak with her at one of the six tables in the room. They would only allow one visitor so Chet had to wait for me at admittance. I'd promised him I wouldn't be long.

Two officers stood near each door, the one for visitors to enter the room and the other for the prisoners to enter. They closely observed the interactions with the prisoners and their loved ones.

Another officer entered through the door at the far end of the room. He was holding Clara by the arm. A sweater was draped over her black-and-white prison uniform, and when she saw me, her face blanched. She turned to leave, but the officer bade her sit down across from me.

She obeyed but wouldn't look me in the eye. Her face had gone sallow, and she gloomily stared at the top of the table.

"Why'd you do it, Clara?" I asked, trying to keep my rage and my hurt feelings at her betrayal in check. "How could you have helped a monster like James Johnson?"

She didn't answer. Still didn't look at me.

"What if he had killed Stevie? A child? Would you have been able to live with yourself?"

Her head swiveled to finally meet my gaze. "I didn't want him to do it. I didn't want him to kidnap the kid. I thought we could keep getting information from you about the egg, but he—"

"He obviously doesn't give a damn about human life. And apparently, neither do you."

Her eyes welled up with tears. "You don't understand."

I scoffed. "You're right. I don't," I ground out. "How could you have betrayed me like that? I thought we were friends."

Her tears stopped, and she looked at me with coldness in her eyes. "Friends? I hardly think so. I was your lackey, your errand girl. Uncle Barney told me that I would have a job as a real designer, but then I come to find out I'd be working for you—as an assistant. He lied to me. Just like all the other men in my life."

My mouth dropped open. "That's usually how it works, Clara. You work as an assistant or an apprentice first—at least until you graduate. Your uncle plays by the book so you probably just misunderstood him." I shook my head with incredulity at her reasoning. "What's the real story?"

She looked away. Her body shook slightly. I gathered it was from her leg bouncing up and down under the table. Was it from nervousness or anger? From the set of her mouth, I gathered it was the latter.

She turned to me again with narrowed eyes. "You're just so perfect, aren't you?"

My brows shot up. "Pardon me?"

"Everyone at the studio talks about how great you are, how talented you are. All the seamstresses love you. You have the ear of all the actors and actresses. Timothy won't shut up about you. You have the perfect husband, the perfect family. You're a do-gooder with all those foster kids, solving all those crimes. And me? I have nothing. The only reason Uncle Barney gave me the job was that I was flunking out of design school."

"I see," I said.

Her resentment of me was shocking. I remembered her telling me her father never paid her much mind, but I didn't know it was so bad for her. I realized I really didn't know Clara, after all. I knew very little about her upbringing, what her childhood had been like, her joys, her sorrows. What she'd done was inexcusable, but I couldn't help but feel a little sorry for her.

"James made me feel special. Like I mattered." She looked down at her hands, which were clasped tightly together on the table. "He said we would get the egg and then we would run away together. He said he would change. But that was a lie, too."

I bit my lip, not sure what else to say. Yes, Clara had betrayed me, but perhaps what was saddest of all was that she had betrayed herself.

The officer appeared at her shoulder. "Time to go."

Without looking at me, she rose from the table and let him lead her from the room.

TWO DAYS LATER, I sat in bed doodling on my sketch pad. The sunlight streamed through the open window, and the cool, late morning breeze cleared my aching head. I had lingered in bed far longer than usual. I picked up a piece of toast from my breakfast tray and took a bite. It had gone cold, but the butter was rich and

creamy, coating my tongue with its delicate flavor. Rose had
been making a fuss over me ever since I'd come home from the
hospital.

I was trying to work out a dress for my Sophia line, but
struggled to see it through. My pencil usually flitted about the
page like it had a mind of its own, but this morning, it was dull
and stagnant—like my mind. The head injury would be the
perfect excuse, but the apathy went deeper. My heart just wasn't
in it.

Timothy had called the previous night with some disturbing
news. He'd been getting pressure from the Steinbergs to let me
go. He'd said they'd claimed my absence from the set of late had
cost them valuable time and money, but I knew that wasn't true.
Timothy had yet to find a replacement for Valentina and was still
in the process of casting the film. We hadn't really even got
started yet, and considering that fact, I was actually ahead of the
game with my designs.

I knew the real reason stemmed from me telling the police
that Clara had been complicit in James Johnson's escape. It
wasn't my fault their niece had been smitten with a criminal
who'd used her for his schemes. Clara was a grown woman
capable of making her own decisions, albeit they were bad ones.
But the scandal had put the Steinbergs in an awkward position,
and they wanted to distance themselves from me, no matter how
talented they believed me to be.

"I'm so sorry, lass," he'd said. "My hands are tied on this
one, darlin'. I need this film. But I'll give it one more try. I have
a meeting with them tomorrow mornin'."

"Thank you," I'd said, my stomach folding in on itself with
the certainty that he'd never persuade them.

"I'll let you know what they say tomorrow. Chin up." And
with that he'd hung up the phone.

I looked at my watch. It was nearly eleven, and I'd had no
word from him. I set the sketch pad down, my hopes dwindling

by the second. The coolness of the breeze from the window raised goose bumps on my skin, and I pulled my dressing gown tighter over my chest, feeling its warmth, feeling Sophia wrap herself around me.

I'd based some of my designs for my Sophia line on this very article of loungewear. It was an eveningwear line, sporting a bohemian style. I'd hadn't much time to devote to the marketing of it, though, as I'd been preoccupied with my job at Ambassador. I'd wanted to pursue a daywear line, but I never seemed to have time. Perhaps if the door to Ambassador was closing . . .

There was a soft knock at the bedroom door. Chet peered in. "Are you decent?"

I gave a chuckle. "Yes."

He opened the door and ushered Detective Baptiste into the room. I straightened up and absently went to run a hand through my hair, forgetting I had a bandage wrapped around my head.

"Detective." Self-conscious at my state of undress, I gave Chet a pointed glare. He raised a shoulder in apology.

"Miss Michelle," the detective greeted me, taking off his hat. "How are you feeling?"

"Oh, you know." I smiled and pointed to my head. "A little sore."

"I wanted to come by to thank you." He ran a hand over the brim of his hat.

"Oh? For what?"

"For Preston Trav— er, James Johnson. I hate to admit it, but we were at a loss. We have Clara Stapleton in custody at the Los Angeles County Jail, as well. She's not talking, though."

Funny, I thought. She'd given me an earful. I didn't feel it necessary to mention I already knew where she was and had been to see her. She'd told me nothing that would have changed things for her or helped in the case. She still had done Johnson's bidding, whatever her reasons.

"He sold her out, though," the detective added. "Said faking his death was her idea."

I scoffed, shaking my head. Stupid, stupid girl. He was still using her.

"What's going to happen to her?" I asked.

"We're charging her as an accessory to murder and accessory to kidnapping. The future doesn't look bright for her. She'll go to prison for a long time."

What a pity. Things could have turned out so differently for her. Her betrayal deeply saddened me. I had enjoyed working with her, mentoring her. I'd had hope of a real partnership, but she had destroyed all that when she'd aided Johnson in both his escape and kidnapping Stevie, which was unforgivable.

"And James Johnson?" I asked.

"Set to hang for his crimes. They've expedited the execution date. Don't want to risk losing him again. He's in solitary confinement."

I nodded. I didn't wish death upon anyone, but James Johnson had used up all his chips. I shuddered to think he'd had Stevie in his clutches. Gratitude washed over me that the boy had been returned to us safely.

"And thank you for tipping us off to the murder of Valentina Baklanova."

My gaze slid over to Chet, who was beaming with pride.

"I regret we didn't get to Anton Belsky before you did," the detective continued. "I sent some officers out to his estate right after you and Deputy Harrison called. You must have smacked him pretty hard. He was still unconscious." He gave a chuckle.

"That was all Madeleine," I said, my lips turning up slightly at the memory. She'd saved my life.

"Turns out he was a fencer for some of the higher-ups in Lenin's Soviet government," Detective Baptiste said. "Laundered money for them through his banks."

I widened my eyes in surprise. "You're kidding." His operation was much bigger than I'd suspected.

He shook his head. "Wish that were the case. The Russian economy has crashed. Millions are starving. The Soviets have been selling the royal family's stolen belongings to international buyers to make some quick money."

"But it was just one egg," I said. "Madeleine's brother, her parents, and Valentina all died for this one egg." It was incredulous.

"Seems ridiculous, I know," he agreed. "But according to Anton Belsky, that Fabergé egg, along with the forty others, belongs to the Russian people. He felt he was doing his duty to get it back."

"All at the cost of human life," I uttered in amazement. "And what about Harold Huxley?"

"Again, thanks to you, we've tipped off the authorities in Hong Kong. They'll be looking for him when that ship docks."

"And the egg?" Chet asked.

"It will most likely be returned to the Soviets."

The thought of that made my mouth sour. The price for one egg was four deaths.

"How did you uncover the true identity of Harold Huxley?" the detective asked me.

I suppressed a nervous laugh. Should I reveal that my dead sister had been trying to tell me I had been deceived into thinking Harold Huxley was my father?

"It was an accident," I admitted. "No feat of intellect. I found a letter from his brother."

"But you thought he was your father?" He asked the question with a tone of condescension—or was it merely curiosity?

"They had been estranged," Chet broke in, protective as always. "Grace hadn't seen her father since she was a child."

The detective flipped his hat back onto his head. "I see. Well, I'll leave you to your rest."

"I'll show you out." Chet gestured toward the door with a tilt of his head.

He shut the door, and I let out a sigh. I surveyed the bed, my sketch pad and crumpled-up papers littering the blanket, and then gazed out the window. Puffy white clouds dotted the azure sky. The pink blooms of the flowering desert willow tree next to the house swayed with the breeze. Detective Baptiste's question about my thinking Harold Huxley was my father burned in my mind. I had been fooled. I had *been* a fool. How could I have not seen through the lie? I tried to comfort myself with the fact that Harold Huxley and my father had looked so much alike.

I threw the covers off my legs. Sick of sitting in bed, I longed to be outside, to get out of my head and forget all that had happened.

WITH FIRM, even strokes, I ran the brush down Goldie's shoulder and then over her back. She stood quietly, her eyes half-closed, basking in the attention. The tangy, earthy smell of the stacked alfalfa bales in the hay room permeated the interior of the barn, and the air was cool against my skin. I felt instantly restored, the ache in my head and my bones melting away with each stroke.

Goldie gave a soft nicker and swung her head around, nuzzling the pocket of my denims.

"Are you looking for a treat?" I asked, running my hand down her forehead.

She nickered again, and I reached into my pocket and pulled out a couple of sugar cubes. "Here you go, girl."

Her lips grazed my outstretched palm as she nibbled the cubes into her mouth and crunched down on them.

A swishing noise at the end of the wide aisleway caught my attention. I looked up to see Felicity striding toward me in her confident, sanguine manner, the fabric of her wide-legged trousers swaying rhythmically with each step. Lenora Lange glided behind her, her silver shoes seeming to barely touch the ground.

"You aren't going to ride are you?" Felicity asked, planting a kiss on my cheek. A cloud of Chanel No. 5 enveloped me.

I gave her a smile "No. I'm just grooming Goldie."

"Good. You really should be in bed."

"I'm all right," I assured her. "Hello, Miss Lange."

She greeted me silently with a nod of her head and a slight upturning of her lips. She surveyed the barn, her nose wrinkling in distaste. I guessed the smell of horses and hay wasn't for everyone.

"Are you sure you should be out here?" Felicity asked, a line of concern sinking between her brows. "I can't believe what you've been through, dear."

I looked directly into her navy eyes. "I'm fine. Really."

Felicity ran her hand down Goldie's forelock. "You're amazing is what I'd say. You got Stevie back and you saved Madeleine. Chet told me all about it. And Anton Belsky? Who would have known he was working for the Soviets? You'd think they wouldn't have gone to such trouble and caused so much damage for just one jeweled egg."

"I know," I agreed. "And my fa— Harold Huxley," I quickly corrected myself, my stomach turning over at my slip of the tongue, "wanted it for himself. In the end, not even Madeleine mattered to him as much as the egg did."

"Poor dear. How is she?"

"She's still in the hospital. They wanted to keep her a bit longer. She was in pretty bad shape. Should be released tomorrow. She's going to stay with us for a while until she figures out what she's going to do next."

"And Harold Huxley gets away with the egg scot-free." Felicity shook her head.

"Hopefully the authorities in China will get him as he comes off the ship. Detective Baptiste said they'll have people looking for him."

"Like that old needle in the haystack," Felicity mused.

"There will be justice." Lenora finally spoke, her voice carrying that otherworldly quality.

A spike of chills ran down my arms. She had been so quiet I'd almost forgotten she was there. Embarrassed I had been so wrapped up in my conversation with Felicity that I had ignored her, I let go a nervous chuckle. "I'm sorry, Miss Lange, what did you say?"

"There will be justice." She looked at me with assuredness in her luminous, wide-eyed gaze.

I sighed, shame settling on me again like a pall. "I'm surprised I was so fooled by him. I actually believed he was my father. He looked so much like him—or at least I thought he did. My memories of my childhood are so fractured."

"He is here." Miss Lange's lips curved to a small smile.

I darted a quick glance at Felicity, who met my gaze with a knowing look on her face.

A trembling started in my gut and spread through my limbs. In the few readings I'd had with Lenora Lange, my father had never made an appearance—only Sophia and my mother. Perhaps, on some level, subconsciously, that's what made me believe he was alive.

"But he's never—"

"He's sorry for that," she said as if she were reading my mind, which, for all I knew, she was. "He wanted to come through, but he was stuck."

"Stuck?" I didn't understand.

"In limbo."

I blinked at her. "You mean, like purgatory?" I had heard of this belief in the Catholic religion.

"In a sense." Her brows pressed downward. "There is no word for it. Sometimes, when a soul is troubled in life, they have a difficult time passing over. They get stuck. Your father had much unfinished business to tend to on this Earth before he left it."

"Business? What business?" Sometimes I wished she would just spit it out. She spoke in circles, and it was frustrating.

"You and Sophia," she said serenely, unbothered by my annoyance.

"But he joined the Army. He survived the train crash. What was he doing all that time before he joined the Army? Why didn't he try to find us?" My voice rose an octave, and Felicity reached out to take my hand.

Lenora smiled at me. "You know."

"What?" I said, exasperated. I wanted to shake it out of her. "Know what?"

She regarded me with her large eyes, softly blinking. A peacefulness washed over her features, but she didn't answer my question.

"You mean, Harold Huxley?"

She slowly nodded her head. My frustration faded, and the tenseness in my shoulders eased.

"He needed to explain," she said.

A strange thought occurred to me. "You don't mean he *sent* Harold Huxley, do you?"

She pressed her hands together at her chest as if in prayer. "There are mysteries we will never understand." She opened her hands and then closed them again. "I do know this: there are no accidents in life. There is a reason for everything."

I thought about the senseless deaths of my mother and my sister. Of the murders of Madeleine's family and Valentina. I wasn't sure I could agree.

Miss Lange closed her eyes, and a smile further softened the tranquility of her features. She nodded, having a private, silent conversation with someone. Was it my father? Her collective, Joshua?

"There is an oak tree," she said, "in a field of grass and flowers."

My mouth dropped open, and I looked at Felicity with wide eyes, remembering the dream. She squeezed my hand in encouragement. I hadn't told her about the dream, but she knew Lenora's ways well enough to know I had experienced a recognition of some kind.

"They are together. They are always with you, and they are at peace." She opened her eyes. They were misty with tears.

Realizing I was still gaping at her, I closed my mouth. A sudden feeling of quietude washed over me at the thought—no, the *knowledge* that my family was together, that my father had been reunited with Sophia and my mother. A renewed energy surged through me, and the stormy turmoil of emotions that had plagued me over the past few years dissipated like the calming of a stormy sea.

"You have a gift and a partnership," she said.

"Pardon?" The mood had shifted, and she pulled me away from the dream.

"For seeking the truth with Sophia's guidance."

"Uh . . . yes?" I wasn't sure what she was getting at.

"You can help many."

I looked over at Felicity again, confused.

"I think she's referring to helping people with your investigative skills."

"Oh, you mean, like, becoming a private investigator?" I laughed. "But I'm a designer. I love what I do."

Felicity shrugged a shoulder. "You know the movie business. It's not a three-hundred-sixty-five-day-a-year job. There are sometimes months with no work."

I offered her a tiny, tight smile. If she only knew. I wasn't quite yet ready to tell her about my imminent unemployment. I thought I'd better wait to hear from Timothy first.

"You'd be a great part-time investigator, Grace," she prattled on. "And you could learn from Chet. Wouldn't it be nice to have some extra pocket change?" She raised her arm, gesturing at the barn, the house, the property.

The extra money would come in handy, but— I shook my head, reliving the events of the past week and the emotional rollercoaster it had created. "It would be nice, but no. I'm not sure I have the stomach for it."

CHAPTER TWENTY-NINE

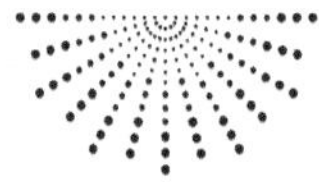

Timothy didn't call until after lunch the next day.

"I'm sorry, Grace. They wouldn't relent."

I sighed into the phone, not surprised. I waited for the wave of disappointment to bring tears to my eyes, but nothing came. Absently, I ran a hand over my hair and winced. I had removed the bandage, and Rose had helped me wash the blood out of my hair that morning, but the bruising was still tender.

"That's all right, Timothy. I understand. Thanks for going to bat for me."

"I hope we can work together again someday, darlin'."

"Me too."

I hung up the telephone and bit a hangnail, staring at the receiver. I'd never been fired before, and I couldn't quite reconcile my feelings about it.

Chet came around the corner from the kitchen. "Everything all right, Grace?"

I smiled and shook my head. I told him, matter-of-factly and without emotion, what had transpired.

He took me in his arms. "You're a wonderful designer, Grace. You'll find something else."

I nodded into his shoulder. "I think I'm going to go out on my own. Pursue the Sophia line."

He pulled away from me and looked into my eyes. "You sure? You love working in the pictures."

"I do," I agreed. "But it's the designing of clothing that I love. The art of it, whether it's costumes or eveningwear or daywear, and since I'll be working for myself, I'll be on my own schedule. It may take a while to—"

Chet pressed his finger to my lips. "I'll support whatever you want to do, Grace." He smiled down at me.

I stood on tiptoes and kissed him. "Thank you, darling." I wrapped my arms around him, grateful for such a supportive and loving husband.

"I'm going to the hospital to get Madeleine," he said. "Want to come?"

"No. I want to stay here and make sure everything is in order for her arrival. She's been through so much. I'm sure she'll need all the cheering up we can give her."

"Right you are. But you're still recovering, too. Don't wear yourself out."

"I'll be fine," I reassured him with another peck on the lips.

CHET ARRIVED with Madeleine in tow two hours later. She looked almost restored to her former self. The fullness had returned to her cheeks, and they had regained some color.

I greeted her with a hug, then took her by the elbow. "Let's get you upstairs to bed."

"No." She raised her hand, loosening my grasp. "I've been in bed for days. I don't want to go near a bed for a while if that's okay."

"Of course," I said. "Come sit on the sofa. I'll get you some lemonade."

Relief swept over her features. "That sounds marvelous."

"Lemonade coming up." Rose had appeared in the entryway. She winked at me and tottered off to the kitchen.

"I'll go to the boarding house and pick up your things," Chet said.

Concern furrowed her brow. "I don't want to be a bother."

Chet smiled. "Nonsense."

We settled ourselves on the couch.

"How are you feeling?" I asked.

"Good." She nodded, as if trying to assure herself. "It's been hard for me to eat, but, you know, hospital food." She chuckled. "I should ask you the same question. How's your head?"

"Better." A surge of emotion clutched at me, and I took her hand. She placed her other hand over mine. I felt a strong connection with this woman, and in her eyes, I could see she felt the same about me. Our ordeal and shared sense of betrayal by Harold Huxley had bonded us, and it was as if we both had just realized it in that moment.

"Thank you," she said with a sudden shyness. "For letting me stay."

I squeezed her hand. "As long as you like."

"I'll stay for a day or two. But then I want to go back to the boarding house. I'll pay you back for the week's rent once I get on my feet again."

"So you're planning to stay in America?"

She nodded. "I've been offered a position."

I pulled my chin back in surprise. "You have?"

"I guess I was a little bossy with the nurses." She giggled. "I couldn't help myself. I wanted to see to it that all the other patients in the room had everything they needed. I think I drove those nurses mad." She laughed again. "Anyway, we actually got along just fine. When they realized I was a nurse, too, they encouraged me to speak with the hospital administrator. Apparently, they are short-staffed there. The head nurse set up a meeting, and the administrator was so impressed with the work I had done at the *Hôtel National des Invalides* that he hired me on the spot."

"That's wonderful, Madeleine!"

Rose came through the kitchen door with a tray, balancing a pitcher of lemonade and two glasses. She set it on the coffee table in front of us.

"Thank you, Rose." I poured a glass for Madeleine and then myself.

The kitchen door swung open again, and this time Stevie pushed his way through. His canvas newspaper tote was slung over one shoulder and rested on the opposite hip. It was full to bursting. When he saw us, he stopped short. His gaze fell to the floor.

"Stevie?" I asked. "What's wrong?"

"Hey, Grace," he said, his eyes darting between me and Madeleine.

"This is my friend, Madeleine," I said. Stevie smiled politely at her and then came over and slumped down in the adjacent armchair.

I exchanged a glance with Rose who shrugged in bewilderment. "What is it, Stevie?" I asked.

He reached into his bag and pulled out a newspaper, rolled and tied with string. He handed it to me. "Early-evening edition. Big story on the front page."

I slid the string off the roll and let it unfurl. Madeleine leaned over to see. I read the headline: SS *VAUGHN* GOES DOWN IN PACIFIC. ALL SOULS LOST.

"Oh my goodness!" I drew in a sharp breath and looked over at Madeleine. Her face had paled.

The article went on to divulge the story of Harold Huxley, aka Peter Michelle, and the theft of a valued Russian treasure, though there was no mention of what that valued treasure was. It told of Valentina Baklanova, her involvement and subsequent murder, and how I had been instrumental in solving the case.

"I can't believe it," Madeleine whispered.

I looked over at Stevie. He plucked at some fuzz on the chair, and his face was set in hard lines. I wondered if he was mourning Harold Huxley.

"What is it?" Rose asked, marching over. She took the paper from my hands and read. "Good Lord," she gasped. "He wasn't your father. Oh, honey. This is awful."

I hadn't yet been ready to divulge the truth of his duplicity to Rose and the others. Chet had respected my wishes to keep it quiet, but now it was out.

"He lied," Stevie said, his eyes clouding over like a thunderstorm. "He was a liar and a thief."

I exchanged a glance with Madeleine. "Stevie had grown quite fond of my—of Harold."

"I hate him," he spat.

"He deceived all of us," I said. "I'm sorry, Stevie."

His eyes met mine, his face coloring with indignation. "I don't care about me. It's you that's been hurt the most. I'd give anything to have my dad come back, and you thought yours had. It's terrible what he did to you."

"Oh, Stevie." I was touched at his concern for me. "It's a shame what he did to all of us." I looked over at Madeleine.

She raised her chin, and her jaw stiffened. "We just have to move on, Stevie," she said. "We can't let anger, or sadness, or fear hold us back. We need to support one another." Her face softened. "Do you think you can do that?"

His mouth turned down, and his chin quivered with emotion. His gaze shifted away from us. "Yeah, I can do that."

I knew it would take him some time to get over the betrayal. It would take time for all of us. Stevie had thought he'd found a replacement father figure in Harold, and he'd suffered the loss of that father all over again.

I reached out and laid my hand on his arm. "He won't be able to hurt anyone ever again."

Rose, standing over us, looked at her watch. "You'd best be off, young man," she said to him. "You've got papers to deliver."

He rose from the chair and left through the kitchen door.

"What a thoughtful young man," Madeleine said with wonder.

I smiled at her. "Yes. He's a special boy."

Madeleine pressed her finger and thumb to the bridge of her nose. "You know, I think I'd like to lie down now," she said. I assumed she was processing the sinking of the ship and the death of Harold Huxley. Although she had been betrayed, I knew she still loved him. Just like an affliction of the body, the love in one's heart didn't vanish in an instant. It took time to heal.

I led her upstairs to the guest room.

Rose had put clean sheets on the bed that morning, and she'd aired the chenille bedspread on the line in the backyard for a couple of hours. The bed was now back to rights, neatly made with some decorative pillows arranged against the headboard. The room was neat, sunny, and tidy.

"Here you are," I said, putting some cheerfulness in my voice.

"It's lovely." Madeleine surveyed the room. She walked over to the bed and sat down, removing her shoes. I helped her get under the bedspread and fluffed the pillows at her back.

"Thank you." She looked up at me with gratitude.

"Get some rest." I tiptoed out of the room and closed the door behind me.

Although the guestroom had been made up to perfection for Madeleine, I felt it needed something to make it even more welcoming. A fresh bouquet of flowers from the garden would do.

On my way to the stairs, I was struck with the sudden urge to put pencil to paper. Often, working on my design sketches helped me sort through my emotions. I veered to the right and stepped into my home studio.

My gaze rested on one of the dress forms adorned with a muslin pattern for a dress in the Sophia daywear line I had started months ago. I walked over to it and surveyed the design. It had been inspired by a piece I'd made for *The Queen of Whitehall*, which had been inspired by a piece I had worked on for Lucile, Lady Duff Gordon when she was with the Follies. Much simpler and more modern in style, of course, but it had the same luxurious opulence.

"Lucile would be proud," came a small voice from the corner of the room. I started and raised my gaze toward the sound.

Sophia sat at one of my worktables, her legs crossed at the knees.

I gawked at the vision, wondering if I'd been hit on the head harder than I'd thought. This wasn't some dreamlike vision. She was so real.

"What are you—" I said, breathless, the sound of my heartbeat whirring in my ears.

"You should pursue this." She pointed to the dress form, a cigarette resting between her ring-clad fingers. A ribbon of smoke curled up toward the ceiling. "Your Sophia line is going to be a real hit. But how could it not, given its name?" A grin spread across her face.

My throat closed up, making me speechless.

"And your friend is right, you know. You should think about the investigation gig." She lifted the cigarette to her red lips. Her cheeks sank deep under her finely curved cheekbones as she inhaled. "We'd make a great team."

"But, I—" I blinked, and she was gone.

I sucked in a breath, my hand at my throat.

Forgetting my sketch pad, I made my way downstairs in a trance. I headed toward the French doors in the living room that led to the backyard and the flower garden.

The door to the kitchen swung open, and Rose bustled out of it, her expression the one she made when she was on a mission to get something done. She startled when she saw me. "Grace, what are you doing?"

I pointed to the backyard, my mind still awhirl after my encounter with Sophia.

"I'm getting flowers for Madeleine's room," I said, my voice barely a whisper.

"With what?" she asked, looking at my hands. "You're not going to rip them from the stems, are you? You need some pruning shears." She placed her hands on her hips, surveying me more closely. "What's wrong with you? You look like you've seen a ghost."

I swallowed and then gave her a delighted smile. "I think I have."

She's a reluctant Broadway star on the hunt to find her sister's killer. Will fame lead her to the truth, or will it be her final curtain call?

[Scan to order *Grace in the Wings*, book 1 of the series!]

I HOPE this book has brought you some entertainment and enjoyment! I am so grateful and honored that you have chosen to spend some time with me.

If you are so inclined, I would appreciate your spending just one more moment and writing a review. It doesn't need to be long, just a few honest words about your reading experience.

You can leave your review on Amazon, Bookbub, Goodreads or all three!

I'D ALSO LOVE to connect with with you on a more personal level. Sign up for my mailing list via my website to participate in special giveaways, and receive news and information about my events and upcoming releases at https://www.KariBovee.com. And, when you sign up you will receive a FREE book! *Shoot like a Girl* is the prequel novella to my Annie Oakley Mystery Series.

ABOUT THE AUTHOR

Empowered women in history, horses, unconventional characters, and real-life historical events fill the pages of award-winning author Kari Bovée's articles and historical mystery musings and manuscripts.

She and her husband, Kevin, spend their time between their horse property in the beautiful Land of Enchantment, New Mexico, and their condo on the sunny shores of Kailua-Kona, Hawaii.

ACKNOWLEDGMENTS

To all of my readers and my awesome A-team, you have my eternal gratitude. Your continued support and encouragement are what makes this endeavor worth all the effort!

To Danielle Poiesz of Double Vision Editorial, it has been wonderful working with you on this and other projects, and I hope we can continue to work together into the future.

Special thanks to my husband Kevin, who reads everything I write. I so appreciate your feedback, love, support, and wisdom. To Jessica, Hunter, Sumiko, Michael and Brita, thank you for always cheering me on and making me laugh. You bring light into my world.

And to my mom, for all your love and support. Thank you.

ALSO BY KARI BOVÉE

Annie Oakley Mystery Series

Shoot like a Girl

Girl with a Gun

Peccadillo at the Palace

Folly at the Fair

Grace Michelle Mystery Series

Grace in the Wings

Grace in Hollywood

Grace Among Thieves

Ruby Delgado Mystery
A Southwestern Stand Alone

Bones of the Redeemed